BOOK OF CANNIBALS 2
THE HUNGER

EDITED BY
REBECCA BESSER

BOOK OF CANNIBALS 2: THE HUNGER

Cover art and illustrations by Gary McCluskey

Table of Contents

EDIBLE AUTOPSY

ADAM P. LEWIS

"Biting into an eye is like biting into a grape–a very firm grape," Joyce said, pushing back the top and bottom eyelids with her index finger and thumb.

Ray's eyeball twitched while he fought her fingers to close his eyelids. His eyeball quivered as the lid only half shut. He looked at the fingers that were prying his eye open, following the wrist, arm, and shoulder until he focused on Joyce's face and stared into her green eyes. She was bent over him, wearing a blue surgical mask, a white cap, and matching apron. Her face and neck were shielded by a clear face shield, and a small lock of blond hair curled out from under the cap and draped over her left eye.

Ray eyes started watering and his vision became blurry, making it difficult for him to see Joyce clearly and guess her age. What he had seen of her though, she looked to be over fifty. Crow's feet spread out from the corners of her eyes. Her voice was old as well—scratchy as if she smoked two packs of cigarettes a day. She continued talking as she positioned her fingers again and held the eyelid back further.

"The outer shell, the sclera, is smooth like grape skin and is tough to bite through. The moment your teeth penetrate it, the eye splits in half through the center. Juices spray out and cover the inside of your mouth. The only difference, in comparison to a grape, is the eyeball excretes a thicker liquid that clings to your teeth and tongue like taffy. Unfortunately it isn't sweet like taffy, but it tastes good nonetheless."

Joyce picked up a knife off the small cart next to the autopsy table. The blade was smooth—three inches long, and thin. She positioned the knife at an angle and pushed it into the corner of Ray's eye. Before the blood flowed, a milky liquid oozed out like molasses.

Ray screamed—the sharp pricks of pain causing him to arch his spine. His back lifted inches off the table and stretched the nylon restraints holding down his torso and neck. His thighs and knees rubbed together as he tried kicking his legs free, but they too were restrained in three separate areas—the hips, knees, and ankles.

Joyce wiggled the knife deeper behind Ray's eyeball until she struck the sphenoid bone located behind it. She then pushed down on the knife handle, as one would a crowbar, lifting it up.

Ray's vision blurred even more and went black. The sensation on the back of his eyeball was like a sharp headache, pounding on the back of his eyes. He tried thrashing his head, but another person, out of view, was holding it still. Even if he wanted to look, he couldn't. His other eye voluntarily shut as the pain radiated across his face and down his neck. He could feel it in the pit of his stomach, making him nauseous.

Joyce picked up an instrument resembling a small ice cream scoop from the cart. It was open at the bottom and the edges that came together inside the cupped center were sharp. She wiggled it behind the eyeball while still pushing down on the knife creating clearance for the scoop. When it was in place, she squeezed the handle. The sharp edges cut through the optic nerve, artery, and vein attached to the back of the eyeball.

Blood seeped from Ray's empty eye socket and drizzled down the side of his face. He felt the blood trickle into his ear and pool for a brief second inside the canal before pouring off the lobe. His screams grew into high-pitched screeches while his heartbeat increased and sweat coated every inch of his naked body.

Joyce plucked the eyeball from the scoop and held it with her fingers, giving it a slight squeeze, testing its firmness. It was stiff, just the way she liked them. She lifted up her face shield and licked the cornea like a child would a jawbreaker.

"It tastes metallic and salty. You'll notice that at first the chewing sounds scratchy just like a grape. Also, you can feel and hear your teeth cutting and grinding into the fibrous tissue. Its consistency is fatty. Here, Mary, try it," she said, handing Mary the eyeball.

Mary released Ray's head and reached forward, cupping her hands to retrieve the eyeball like one would under the opening of a gum ball machine. Joyce dropped it into Mary's waiting hands. Mary pinched the eyeball between her fingers and popped it into her mouth like candy, biting down. The eyeball reacted between her teeth just as Joyce described. It popped and chewed like fat. It sounded like she was chewing on grass as her teeth ground through the fibrous tissue. She didn't gag, but smiled as she rolled the thick juices and particles of eyeball around in her mouth with her tongue.

Ray's eyelid twitched over his empty eye socket. He continued screaming, turning his voice hoarse.

"Well, Mary, what do you think?" Joyce asked.

Mary smiled as her eyes rolled back in her head and her eyelids shut in pleasure. "I love it! The juice trickling out reminds me of that bubble gum with the liquid center that seeps out during the first bite."

Ray wept and begged, "Let me go, please!"

Joyce smiled down at him. "And not get our fill? You selfish man, you!"

"Please, I've done nothing to you!"

"You have terminal cancer. It's wrapped around your spine. You're going to die in just weeks. We're just helping the process along," Joyce said in a caring voice while she patted his cheek. "Think of me as Hospice."

Ray begged. "Please! I have a wife and children. I want to say goodbye."

Joyce ignored Ray's pleas and picked up a scalpel. "Next, we'll open the trunk. It's traditionally the first area of the body we open, but I wanted to treat you to a little appetizer before we did so. What I need you to do for me, Mary, is place the block under his shoulder blades. It will lift the chest, dropping the arms down, and allow us maximum exposure to the chest cavity."

Mary loosened the straps slightly, allowing the slack needed to push the block under Ray's body, lifting his back off the table and pushing his chest upward.

"The incision is Y-shaped. It extends from the front of each shoulder down to the xiphoid process located at the inferior end of the sternum. In other words, cut from the top of each shoulder to the bottom of the rib cage, stopping just above the pubic area. Observe," Joyce said, pressing the scalpel into Ray's left shoulder.

Ray's shoulder buckled as the cold blade of the knife pricked his skin. He yelled out indecipherable words of agony while trying to flail his chest and disrupt the incision.

Joyce flinched back. "Hold him down, please."

Mary pressed her hands down on Ray's shoulders with all her upper-body strength, making his body immobile.

Joyce pushed the scalpel back into Ray's shoulder, puncturing down through his skin and into fat and muscle. She then dragged the blade toward the center of his chest below the sternum. She repeated the same incision on the opposite side of the chest, all the while Ray's hips bucked and his legs squirmed.

Ray filled the room with pain-ridden screams and swore between inhales, "Damn you, bitch, please…fucking stop!"

Joyce and Mary acted as though Ray were dead; his begging fell on deaf ears.

"Now," Joyce said, "I'll continue the incision from where the first two meet at the center of the chest. This cut will continue down to the pubic area and cut around the umbilicus. In laymen's terms, that would be the bellybutton. Oh, and remember that the Y-incision should be made deep enough into the chest to reach the rib cage and deep enough into the abdomen to reach the abdominal cavity. But be careful not to cut into the intestines, unless you clean them out first–they spoil the other organs."

Every inch of Ray's body began to spasm. His fingers curled against the metal autopsy table–the pressure breaking his fingernails. His teeth ground together as the Y-incision was made. Pieces of his teeth broke off and covered the insides of his cheeks with grit. His breathing stuttered, breaking apart his cries, turning them into whimpers.

Blood cascaded over the sides of Ray's chest and torso. It pooled until gravity pulled it down the table where it drained through a hole into a collection bucket.

"Will the bleeding stop?" Mary asked, concerned that its salty tastes would drain from the organs, ruining their natural flavors.

"Once he's dead the bleeding will stop, which won't be too much longer. He'll die from the shock of blood loss before we remove any organs."

Joyce placed the scalpel back on the tool cart and turned back to Ray. She looked at his chest and smiled. "His chest muscles aren't moving anymore. He's dead. You can release your grip on his shoulders now."

Mary removed her hands.

Joyce continued, "The next step is to fold back the flaps of skin created by the Y-incision, exposing the neck muscles, rib cage, and abdomen."

Joyce lifted the flap of skin and tissue around the neck and flipped it over Ray's face. She then pulled back the incision that ran down the center of Ray's body, stretching and folding the skin over the sides of his torso.

Mary's mouth salivated as she looked down at the exposed organs. She walked around the table, licking her lips.

Joyce noticed the excitement on Mary's face. "Relax. We still have to saw out the rib cage, cut through the pericardial sac containing the lungs and heart, and cut away the abdomen muscles, exposing the remaining internal organs."

Joyce retrieved a Stryker saw and turned it on. She lowered it to the ribs and looked up at Mary. She turned the saw off and handed it to Mary. "You may do the honors of cutting out the ribs."

Mary smiled. "Thank you."

"Remember, cut around the outer edges of the rib cage, leaving the sternum intact. Once the cuts are made, I'll lift the rib cage and sternum out as one piece."

"What are you going to do with it?" Mark asked.

Joyce laughed. "Barbeque them later."

A grin spread across Mary's face. She turned on the saw again and began cutting through the ribs. Once removed, Joyce placed the ribs in a plastic bag, opened a cooler filled with ice, and dropped the rib cage inside. She closed the lid and returned to the autopsy table.

"Okay, Mary, I want you to use the scalpel and cut through the pericardial sac."

Joyce watched Mary cut through the sac. As Mary did so, she instructed, "Be careful now. Watch what you are doing so you don't cut yourself. Cut the sac like you would wrapping paper–long, single cuts."

Mary cut as Joyce instructed. Once the sac was cut away, Joyce took over. She cut through the pulmonary arteries, loosened the heart, and removed it from the chest cavity. She carried it over to a metal tray and began dissecting it. With her fingers, she pushed fatty deposits stuck to the interior sides of the veins out and onto the tray. With a knife, she scooped up the fatty deposit and licked the knife clean. She squeezed another vein, pushing out more fat. She scooped it up with the knife and handed it to Mary. She placed the knife in her mouth, closed her lips down on it like she would a lollipop, and pulled the knife out; the knife was now wiped clean.

Mary gagged.

"Sorry," Joyce said, "it's gooey and sticky–hard to swallow and doesn't taste the best. It's an acquired taste, like caviar. I should've spread it on a piece of liver for you."

Joyce walked over to the blood collecting bucket. She dipped a Dixie cup into the blood, filled it up, and handed it to Mary. "Here, wash it down."

Mary lifted her face shield and kicked back the cup of blood like a shot of Tequila. She wiped her lips dry with her sleeve and said, "Thanks, I needed that."

Joyce stepped back to the autopsy table and cut into the stomach. With a ladle, she scooped out the contents and poured it into a bowl. Bits of undigested food plopped into the bowl and floated in thick stomach bile that clung to the lip of the ladle like maple syrup dripping slowly from a jug spout. She shook the ladle until the bile let loose and dripped into the bowl.

"Did you get the plasticware set from the hospital cafeteria like I asked you to?"

Mary nodded and proceeded to unwrap the plasticware. She handed Joyce the spoon. Joyce dipped the spoon into the bowl, scooping up a spoonful of bile and partially digested food particles. She raised the spoon to her face and sniffed. She then opened her mouth, closed her lips around the base of the spoon handle, and pulled it out from between her lips–a small smear of bile remained on the spoon.

Joyce dipped the spoon back into the bowl and scooped up more bile and food. She held it up to Mary's face with her other hand underneath Mary's chin, waiting to catch anything that might drip off the base of the spoon.

Mary opened her mouth and shut it around the spoon. She pulled her head back, removing the spoon from her mouth. She swallowed and said, "His last meal must've been chili; that was spicy and bitter, but I like it."

Joyce smiled. "Good. I'm glad."

She ladled the remaining stomach contents into a bed pan and cut pieces of lung into squares the size of bread and handed a piece to Mary. "The lung is porous like a sponge. You can use it to dunk into the bile like soup."

Mary dipped the piece of lung into the bowl and absorbed some bile. She then bit down, tearing off a bite, chewing and swallowing. "Has a cornbread-like texture to it. I like the stomach bile better without the lung though. The lung makes it feel a bit heavy in my stomach."

Joyce dipped her piece of lung into the bile, swirled it around, and placed it in her mouth. She bit down, chewing and swallowing as well. "I think it all depends on the persons' last meal. The lung doesn't pair well with the spiciness of what he last ate. Also, we're lucky. There isn't any tar from cigarettes clogging up his lungs. If there was, I wouldn't eat it. The smoky tar flavoring makes the lung taste burnt—sort of Cajun style."

Mary wiped her mouth on a napkin and asked, "What are we going to eat next?"

Joyce looked up and down Ray's body. Her eyes affixed on his scrotum. "There isn't much left that is really edible raw. How about the testicles? Those are easy to remove and taste good."

Mary nodded. "Let's do it!"

Joyce pushed Ray's penis to the side and lifted up on his scrotum, stretching out the skin to make it easier to drag a knife through the sack. With a scalpel, she cut from the base of the penis, down through the center of the scrotum and stopped the incision just above Ray's anus; blood oozed from the scrotum. She pushed on the scrotum, inside-outing it until a testicle rolled out and rested in her palm. With scissors, she cut the arteries and ducts that carried the sperm from the testicle to the penis. Once freed, she squeezed the testicle between her fingers.

"It's firm—firmer than an eyeball," Joyce said. "Squeezing the testicle this hard would send a dull pain throughout his body if he were alive. It would've felt like he was kicked."

Joyce handed the testicle to Mary and then cut the other one free. Mary bit into it like it was a large cherry tomato. Her teeth raked back and forth, sawing through the layered tissue until it was severed. Blood drizzled over her chin and down between her breasts.

"Tastes gamey–similar to rabbit," Mary said, picking up the napkin from the plasticware set to wipe her mouth, chin, and chest.

Joyce laughed. "I always thought testicles tasted fatty." She then bit down into the other testicle, chewing and swallowing.

After the women finished eating the testicles, Joyce turned her attention to Ray's skull. "Now we'll eat his brain."

Mary held Ray's head still as Joyce made a circular incision around his crown. She rolled the skin back away from the incision, exposing the skull. She then turned on the saw and started cutting through the bone. Skull dust plumed from the saw blade as it ground through the bone. Mary covered her ears as the high-pitched whirling sounds intensified. After the sawing was complete, Joyce pulled off the skullcap, exposing the brain–the folds of the brain were darkened by blood. The rest of the brain was yellowish with veins traveling from fold to fold like spider webs woven between fence posts.

Joyce handed Mary a spoon. "Dig in! It's like eating a bowl of pudding, except it's chewy because of the veins. The texture is similar to scrambled eggs, but with more density. Monkey brains are considered a delicacy in some parts of the world; people just crack open the monkey's skull and start eating. Sometimes the monkey is still alive when served. I've never tried that on a human before–should've done so today. I would've loved cracking open his skull like a nut and digging into his brain. It would've made a great scientific experiment. No one knows how long a person would live if their brains were being eaten."

"What's the brain taste like?" Mary asked. "I hope it doesn't taste anything like the fatty deposits from the arteries."

"Nope, it doesn't taste anything like that. The best way to describe how the brain tastes is to compare it to sweetbread."

Mary shook her head. "I've never had sweetbread before. I smelled it cooking once and I thought it was gross."

"Well, at least try it so you can form your own opinion–I think you'll like it."

The women dug their spoons between the folds of the brain–the spoons digging in made a squishing sound similar to macaroni salad being stirred. They lifted their spoons and slurped the brains into their mouths. They chewed through the softness of the brains and the rubbery veins and swallowed. They ate spoonful after spoonful until half the brain was consumed.

Joyce smiled at Mary. "You ate so much of the brain and at such a fast pace, I think you enjoyed it."

Mary dropped her spoon onto the autopsy table and leaned back in a chair. She unbuttoned her pants and rested her hands atop her stomach and grunted. "I did. I enjoyed every bite. Tastes like veal to me, but chewier. I don't think I can eat another bite. I'm stuffed. If this was Christmas, I'd fall asleep on the couch!"

"Like I said, there isn't much left to eat raw," Joyce said, wiping her mouth clean on her apron. "The limbs are better eaten after cooked on a grill. I like to deep fry the toes and fingers and eat them like chicken wings, but you have to remove the fingernails. The boiling grease makes them explode like popcorn and sends grease shooting into the air. I've burnt myself doing so a few times."

Joyce butchered Ray's body like he was a side of beef hanging on a meat hook in a slaughterhouse. She sliced different cuts of meat from his body—chuck, shoulder, sirloin, and flank, and wrapped it up to freeze and cook later. With sheers, she sniped off his toes and fingers. After she was done carving, she filled Ray's body cavity with the scraps and sewed up the Y-incision and replaced the skullcap.

*   *   *

A week later... Joyce pulled her car up in front of a white ranch-style home. She parked, unbuckled, and walked up to the porch. She breathed deep, cleared her throat, and adjusted her bra strap before ringing the doorbell.

A woman answered. Her hair was curly and she wore a long, black dress; her eyes were puffy and red. The woman's eyebrows rose in confusion upon seeing Joyce, whom she didn't know. "Can I help you?"

"Hi, we haven't met, I'm Dr. Joyce Myerburg," she said, extending her hand in friendship.

"I'm Ray's wife, Sara," she said, shaking Joyce's hand.

Joyce said, solemnly, "I was present when your husband passed. I'm sorry for your loss. I wish I could've done more. I don't want to sound like I'm making excuses, but given his terminal cancer, I can't say for sure that he would've lived more than a week—that's how advanced his cancer was. I think him dying was the best for him."

Sara smiled. "He'd been sick for a few years. I expected this day to come. I'm sure you did everything in your power to save Ray. I just wish I could've said goodbye."

"And I know for a fact he would've wanted to say goodbye to his family as well. But, if it means anything to you, he passed quickly. Sometimes it helps knowing a loved one didn't suffer too long."

Sara sniffled and dabbed her eyes with a tissue. "Thank you, knowing that will help me sleep better tonight–God knows I need it. It's been a rough week without him."

"You're welcome," Joyce said, placing her hand on Sara's shoulder and squeezing it lightly in compassion. "You have the support of your family to see you through this rough patch in your life."

Sara smiled. "I suppose you're right."

"I lost my husband, too. I know what you're going through."

Sara stepped to the side and held the door open. "Please, won't you come inside and join my family and friends."

"I don't want to be intrusive," Joyce said, "or bother anyone. Sometimes doctors at gathering likes these create mixed feelings–sometimes arguments happen. I wouldn't want to cause a scene."

"Nonsense, we're all adults here. Besides, you've come all this way to give your condolences. We'd love to have you join us."

"Thank you." Joyce stepped inside and handed Sara a tray covered with tin foil. "I've brought you food. It's the least I could do. I just wanted to stop by and say I'm sorry and help out anyway I could."

Sara smiled. "Thank you. You didn't have to go through the trouble." She lifted the foil and peeked underneath. The sweet scent of honey barbeque sauce made her mouth water.

"Oh, it wasn't any trouble at all."

"Smells great, what dish is this?" Sara asked.

Joyce smiled. "They're barbecued ribs. I hope you like them. I used an old family recipe."

Sara set the ribs on the table. She removed the foil and lifted a rib from the tray–steam rose and dissipated into the air. She placed a rib on a plate and licked her fingers clean. She sat down at the kitchen table and began nibbling on the rib. Barbeque sauce dripped down her chin and she wiped it clean with a napkin.

Joyce placed a rib on a plate and sat across the table from Sara, smiling as she bit into the flesh and pulled it free from the bone with her teeth.

HOMEGROWN

MARIAH DEITRICK

Jen slumped down in a chair at the dining room table with a plate of food in front of her and sighed. It had been a long day, and it wasn't over yet. She still had to finish her case file notes before preparing a new case for tomorrow.

"Do I even need to ask how your day was?" her husband, Chris, asked.

"Horrible," she groaned. "I wish people would stop calling us just because they're mad. Today, I had to investigate a reported abuse on a six-year-old boy. His parents are going through a custody battle. The boy's dad thought calling us would help him win."

"Sounds bad," he said.

"That's not even the half of it," she grumbled. "Tomorrow I have the biggest case of my career. There are twelve kids in this family. If it's founded, where are those poor kids going to go? There aren't any openings in foster care, and some are too young for a group home." She shoveled a spoon full of corn into her mouth. "Not to mention, this is going to take me weeks to investigate."

Jen didn't mind the work; she just had an overload right now.

"I know you can do it," he said supportively.

She finished her supper in silence. She had to work on her files and prepare for tomorrow. There where several people she had to meet with—the detective on the case, the entire family in question, as well as the claimant.

After working until three in the morning, Jen still managed to get up at five to get started on her new case.

She grabbed an apple on her way out the door and rushed to an appointment with the detective at eight. After a quick stop at the office to drop her files from yesterday off to her boss for review, she was on her way to the house that was going to be her focus for the next few weeks.

When she pulled up to the old farm house, the detective was waiting for her. She grabbed her briefcase and headed toward him. She needed as much information as possible on the case. All she knew was that it was an abuse case, but she also knew there was more to it. This time she was doing her interviewing backwards. Normally she'd talk to the claimant first, but this time she was instructed to speak with the family and the detective first.

"I'm Jennifer Blake," she introduced herself. "You can call me Jen."

"William Murphy," the detective responded, holding out a hand to shake hers. "Bill, please. You're the social worker?"

"Yes."

"I haven't found much," he said, flipping through pages in a pocket sized notebook. "Miss Johnson claims there were two more children living here. She stated that the two boys were here when she came last week, but gone this week. I haven't found anything to support her claim, and both parents deny it." He closed the notebook and stuffed it back into his pocket.

"So, why was I called?" Jen asked–she'd been told it was abuse, not a missing person's case.

"Miss Johnson stated she received a letter from one of the missing boys begging her for help. It's being fingerprinted now, but I'm not holding my breath."

She nodded. "Thanks. I'll see what I can come up with. Let me know if anything turns up."

"Will do," he answered.

When Jen reached the front door, a woman in her mid-forties answered. To Jen's surprise, the woman looked pregnant. She didn't say anything because she couldn't be sure, but there was a distinct bulge protruding from the center of her body.

"Hello. I'm Jennifer Blake. I'll be the social worker handling your case," Jen introduced herself.

"Annette," the woman said, and with a smile she led Jen to the kitchen.

Jen took a seat at the table and pulled a legal pad out of her briefcase. "I have to ask you before we begin, if you understand why I'm here?"

"Yes," Annette answered.

"Can you tell me why you think I'm here?"

"Miss Johnson told you we had more kids," Annette replied with a chuckle.

"Did you have two other kids here?"

"Of course not!" Mrs. Wilson snapped—the smile on her face gone.

Jen changed her line of questioning because she could see Annette was getting irritated. "How old are your children?"

Annette told her all the ages of the children, their names, and grades in school. She explained that she home schooled them and she seemed very proud of that fact, but she admitted Miss Johnson came in to help.

"I just can't believe she would do this," Annette said sadly. "We've been very good to her, and the kids love her. I don't know why she would want to hurt our family like this."

"It's hard to say. People do strange things sometimes," Jen said, trying to comfort her. She felt bad for the woman, but she still needed to get answers from her. "Can you tell me exactly what happened when Miss Johnson questioned you about the two children?"

"She came over, just like she does every week, and when I rounded up all the kids for their lessons, she started yelling. She grabbed a hold of one of my younger children and started shaking him; Miss Johnson wanted him to tell her where the boys were. I think she went crazy." Annette sounded concerned about Miss Johnson. There was no irritation when she talked about her, like Jen had expected.

In the middle of the questioning, Annette's husband, James, walked in. Jen was a little intimidated by the man. He was around six-foot-five and three hundred and fifty pounds, but she had to interview him, too.

Jen asked him the same questions she'd asked his wife, and after the interviewing was over, Annette gave Jen a tour of the house. It wasn't overly clean, but it wasn't disgusting either. Jen had seen much worse. In fact, you couldn't even tell twelve children lived there. The bigger kids seemed to keep their belongings picked up very well. The only toys lying around were baby toys. The laundry was kept up, dishes cleaned, and beds made. Nobody could say this woman's house was a danger to the children. All the cleaning supplies were safely locked under the cupboard and the medications were put up on a high shelf out of reach. From the look of the house, Annette seemed to be a very caring mother. So, why would anyone say she'd harmed her children? Jen wondered.

There was, in fact, no sign of any other children. Jen decided to wait to talk to the kids. She didn't want to bother them if there was no need, and at this point, she didn't see anything out of the ordinary.

"Thank you for your time," Jen said on her way out the door. This felt like yesterday all over again—another case of revenge.

"Thank you," Annette said. "I hope we've helped clear this matter up."

"I still have some investigating to do, but I'll keep in touch," Jen said in her professional tone. She wasn't allowed to say things that might indicate she was going to throw out a case. She had to make them believe it wasn't over, and really it wasn't; Jen still had to talk to Miss Johnson about her allegations.

Jen hopped into her car and drove to Miss Johnson's house. She hoped to get all the information she needed to close the case. She wouldn't be able to officially close it until Bill finished his investigation, but she could move on to another case in the mean time. Jen didn't like to waste time and that's all she seemed to be doing lately with all the false reports she'd been dealing with. If this one was out of the way, she might actually be able to get caught up on her work load.

When Jen arrived at Miss Johnson's house, she was sitting on the porch. Jen walked slowly up the brick walkway. "Hello," she greeted the gray-haired woman.

"Are you here about the missing Wilson children?" the woman asked, unsurprised.

"Yes. I'm Jennifer Blake, but you can call me Jen—you must be Miss Johnson."

"Yes, I am. Did you go there?" Miss Johnson asked as she stood and opened the screen door.

"I did," Jen answered, and Miss Johnson nodded.

"I bet they told you I was crazy, huh?" she chuckled to herself.

"No," Jen lied.

Miss Johnson sat down in a chair and gestured toward the blue and white striped couch across from her. Jen took the offered seat and pulled out her notebook.

"How long have you known the Wilson family?" Jen began her questioning.

"I started working with them two years ago when they moved here."

"Where did they move from?" Jen asked.

"I'm not sure," Miss Johnson said, frowning. She didn't even look at Jen when she began, staring past her at the wall. "They were sweet boys. Always very polite when I came," she stopped and looked Jen right in the eye. "Those boys were scared to death. I could see the fear on their faces whenever their mother came close to them."

"Have you ever seen her harm the children?" Jen asked.

"No. When I'm there she's a loving mother," she shook her head in disbelief.

Jen looked at the woman for a long moment. She'd just admitted that she hadn't seen anything out of the ordinary and Annette seemed to be a loving mother. There was no indication anything had happened to any of the children, and there was absolutely no sign of any *other* children. "What do you think happened to those boys?" she finally asked.

"I don't know," Miss Johnson shrugged. "All I know is they were there the other day and now they're gone. Annette and James laughed at me when I asked about the boys." She looked away again. "I'm not crazy. I know they were there."

The two women sat quietly for a few minutes before Jen started in on her routine questioning. She didn't think the woman was crazy, but maybe she was confused. She may even need some medical attention, Jen thought. She made a note to contact someone to visit Miss Johnson thinking perhaps she was remembering some boys from another family she'd worked with.

By the time Jen was finished talking to Miss Johnson it was noon. She decided to stop off at the Mental Health Clinic before heading back to the office. She was truly worried about Miss Johnson and wanted to get her help right away. It bothered her that the woman had truly believed there had been more children.

Back at the office, Jen retrieved her messages and flipped through them quickly. Some of the messages were normal—people calling about their case, others reporting new information on cases–but there was one that was out of the ordinary. The last message slip she came to had Detective Bill's name on it.

He must need to know what I found, Jen thought.

She started to pick up her phone to call him back, but her line was already blinking, indicating she had a call coming in.

"Jennifer Blake," she answered in her professional tone.

"Detective Bill, here."

"I was just about to return your call."

"Well, this is kind of important," Bill said. "We got a hit on the fingerprints. It turned up a seventeen-year-old named Evan Wilson."

Jen tried to remember if Miss Johnson had said the boys' names, but she couldn't recall offhand. She flipped through her notes, but found no names for either of the boys–she hadn't even asked for them. "Is he their child?" Jen felt horrible now. She'd been so concerned about Miss Johnson's confusion that she hadn't done her job thoroughly.

"I'm not sure," Bill answered, "but he does have the same last name."

"Is there any way to find out?"

"Not with the fingerprint alone–I was hoping you could help. Did Miss Johnson mention the names to you?" Bill asked.

"No, she didn't," Jen said with a sigh, feeling slightly better knowing that she wasn't the only one who hadn't asked for names.

"I'll see what I can find out," Bill said. "I'll keep in touch."

They hung up and Jen sat wondering what to do next. Nothing had turned up on the family when she'd done her database search before her investigation. She was sure she wouldn't find anything on Evan either. Instead of searching again, she decided to call Miss Johnson and ask her for the boys' names. She still couldn't believe she'd forgotten to ask her when she'd been there, but now wasn't the time to dwell on that. She needed to figure out who this boy was, who wrote the note.

Jen picked up her phone and dialed Miss Johnson.

"Hello," she answered.

"Miss Johnson?" Jen asked.

"Yes."

"This is Jennifer Blake. I have a couple more questions if you have the time."

"I'm not talking to you anymore," Miss Johnson snapped. "You think I'm crazy just like they do. Because of you, I have doctors coming to my house."

"I'm really sorry about that, but this is important," Jen said, biting her bottom lip–she'd forgotten about her stop at the clinic.

"I have nothing more to say. You don't believe me anyway..."

"I just need to know the names of the boys," Jen interrupted.

"Eric and Evan," Miss Johnson blurted before hanging up.

Jen jotted the names down on a pad of paper and picked the phone up again. She was going to call Bill, but decided against it–she needed more information before she called him.

She started up her computer and began a new search. This time she didn't search the parents, but searched the children. If Bill could get a hit on a fingerprint, they had to be in the system somewhere.

Starting with Evan's name, Jen worked her way down the children's names until she finally got a hit on one of the younger boys–Nathan; he was born in Kansas. Jen knew that had to be the last place they'd lived because he was only three.

With her new findings, Jen called Bill, thinking he should be able to get a warrant for Annette's medical records–her records would say how many pregnancies she'd had.

Bill agreed to work on getting the records, but he said it would take some time to arrange. So, in the mean time, the two decided to make another house call.

Jen agreed to meet him at the police station in twenty minutes. She wanted to look one more place for information before she headed out. This time she looked for newspaper articles in Kansas. Having another baby in a family of that size would surely have made the paper.

Instead of finding an article on the baby, she found one on the entire family. The headline read, ***Tragedy Strikes Local Family***. James and Annette's names stood out, but their last name appeared as Fisher. It wasn't until the end of the article that she was sure it was the same family–at the bottom was a picture of the entire family. Jen counted the children in the photo and then counted them again to make sure she'd counted right the first time. Miss Johnson was wrong. There hadn't been two more children. There had been *five* more children. Jen looked at the date on the article–it was only three years old. How, in that short amount of time, had the Wilson family *lost* five children? In fact, the article was about one of their children having gone missing. He was seventeen then—the same age as Evan Wilson now.

Jen quickly printed out the article for Bill and shoved the article in her briefcase–she was in a hurry to see him and share the new information. There was no longer a need for medical records when Jen had all the proof she needed. The article was full of quotes from James and Annette about their *seventeen* children. There was no way they could deny it now.

The police station was busy when Jen arrived, but she pushed her way up to the front desk and asked to see Bill. The woman behind the desk was reluctant at first, but agreed when Jen told her who she was.

Bill came around the corner in a matter of seconds after the woman called him. He waved Jen forward to his office.

"I've found something," Jen said excitedly.

"Really?" he sounded surprised–it had only been a few minutes since he'd talked to her last.

"You're not going to believe this," Jen said, pulling the article out of her briefcase and handing it to him–she wanted him to read it for himself.

Bill took the article and settled into his chair, behind his desk. Jen sat in the chair across from him and watched his reaction as he read. She was sure his face looked the same way as hers had when she'd counted the children. She could even see him recounting, just as she had.

"Is this real?" he asked. "Where are those other children?"

Jen shrugged. "I found it on the internet in the newspaper's archives, after getting a hit on their three-year-old."

Bill stood and left the office without another word. When he returned, he was holding several copies of the article. He handed the original copy back to Jen. "Thanks."

Jen shoved her copy back into her briefcase and waited for him to speak. She couldn't do anything yet. There was still no hard evidence that the children had been harmed, and there wasn't a judge in the world who would take those children at this point.

"Let's go confront our friends about this," Bill said.

She jotted down notes on the way to the old farm house, and questions she wanted to ask the family. Jen was sure Bill had his own questions, but she didn't want to miss anything this time around. She'd already messed up with Miss Johnson—the only eye witness they had.

As they drove up the drive and stopped by the front door, Jen noticed a blind in the window shift. Someone had looked out to see who was coming.

Good, they're home, she thought.

Bill walked ahead to the door and used the side of his fist to pound on it. They could both hear commotion and voices coming from the other side, but no one made any attempt to answer.

"James...Annette!" Bill called out and the commotion got louder, and the words coming from behind the door became clearer.

"Don't open it," James whispered.

"I have to," Annette whispered back.

"You can't," James hissed.

"I'm afraid you don't have a choice," Bill yelled, letting them know he could hear them.

Everything got quiet; the voices and commotion stopped. Bill put his fist up again, ready to knock, when Annette pulled it open a crack–she only opened it enough so her head would fit through.

"Can I help you?" she asked, trying to keep her voice polite.

"We have a couple of questions," Bill said. "Can we come in?" He was trying to peek around her, but that only made her pull the door in closer to herself, narrowing the opening even more.

"I'm afraid now is not a good time," she looked apologetic.

"It won't take long," Jen said.

Annette glanced behind her and shook her head 'no'. Jen assumed it was James she was silently conversing with because his was the other voice they'd heard.

"Please," Jen pleaded. "We only have a couple of questions."

Annette glanced behind her again and then pulled the door open wide for them to enter. She didn't seem worried anymore–her expression had shifted to excitement. Jen looked at the woman, frowning as she passed. *Strange*, she thought. *What would change her expression so quickly?*

"I'm afraid you've caught us at a bad time," James said, bringing Jen's attention to him.

"What's going on here?" Bill asked.

Jen gasped when she saw James standing in the doorway of the kitchen. He was wearing an apron covered in blood and was holding a slab of meat in his bloody hand–a pool of the red liquid gathered at his feet where the meat was dripping.

"We're fixing dinner," James smirked. "Come on in and have a seat." He turned toward the kitchen.

The two followed him slowly, not sure what they were getting into. Bill's cop instincts kicked in and he put his hand on his gun. Something was very wrong and neither of them knew what it was, but Jen wasn't taking any chances–she stayed as close to Bill as she could.

When the two reached the kitchen, Jen's stomach lurched. She couldn't hold back the vomit that escaped her lips; Bill turned his head and gasped at the site. The kitchen was covered in blood and a mangled human body was sprawled out on the kitchen table.

"What's going on here?" Bill asked after composing himself.

"I already told you," James answered. "We're fixing dinner."

Jen took a closer look at the body despite herself. To her horror, she recognized the boy—it was their oldest, Ben.

"James Wilson," Bill said, now all detective again. "You have the right to remain silent..."

"Oh, please," James rolled his eyes. "You're not arresting me for cooking, are you?"

"I'm arresting you for murder," Bill said, grabbing for his gun.

Jen closed her eyes, not wanting to watch him shoot James, but the sound that followed was not a gunshot. Instead, she heard a loud clunk. When she opened her eyes, Bill was lying on the floor unconscious—Annette had hit him in the head with a cast iron frying pan.

"Have a seat," Annette said and gestured to the table with the pan.

Jen sloshed through the blood on the floor to the seat at the end of the table. She pulled the chair as far away from the body as she could—if she had to sit there, she didn't want to be close to the body of the boy she should have been able to save.

Annette sat the frying pan on the counter and grabbed a large stew pot from under the cupboard and began chopping the flesh and meat that was lying on a cutting board. It looked to Jen as though she was making some sort of stew. Jen cringed at the thought of eating it, or worse, being in it.

She brought her attention back to Bill, who was still lifeless on the floor, hoping he would wake soon. She hadn't been trained for anything like this. Not that Bill had been, but he surely had far more experience in dangerous situations than she did. What was going on here gave a whole new meaning to the word 'homegrown'.

"Where are the other children?" Jen asked. She didn't really want to bring attention to herself, but she was worried about them.

"Don't you worry, they'll join us soon," Annette answered absently.

Jen sat quietly watching them work. They used every part of the body, obviously trying not to leave any evidence behind. The bones and teeth were put in a grinder and then added to the stew pots cooking on the stove. Annette had a large pot placed on each of the four burners, and two more were sitting on the counter. Every now and then, Jen would see her sample her creation.

"This is going to be so much better than the last batch," Annette told her husband with a smile.

"This one wasn't as well fed—not as much fat this time," James replied, stuffing the last of the meat into large freezer bags.

The way the couple talked about their son made Jen sick again. They sounded like they were talking about an animal they'd caught and butchered, rather than their *child*. She couldn't believe someone could be that callous. After all, Annette had given birth to these children. She, of all people, should feel wretched about what they were doing, but instead, she seemed to be enjoying it.

Bill began stirring on the floor.

"Our guest is waking," James said with a smile. "He'll have to sit patiently—we have cleaning to do."

James and Annette pulled Bill off the floor and sat him in a chair at the table. He was disoriented and had a hard time sitting on his own. James laughed as he pushed Bill back into an upright position.

Once Bill was stable in his chair, the couple began cleaning up their mess. Annette extracted a bottle of bleach from under the sink. James left the room, and when he returned he had a bucket of paint and rollers.

"Clean up time!" Annette yelled, and instantly loud footsteps thudded down the stairs.

With all these people crammed in this little kitchen, it would be easy for us to make our move and escape, Jen thought, wishing she could communicate with Bill, but he still wasn't fully awake. She didn't know exactly what to do, but she was sure the older children would help take their parents down—they had to know they were next.

The children had the kitchen almost done by the time Bill fully regained consciousness; there was no time left to come up with a plan. Jen's heart sank.

"Supper's almost ready," Annette announced. "Set the table."

Two of the girls stopped scrubbing the floor and grabbed dishes out of the cupboard.

They set a bowl, spoon, and glass at every place. Jen eyed the dishes as though they were snakes about to jump up and bite her in the face. She'd never been so afraid of eating in her life. Any other time Jen would say she wasn't hungry, but that wasn't going to work with this family. Unless she came up with something quick, she would have to eat; her stomach churned from the thought of it.

James and the kids took their seats at the table and Annette started dishing out the stew she'd made. The smell wasn't horrible, but Jen gagged as chunks slopped into the bowls.

Jen watched the children's reactions. The younger ones dug right in, clearly not understanding what was going on, but the older ones hesitated.

She could see the fear on their faces. If they didn't eat, they would probably end up as a meal sooner. Jen couldn't blame them for eating. It was the only thing they could do to survive.

"You're going to love this," James said, glancing back and forth between Bill and Jen. "You'll never want anything else once you've had this meat."

"I doubt that," Bill argued, and Jen shot him a disapproving look. She didn't think it was wise of him to provoke someone who obviously had no problem killing people.

James laughed. "We'll see."

"No, we won't," Bill said. "I'm not eating."

Jen was truly frightened now. James was getting irritated–the veins in his forehead bulged. He slammed his spoon down on the table and stood. "You will eat," he said, hovering over Bill.

Annette walked over to the two men and slopped some stew into Bill's bowl with a smile. She seemed untouched by her husband's anger and went about filling the last three bowls—hers, James', and Jen's. "Let's eat," she said, tapping James on the shoulder, but he kept his position over Bill.

Jen looked down at the bowl in front of her–an eyeball was floating on top, looking at her. She gasped and shoved away from the table. Her chair squealed across the floor, bringing James' attention to her.

"What? You don't want to eat either?" he asked.

Jen shook her head 'no'.

"Why don't you sit and enjoy the meal?" Bill said, trying to bring the attention back to himself and off of Jen.

James smiled and nodded toward Annette. In one swift movement, he had Bill in a choke hold and Annette was shoving a spoonful of stew into his mouth. Bill pursed his lips together, but Annette shoved harder–bloody juices from the stew ran down his face and chin.

"Stop!" Jen yelled and instantly regretted it.

The two snapped their heads up toward her. James sprinted around the table, grabbed the eye that was floating in her bowl, and shoved it into her mouth. Jen wasn't strong enough to fight him off, and he got it into her mouth with little effort; he pushed on the bottom of her chin to make her chew. Tears filled her eyes as she gagged on the juice that filled her mouth once the eye popped.

"Now eat," James said and shoved her away from him, knocking her out of the chair.

She looked up at the children she'd landed behind, but they didn't even turn around. "Ah oh," one of the little kids said, but it was the only reaction from the children. Evidently, they had been through this before.

Sobbing, Jen pulled herself back to her feet and sat back down in the chair. Bill shot her an apologetic look, but Jen knew there was nothing he could do.

When everyone was done eating, James ordered the children to their rooms. Jen was thankful he'd let them leave, but she was afraid of what he'd do next. She looked at the clock hanging over the window in front of the sink. It was now 7:30 in the evening. Chris would surely be worried about her by now, and Bill could have someone worried about him, too. Would they come looking for them? The thought frightened her. She didn't want anyone else involved in this mess.

"It's time for bed," James said, motioning for Jen to stand up. "Not you," he added when Bill got to his feet.

Jen followed James down the hallway toward the basement door, hearing a thud behind them as if something heavy had fallen in the kitchen. Fleetingly, Jen thought about Bill, but knew there was nothing she could do to help him. When they reached the door, James pulled a needle out of his pocket. Jen took an automatic step back, but she hadn't counted on Annette being right behind them. A sharp pain filled Jen's side–Annette had shoved another needle into her with all her force.

"You'll sleep great now," Annette laughed.

"Now get moving," James pushed her forward.

Reluctantly, Jen did as she was told and started down the basement steps. As soon as she cleared the doorway, James slammed the door shut— with a click, it was locked.

With tear-filled eyes, Jen made her way to the bottom of the stairs. This was the first time she'd been left alone–she had to use that to her advantage. She scanned the dark area, thinking there had to be something she could use to defend herself.

The medication took effect quicker than Jen had anticipated. Soon, she was lying on the floor unable to move. She felt paralyzed, but she was tired too. Unable to fight it, Jen fell fast asleep.

*　*　*

Groggy from the medication, Jen was pulled to her feet and dragged back up the stairs. She had no idea how much time had passed or what had happened to Bill. All she knew was she was in no shape to fight them. Her head bobbed back and forth, and her legs felt like limp noodles under her; she couldn't run even if she had the chance to.

They placed her in a chair at the table. Bill was still sitting in the same chair, but there was something different about him and Jen's blurred vision wouldn't allow her to see exactly what it was.

"We don't have much time," Annette warned her husband. "Someone will come looking for them soon."

"I know, I know. I'm taking care of it," James replied in a tone that was clearly intended to shut her up.

"Sorry," she muttered.

This time James didn't say anything as he pulled a large grinder from under the cupboard and slammed it down on the counter top.

Jen, still trying to shake off the remaining medication, sat slumped over in her chair. She tried keeping her head up, but she was still too weak. She wanted to yell over to Bill for help, but she couldn't even get her mouth to move; she could only get out a groan every now and then.

"Looks like the kitchen will be getting a new coat of paint again," James laughed.

His loud footsteps made Jen cringe—every step he took amplified as he came closer to the table. Her heart raced and she began shaking violently. Repainting meant they planned on another slaughter in the kitchen. She was sure it was going to be her and there was nothing she could do about it— she couldn't even hold her own head up.

She struggled with the weight of her head and tried to look at Bill—she wanted to get his attention. They were going to have to try something. There was no other option at this point. They could either try and fight, or do nothing and become a meal.

"B…B…Bill," she managed to choke out, but there was no answer— well, not from Bill anyway.

"I'm afraid he can't talk right now," Annette answered for him.

Jen finally forced her head up and squinted to clear some of the blurriness from her vision, and instantly wished she hadn't. Bill was sitting up in the chair with his mouth sewn shut. Jen gasped in horror and let her head fall back to her chest.

"He just wouldn't shut his big mouth when he regained consciousness again," James said. "This is what happens to people who can't mind their own business."

Annette handed him a tray full of utensils, and Jen tried to focus on anything other than what James was doing. She didn't want to watch him mutilate Bill. She would freak out, and now was not the time for that. She needed a plan, and she needed it quick.

Annette paced back and forth across the kitchen while her husband prepared the items on the tray. Jen couldn't believe how nervous the woman was—she had always stayed so calm before. *What's making her so anxious now?* Jen wondered. *Does she know something I don't? Is someone coming?*

Jen tried to think of a way to use Annette's anxiety to her benefit; there had to be a way to make the woman see reason. Obviously if she was that concerned, the woman felt something. If Jen could get her to turn on her husband, then they still had a chance. She was still positive the children would help.

With a small glimmer of hope, Jen raised her head to look at the woman. Annette was too busy pacing to even notice her stare. Jen waited patiently for Annette to glance in her direction. When she finally did, Jen gave her a pleading look.

"Annette," James called to his wife, interrupting the glance the two women shared, "come help me with this."

Annette stopped her pacing at once and hurried to assist her husband. Jen followed Annette to James' side with her eyes—her eyesight was much better and she could see everything more clearly. Bill was worse than she'd originally thought—he was sitting limp with his eyes wide open, staring at her.

The couple picked Bill up, laid him on the table, and began to pull his clothes off. Jen closed her eyes. She didn't want to watch. It would only be a reminder of what they were going to do to her next.

"I'm thinking about a cook-out tonight," James said. "How about grilled burgers?"

"That sounds wonderful. We haven't had those for ages," Annette agreed, her nerves seeming to calm instantly while talking about food.

"Looks like we should be able to get a good meat supply from this guy," James laughed, patting Bill's bare stomach.

"That's good," Annette said, joining in the laughter. "We have a lot of mouths to feed."

James went back to work on Bill's body. Jen could hear a horrible sucking sound as James cut and pulled the muscle away from the bone on Bill's leg. It was the most disgusting noise she'd ever heard, but it wasn't as disturbing as the tears that ran down Bill's cheeks.

"He's alive!" Jen shouted in horror.

Annette jumped, startled by Jen's outburst. "Of course he is. We only gave him something so he couldn't move. James thought he might enjoy seeing how this all works."

"Grinder," James instructed, paying no attention to their conversation.

Annette placed the large grinder on the table in front of Jen, and held it in place while her husband started feeding meat through the opening on the top–James turned the handle with little effort.

As the ground meat came out, Annette scooped it up with her free hand and slopped it into a large bowl. Once it was filled, she took the bowl to the counter, and James continued to butcher Bill, paying no attention to the tears streaming down Bill's face as he worked.

"Stop!" Jen yelled–she couldn't take it anymore. She didn't care if they killed her now, she just wanted it all to stop.

James laughed. "Oh, do his tears bother you?" he asked, pretending to be sympathetic. "I can fix that." In smooth, swift motions, Bill's eyes were plucked from his head. "See. No more tears."

"You're sick!" Jen yelled. "Killing us isn't going to help you. People know we're here," she lied, but that was all she had.

"James..." Annette said anxiously.

Jen could tell what she'd said had bothered her, but James wasn't as concerned as his wife.

"She's lying! Can't you see that?" he asked, waving a knife at his wife. "Don't worry. If someone was coming, they would have been here by now."

Annette put her head down and didn't say another word. She left the kitchen and returned with the children to start clean up. James shot her a disgusted look, but he didn't argue. In an odd way, the children in the kitchen, cleaning, made Jen feel better. If they were cleaning, it meant she wasn't going to die yet. There was still time for a plan.

"Don't miss anything," James instructed, pulling Jen to her feet. "And when you're done, come outside."

Once outside, Jen noticed something she had paid no attention to before—corn fields. The house was surrounded by them. She'd heard stories of children getting lost in corn fields. Even with a team of volunteers, it took hours to find them. If she got into one of the fields, there was no way James and Annette would be able to find her.

"Sit here," James said, pushing her down at the picnic table, "and don't try anything funny." He waved a finger at her like he was scolding a child.

Watching the couple carefully, Jen planned her escape. She looked around nonchalantly every couple of minutes trying to find the closest route to the field. There was no doubt in her mind James was faster than she was—her only chance was to become invisible in the fields.

In a matter of seconds, Jen had her plan and was ready to go—she just needed the couple to move out of her way. They were standing right next to the picnic table, seasoning the meat they were going to grill, and there was no chance of her making it past them if they stood there the entire time. At some point they would have to put the food on the grill; Jen would just have to wait until they did.

"Grills ready," James said, and Annette instantly carried the plate of hamburgers over to him.

Trembling with fear, Jen kept reminding herself this was her only chance and she couldn't blow it. She leaped off her seat and darted for the closest field.

"Hey!" James shouted, and burst into a full sprint after her.

Jen could hear his footsteps behind her, but they were a good distance away still. Pushing the corn out of her way, Jen used the sun to guide her in the right direction. It was all she had to keep her from getting lost and winding up back at the Wilson house.

"Children!" Annette bellowed, and the screen door creaked and loud thudding footsteps tromped down the stairs.

Jen knew they were all after her now, but she had a good head start on them. If she could keep up her pace and go in the right direction, she would make it to town in no time. *I just have to make it to town*, she told herself over and over. *They won't dare try anything in town.*

Ignoring the burning in her legs, Jen pushed herself harder; the fear of being caught was far worse than the pain. It would be very unpleasant, to say the least, if they caught her now. She had just pissed James off and he was not a forgiving man. He would probably cut her legs off and feed them to her as punishment.

A loud roaring sound vibrated through the air and shook the ground, making Jen flinch with dread. They'd decided to come after her in their old, beat up truck, and they weren't taking the roads.

Corn stalks snapped as the truck plowed them over. It was getting closer behind her; the truck protested as the driver forced it faster.

Jen leaped to the side just as the truck flew past. The truck's brakes squealed in protest as it was forced to a stop. The engine revved—they were turning around. James wasn't worried about making her a meal anymore, he just wanted her dead.

The old truck continued to fly past her over and over again; Jen only made it out of the way by seconds each time as she was forced farther and farther in the wrong direction. She was getting deeper into the middle of the field, because she hadn't counted on James destroying his own crops to catch her.

Trying to dodge out of the way, Jen changed her direction. She knew it was going to put her right in the path of the truck, but it was the direction she needed to go. The neighbor's field wasn't far, and thanks to James thinning his field, she could see the road.

Taking in a deep breath, Jen darted in front of the truck, but she wasn't fast enough. The truck nicked her foot, sending her face first into the dirt. Trying to control her screams, Jen pulled herself off the ground. There was no time to stop now—not with the road that close.

The truck tires spun in the dirt as the driver floored it and she could hear the mud hit the corn stalks that were left standing, which wasn't many.

She struggled on her foot—fighting the pain—until she finally reached a road and burst into tears, because she'd made it out of their field. She was sure James wasn't stupid enough to drive through someone else's field to find her because it would bring the cops for destruction of property and they couldn't afford to bring that kind of attention to themselves now.

In the cover of the new corn field, Jen dragged her foot behind her, making her way to the next road. It was so close, but it was taking forever; the throbbing in her foot was slowing her down.

Pushing herself harder, Jen heard the sound of corn stalks snapping again and slowed to listen more carefully. The sound of the truck was gone, so someone was following her on foot—her heart raced when she realized they were as invisible as she was.

Trying to force that thought from her mind, Jen hobbled faster. Her foot was numbing, and she was picking up more speed by the time she reached the next road. Without hesitation, she darted across it and into the last field she'd have to get through before reaching the city limits.

The sound of corn shuffling got louder and louder. Whoever it was, was right behind her—she didn't turn around.

When Jen reached the beginning of street lights leading into town, she turned to see James standing at the edge of the field watching her. He only hesitated for a moment before disappearing back into the corn stalks.

Jen made her way down the streets of town toward the police station, pushing people out of her way as she went. Most of them yelled out to her, but Jen ignored them and kept pushing forward. No one but the police could help her now.

She reached the police station just as the sun had completely disappeared, and she started sobbing. The tears fell uncontrollably–her foot ached and her body became weak, and she felt like she was going to faint any second.

With the last bit of energy Jen had, she hobbled up to the front desk where a young officer was sitting; he looked horrified when he saw her. Jen knew exactly what he was thinking that—she'd been raped.

The officer hopped to his feet and offered her support, which she gladly took and sat down in a chair–he sat next to her.

"What happened to you?" he asked in a gentle tone.

Jen could hardly talk, but she fought back sobs and began her story. "I'm Jennifer Blake," she started. "I'm a social worker. I was out on a case with Detective Bill Murphy..." Jen went on to tell him all the horrific events that followed.

The young detective was beside himself because he didn't know what to do, so he went to get help. He knew Bill hadn't shown up for work, but nobody was concerned. They all assumed he was out working on a case and didn't need to come in for anything.

An older officer came to assist. "Come with me," he said, helping Jen to her feet.

Once inside his office, she started over, telling the new officer everything. He waited patiently as she cried hysterically. When she finished, he called an ambulance for her.

"If I have any more questions, I'll contact you," he said, grabbing his gun and radio.

The young officer at the desk was ordered to keep an eye on her while the others went out on the case.

Ten officers went to the Wilson house, and when they arrived Bill's cruiser was still in the driveway–they hadn't even finished cleaning the kitchen from his slaughter. And the only thing missing in the investigation was the Wilson family.

CASA SUSTANTIVO

BRIAN J. SMITH

1887

The horse gave an exhausted sigh as it lunged forward—its left leg snapping like a carrot. Tom and Wayne Fullerton leapt off, hit the ground, and rolled out of its path—nearly swallowed by the ball of dust growing around it. Once the dust settled, they brushed the dirt from their clothes and stared around the wide, brown desert. The horse lay on its side, kicking and clawing at the ground to regain its balance; Wayne slipped his Peacemaker from his holster and finished off the horse. Tom jumped at the sound, flipped his Navy Colt .45 from his holster and scanned the desert for hidden snipers.

When he realized Wayne had pulled the trigger, Tom tucked his pistol away and said, "'Bout you tell me next time you do that, cuz?"

"I'm sure the horse feels the same way, Tommy Boy."

"I told you about..."

"I know, I know," Wayne said, flapping his palm in the air to silence him. "You

don't like it when I call you that."

"My daddy kept calling me that and it still gets on my nerves."

"Do you have the satchel?"

"Right here," Tom said, slapping the scarred brown satchel resting against his hip. "You think I'd leave all that gold behind?"

"Stolen gold, remember?"

"I wonder when they'll find that stagecoach we left behind."

"You heard the guy. He said it's a two day ride before they would find them, and by the time that happens..."

"We'll be long gone."

"Hell yeah!" Wayne said as they trotted away from the dead horse, their spurs jangling in rhythm with the gold in the satchel.

The sun was sinking on the horizon, painting the sky with a vibrant layer of multicolored twilight. Cactus and sagebrush shadows bled across the desert like stretched oil stains, while a warm breeze cut across the landscape from the west, tousling their jackets.

"Hey, cuz," Tom said, feeling the satchel rubbing against his right hip. "It's colder than a witch's tit in a brass bra."

"It sure is."

"Can we set up camp now?"

"We can't. They'd know we were here and where we were going."

"What the hell is that?" Tom asked, pointing to a red-orange orb glowing in the distance.

"Let's go see," Wayne replied, walking around Tom.

Tom shifted the satchel from his right hip to his left and followed Wayne toward the light. The closer they got the bigger the light grew and began to flicker and dance like a thousand candles. When they peered over the tall, sandy incline, they saw an old Mexican army fort sitting in the midst of a barren wasteland nearly darkened by the approach of dusk. A necklace of long brown torches flashed in the night and embraced the building in a jittery red-orange halo. Spanish tiles made up the roof of an old guard's tower—a larger room that sat off to the right beside of a large open area bordered by a high stucco wall.

"What the hell is that?"

"Looks like," Wayne said, squinting his eyes for a better look, "a damn cantina."

"Then what the hell are we waiting for?" Tom asked excitedly.

If there was one thing Tom and Wayne had in common, it was that they'd always fought as kids. One would give just as much as the other, but it would take the adults to tear them apart. It wasn't until after they'd snatched a bag of assorted gum drops and jelly beans from a store in Dodge City that they'd thought they were fit for a life of crime; they'd traded their Nebraska farming days for pilfering and cattle-napping. On their wanted posters, which were spread out from Phoenix to Abilene, Tom was on the left with the clean-shaven head, blue eyes, and broad shoulders, and Wayne was on the opposite side, baring a mad-dog growl, heavy cheeks, short dark hair, and green eyes.

Their first job in Flagstaff got them a reward value of a thousand dollars. Three years later it was increased to a staggering twenty-five thousand.

They followed the edge of the incline until they came to a winding dirt trail leading straight to the fort. A finger-shaped wooden sign pointed at the building like a tour guide; it was covered in the colors of a Mexican flag with the words **CASA SUSTANTIVO** stamped on the front in black block letters. They passed the sign and followed the rest of the trail to the fort's gate. A squat, bald man in gray pants, black boots, white blouse, and a ten-gallon hat stood between them and the wooden door beside the large barred gate.

"Can I help you?"

"We'd like to go inside."

"I don't think so," the doorman replied, placing his hand on Tom's chest. "Your kind isn't even…"

Something rattled from beyond the door; hypnotic blue eyes peeked out at them from a square peephole before they disappeared and the door opened. A beautiful senorita in a billowy white dress, hugged by a roller coaster of red and green hills, stepped out. Her crescent-shaped smile radiated in the moonlight, her elegant dark hair was tied to the back of her head by a walnut brown clip, and her skin had a brown tint that made Tom think of beautiful sunsets. She was more gorgeous than Peggy Ladson, the daughter of his daddy's best friend. He didn't know what had happened to her after he'd left town, but that wasn't important right now—this woman was.

"Luis," the senorita purred. "What's going on?"

"They wanted in, but they don't have passes."

"I think we can make an exception," she said with a wink, watching Tom blowing hot air into his cold, cupped hands. "Besides, the sun is setting and it gets cold out here. We can't leave them to freeze."

"Look, if we can just get a room for tonight," Wayne implored, "we'll be out of here by sunrise."

"That's okay. The rule here in Casa Sustantivo is that no one gets left behind."

"I still don't like them," Luis growled with a shield of sweat beads glistening off his forehead and brow.

"Come on, gentlemen," she said, taking Tom's hand with another wink. "You can come on in. Everyone is welcome at Casa Sustantivo especially you, senor."

She led them down a short corridor as the door shut behind them with an angry thud. After they left the corridor, they passed six open archways leading out onto a wide, sandy courtyard to the right. Three wooden doors stood along the opposite wall, but only two of them were marked by the same black block letters they'd seen on the sign. **ROOMS** was posted above the first door, and the words **GEN. QUARTERS** was posted above the door at the end of the hallway. In the courtyard, three long, wooden tables with matching bench seats, filled with rowdy people, sat three feet apart. The tables were decked out with elegant dinnerware, and on the far left side of the courtyard a bonfire threw a twitching red-orange light across the ground and up along the walls.

"Looks like you've got a good one going on here," Wayne commented, motioning to the activity.

"It's the anniversary of the death of General Escobar's family," she said. "Every year on this exact date, he honors their memory by holding a great feast."

"Could we be shown to our room?" Tom asked, itching to get changed and join in the fun.

"Right this way."

She led them through the door marked **ROOMS** and left the crowd, and the noise, behind. They followed a long dark-and-light stucco corridor, past oaken doors with black iron numbers before turning right. She stopped at the end of the corridor, slipped a key from the front of her dress, and opened the door to room number 17; a Mexican pronunciation of the same number was below it.

"Here's your room, gentlemen," she said. "Don't worry about locking your door at night, it's a service we provide free of charge. The room is two schillings a night."

Wayne gave Tom a slight nod. Tom opened the satchel, flipped a gold coin into the air, caught it in his left hand, and dropped it slowly into her waiting palm. When their fingers touched, a blanket of gooseflesh sheathed his arm and the hairs on the back of his neck stood up.

"That's for you, senorita."

Smiling, she said, "Just call me Rita."

"Will do," Tom said, as both parties went their separate ways.

As Wayne fell onto the bed, resting his head on the pillow, he said, "Somebody wants your ass on a platter, cuz."

"I don't think she'll bother with the platter," Tom said with a laugh, setting the satchel at the foot of the other bed. "We going to that little shindig outside?"

"You bet."

"Let's get ready, then."

Wayne shed his jacket and replaced his dirty blue shirt with a white shirt that had ruffles around the wrists; Tom traded his dirty white shirt for a maroon silk shirt he'd bought in Paris two years before. Dressed and refreshed, they left the room and walked out to the courtyard. The three tables were almost completely occupied; two Mexican guards were posted by the **GEN. QUARTERS** door, six were pacing the courtyard, and two more were posted on each side of the main corridor. A trio of mariachis roamed the tables, strumming their guitars while singing sweet Mexican songs.

"The tables are getting..."

"'Cuse me, senor," a heavyset Mexican soldier said, placing his hand on Tom's shoulder. "You need to give me your guns."

"What?" Wayne asked, peering around his cousin's shoulder.

"You need to hand over your guns until after the fiesta."

"That's okay, we can handle our drink—we'll keep our guns."

"The General asks that you do so," the soldier said sternly, taking his hand off Tom's shoulder. "It's required of all the guests."

Sighing, they unbuckled their holsters and reluctantly lay them in the soldier's hands. He thanked them, smiled, and walked away. They stepped through the open archway and scanned the courtyard. People were dancing, laughing, and drinking or sitting at a table, deep in private conversations; the smell of wood smoke, tobacco, liquor, and coffee was thick in the air.

"Is this a fiesta or what?" Tom asked, baring a mischievous smile.

"Hi, guys."

Two women in brown leather vests, matching pants, and dirty brown boots, waved at them. The one on the right was stocky with boyish cut dark hair, brown eyes, and beige skin; her partner had shoulder-length russet brown hair, green eyes, and pale skin. They both had muscular arms, flat stomachs, and stunning-white smiles. Wayne waved at the brunette and led Tom to a wooden kiosk between the bonfire and the left corner of the wall. They bought a cup of coffee from an old, scarred senorita, took a sip, and thanked her in their best Spanish.

Tom made eye contact with Rita and waved her over; she wiped something red from her mouth with the back of her hand as she headed in his direction.

"Hi, handsome," she purred.

"Hello, Rita. Too much lipstick?" Tom teased and then kissed her left palm. "You look beautiful."

She wore a red, green, and white billowy dress like the one they'd seen her in earlier. Her hair fell down to the middle of her back and draped evenly across the tops of her shoulders.

"Shall we go over by the bonfire to warm..."

A loud choir of bugles shot rang out across the patio, drawing everybody's attention. The same heavyset Mexican who'd took their guns away parted the line of bugle players and stood in front of them. The **GEN. QUARTERS** door opened but the bugle players blocked everybody's view of who was coming out.

"Thank you all for coming tonight. I'll now turn you over to our gracious host, General Philippe Escobar."

The heavyset Mexican stepped aside for a middle-aged man with short, salt-and-pepper hair, scarred tan skin, and bright blue eyes. His hands were large and weathered, his mouth had a soft pink tint, and his posture was military perfect. Two more soldiers, both big enough to lift a cow, flanked the General. The one on the left was bald and the other had long black hair and a cleft chin.

"Thank you, Reynaldo," the General said, patting the heavyset Mexican's shoulder before turning to face the crowd. "Thank you, everybody. This is a night that I'll never forget. Tonight commemorates the death of a great and wonderful woman. A woman I'd taken into my arms from sunrise to sunset and loved with all of my heart. But tonight is also a celebration of mi familia's passing, and if it was one thing they prided themselves on it was plenty of food and laughs. So eat up!"

When the General finished, the coffee lady leapt out of her kiosk and tackled an old woman to the ground. She clamped her teeth onto the other woman's throat and pulled her head back to stare up at the sky—her lips red with blood as she chewed on the flesh she'd torn off. By the bonfire, Rita slipped a small, curved dagger from the front of her dress and lunged at Tom; he dodged out of her path and stumbled to the ground ass-first. He scrambled to his feet just as Rita swung the knife at his stomach in a whistling arc–his hands bracing the wall with white knuckles. Screams of the fallen pierced the night, rising and falling, rising and falling.

Wayne reached for his gun and cursed under his breath when he realized it wasn't there. Something collided with the back of his head, throwing splinters everywhere and knocking him to the ground; he rolled onto his back to see the heavyset mariachi standing over him, eyes wide, baring a pink-white grin.

"Dinner's served, hombre," the mariachi said, raising the severed guitar bridge in both hands.

Wayne pulled his foot back and kicked the mariachi in the stomach, throwing him backwards across the patio. When he sat up–fists poised and ready–the party had turned into a playground in Hell. The remaining mariachis tackled a tall cowboy to the ground and tugged on his arms and legs until they snapped off, spraying blood everywhere. People were being dragged down, their necks, cheeks, legs, and thighs gnawed by the Mexican waitresses clamped onto their backs. As the mariachis fed on the arms and legs of their first victim, Reynaldo jumped over a table, tore an old woman's ears from her head and chewed them like tobacco while he forced her down on a nearby table where he gutted her and pulled out her intestines like a magician plucking colored scarves from his hand.

One of the General's guards shoved a wounded woman back onto the patio and into the hands of the ravenous mariachis who tore at her clothes and skin. The General's long haired guard joined the crowd. He slipped a long Bowie knife from the sheath at his hip and sliced an old man's throat, staining his shirt with blood.

Tom dodged another swipe of Rita's knife, spun to the left and tripped her, sending her into the bonfire. He ran across the courtyard, ducking away from other fights and pulled Wayne to his feet. The coffee lady jumped onto Tom's back and filled his ear with animal-like grunts–her hungry mouth openly poised over his neck. Wayne spun on his right foot, swung a hard left and clocked her in the jaw, knocking her to the ground.

"What the hell is going on here?" Wayne asked.

"Beats me, cuz," Tom said, sweat sliding down his face. "I had to kick a beautiful woman into the fire."

He peered down the courtyard, watching Rita's body burn. Her screams of agony were drowned out by the others, but he could see her brown skin as it bubbled, blistered, and turned black.

"Hey, guys!" Someone yelled, getting their attention.

The two short-haired girls waved them over. The dark-haired girl punched a mariachi in the mouth, knocking him against the wall, causing him to bite his tongue and spill blood down the front of his shirt.

Instead of asking them if they were okay–since the dark-haired girl could take care of herself–Wayne hollered, "Let's get the hell out of here!"

Tom and Wayne took one step before something struck their legs, sending them to the ground on their chests. They were rolled over onto their backs, only to stare up at Luis and Reynaldo's blackened teeth and fetid breath. Luis held a severed bone in his hand like a knife and Reynaldo wielded a blunt wooden instrument with a nail sticking out through the top of it. Tom gripped a ball of sand in his left fist while Wayne raised up on his elbows.

"Maybe you should've listened to me when I said you couldn't come in," Luis laughed.

"Less talkin'," Reynaldo said, "more eating."

When Reynaldo raised the club, the raven-haired girl leapt off the nearby table, spun like top, and kicked him in the face. The club flipped through the air for a second before the dark-haired girl caught it in her left hand and planted the nail into his right eye and tugged on the club, snapping his neck.

Tom threw the ball of sand into Luis's face, blinding him instantly. Wayne kicked the bone out of his hand, drove his boot heel into Luis' groin and rammed a fork into the Mexican's throat as he stood. Tom could see out of the cover of his eye that Rita's arms and legs had stopped kicking and she was finally dead.

"Let's go," Tom said, pulling on the russet-haired girl's left hand.

The four of them ran through the chaos, through a nearby archway, and down the main hall toward the front door. Wayne and the dark-haired girl pushed on the door and the gate, but they wouldn't budge.

"Son of a bitch!" the raven-haired girl screamed. "They shut us in from the outside."

"How do we get out?" Tom asked frantically. "What do we do now?"

"We fight these bastards," the russet-haired girl replied, marching back down the corridor.

They jogged back down the main corridor and stopped dead in their tracks when they saw that General Escobar was sitting at the head of the nearest table, munching on a giant brown foot. The screaming had stopped but the carnage hadn't–bodies either crawled with their last breath or were flanked by their ravenous attackers. Puddles of blood glinted in the moonlight while severed limbs and heads were strewn about like litter. The General's dark-haired bodyguard stood by the bonfire, watching solemnly as Rita continued to burn.

"Don't move," the russet-haired girl whispered. "They can't see us."

They carefully crept down the hallway; the remaining seven cannibals were spaced out at different areas and tables, gnawing on the body part of their choice.

"Hey, Javier," the General's bald bodyguard said to his dark-haired co-hort still standing by the fire. "Cat got your tongue?"

A chorus of laughter erupted from the tables. Javier turned his attention to the laughter, his jaw tight with anger.

"That punta killed my wife," Javier said, slipping his knife from his hip. "And if you don't shut your mouth, Hector, I'll put your ass..."

"At ease, soldier," Escobar said, then plucked a toe from the foot with his teeth and continued, "just sit down and eat something before the others get out here."

"Don't you mean 'someone'?" Hector asked, smirking.

After he laughed, General Escobar held the half-gnawed foot in one hand and a pale foot in the other and asked, "What do you prefer, Javier? White meat or dark meat?"

Another chorus of laughter exploded across the courtyard. Tom stepped around Wayne and tripped over the raven-haired girl's foot. He fell face first and hit the ground, his spurs scratching the ground. The remaining seven stared over at them. Tom and the girls stared at them like trapped mice. Javier pointed his knife at Tom and the others stood up from their tables.

"They're still alive," Hector said, running toward Tom.

"Get him!" Javier yelled. "He killed my Rita!"

Tom clambered to his feet and followed the others down the hallway before Hector could touch him. Something flipped through the air and scratched his right cheek, but he kept pace with his comrades. Wayne threw the **ROOMS** door open, hurried them inside, and shut it behind them; a sharp curved tomahawk broke through the door, spraying splinters everywhere just as the door closed.

"Where are we going?"

"Our room," Tom said, leading everyone to room seventeen.

When they got into the room, the raven-haired girl dragged the trunk from the foot of Tom's bed–she tipped it over onto its left side and wedged it under the doorknob.

"That should keep them out," she said, placing her hands on her hips.

"Let's hope so," Wayne said, then pointed at the girl and asked. "What's your name, darling?"

"It's Harley-Jane–not darling," she said, then pointed a thumb at her raven-haired partner. "This is my sister Peaches."

"My name's Wayne and that's my cousin Tom."

"Nice to meet you both," Peaches said. "How about you tell us how we plan on getting out of here in one piece."

"That's gonna take some time since we don't have any guns."

"Guns?"

"We had pistols when we came in, but they made us give them up."

Something leapt through the open window, letting out an animal-like grunt; the old lady who ran the coffee kiosk was hanging onto the window pane, swinging an axe at them. Peaches spun away from the window to avoid getting hit and slid something out of her left pocket and flipped it across the room–it winked in the dim amber glow of the lanterns above the bedside table. The cross-handled-stainless-steel-knife caught the old woman in the neck; blood sprayed the window pane and cascaded down the wall.

Grabbing the axe from the dead woman's limp grasp, Harley-Jane said, "Bye, bitch."

She kicked the woman in the face and sent her tumbling away from the open window and into the night. Peaches and Wayne stripped the first bed while Harley-Jane and Tom moved the bedside table and the lantern. They shoved the bed frame against the window, blocking out their view of the woman still dying outside, and Peaches pushed the other trunk and the bedside table against the barrier for support.

"If we could only get to our weapons," Tom said, "we could take these bastards out."

"That's easier said than done."

"I saw them put our weapons in that other room," Harley-Jane replied, putting her hand to her forehead.

"The one marked 'General's Quarters'?"

"No, the other one–the one that isn't marked," she said, nodding her head.

"Do you know they're really there or do you think they're there?"

"What's that supposed to mean?" Peaches asked, walking toward Tom, her hands balled into tight fists.

Standing up to meet her, Tom said, "All I'm saying is that we don't know for sure. What if we open that door and there's more of those cannibal bastards in there just waiting to come out?"

Pushing them apart, Wayne said, "We're not gonna know unless we actually open it, now do we?"

"True," Harley-Jane said from the other side of the room. "But like Wayne said, we need to stick together if we plan on getting out of here."

"How do we fight them off?" Peaches asked.

"We're gonna have to find something to use as weapons and get to that room."

Harley-Jane screamed *hi-ya* and shattered the mirror on the wall above a small wash basin with a well-aimed side kick—it broke into three pieces and fell into the wash basin below. She slipped her knife out of her boot, snapped one of the bedpost from the bed-barrier, and dug a hole inside the top. A minute later, she picked up a piece of glass and stuck it into the notch, then tied it in place with a red scarf and held it in her left hand.

"I'm ready," she said. "Are you?"

"How did you do that?" Tom inquired.

Rolling her eyes and smirking, she asked, "Want one?"

"If you don't mind."

After Harley-Jane fashioned the same weapon for Tom using Peaches' dark blue bandana, they stood in front of the door; Peaches held the axe in her left hand, Harley-Jane and Tom wielded their mirrored clubs. Wayne suddenly realized he was empty handed and he looked around to see what he could find, but didn't see anything he could use.

"You want..."

"I'm cool," he said to Harley-Jane. "I just want to get my guns and play 'Oh Susanna' with these bastards."

"You gonna go barehanded?"

"My daddy taught me how to fight fair and if I go down..."

"Then what?" Tom asked, shocked by what Wayne had said.

Thinking about the right answer, Wayne said, "Then I guess I go down."

"You haven't lost a fight since that time I kicked your ass in Grandpa's..."

"You didn't win that fight," Wayne said. "If I remember right, I broke your..."

"The only thing you broke was..."

"How about the both of you just shut up," Peaches said, holding up her hand, fingers spaced wide apart. "Let's get out there and kick some *sustantivo* ass."

Wayne removed the trunk from under the door and stepped out into the main hallway with Peaches by his side. Tom and Harley-Jane followed–their mirrored clubs held in their white-knuckled hands. They crept down the hallway toward the courtyard; something inside the hotel room they'd just exited fell to the floor with a catastrophic crash.

"What the hell was that?" Tom asked.

"The bed must've fallen over," Peaches said.

"They got inside," Harley said. "Shit, Tom. Put your backs to us and cover the rear in case they try to jump us from behind."

Tom did as he asked and put his back against Peaches'; his mirrored club winked under the lantern's brass-amber glow.

"We're almost there," Peaches whispered. "What's our plan?"

Wayne tried to pry the tomahawk from the door but it was lodged in too tightly. He cursed under his breath, snatched a lantern off the wall, held it behind his back, and opened the door. Hector and Javier were standing between them and the courtyard, flanked by the remaining five men. Javier swung his knife in front of his face in a strange hypnotic dance, letting the moonlight wink off the blade.

"I'm gonna kill you, puntas," Javier said. "But I'm gonna kill him first." He pointed the tip of his blade at Tom. "You killed my wife, you bastard."

"Just go peacefully," Hector replied, "and we'll make it quick."

"Try me, you little son of a bitch," Wayne snarled.

The closer they got to the courtyard, the farther the cannibals backed up, creating a ring around the four survivors. General Escobar stood in the middle of the courtyard with his arms crossed across his chest.

"You're outnumbered," Escobar said. "Give up now while you still can."

"Not yet."

"You should give cannibalism a chance–it's not so bad after the first time," Escobar said, then shrugged his shoulders. "After a bunch of Confederate soldiers found me and my family, they left me out in the desert with the dead bodies of my loved ones. I had to do whatever I could to survive, so I ate them. Ever since then I've never asked for anything else but a nice, fat slab of human flesh."

"I'm a vegetarian," Harley-Jane snapped. "No, thanks."

"Too bad."

"For you it is," Wayne said and tossed the lantern through the open archway.

The lantern flipped through the air and struck Escobar in the face with a violent mist of sharp glass and fire. The flames caught his clothes and crawled up his arms, neck, and hair; smoke drifted from his shoulders and he threw himself to the ground. Peaches swung the axe, hacked off the right arm of a nearby cannibal and kicked him across the courtyard, sprinkling blood everywhere. Harley-Jane and Tom jabbed at the air with their mirrored clubs, hitting other cannibals in the face, neck, and chest. Wayne ran around Hector's well-aimed jab, came back with a left jab and knocked him into the **GEN. QUARTERS** door. Harley-Jane spun on her left foot, swung her club in a downward motion, and sliced the chest of a skinny Mexican, pushing him backward into the courtyard. Escobar rolled back and forth, still attempting to put out the flames. Javier swung his knife at Tom's face, but the blade whistled past him; Tom kicked him against a pillar, pulled the mirrored club back with both hands, and rammed it into Javier's chest—his blood painted the wall as he slid to the floor. Wayne kicked down the unmarked door and walked in, marveling at the shelves of ammo and guns on racks affixed to the walls. He grabbed two bolt-action rifles and his and Tom's holsters, while shoving bullets into his front pockets. Harley-Jane, Peaches, and Tom scampered into the room and closed the door behind them.

"What the hell happened?" Wayne asked.

"Escobar put out the flames and three more of them came out from the main hallway."

"Get everything?" Tom asked.

"Everything," Wayne said with a nod and jabbed his thumb at the back of the room. "They got a fuckin' arsenal. Everybody okay?"

"Not all of us."

"What's the matter, Tom?"

Tom pulled his shirt open to reveal the left side of his stomach—a long splinter jutted out of a deep wound. Harley-Jane and Peaches gasped.

"How did that happen?"

"When the tomahawk hit the door this splinter hit me."

"Why didn't you say anything?" Wayne asked.

"I tried to pull it out, but that little bastard's in there too deep—if I pull it out, I'm a goner."

"You're bleeding to death."

"That's why you're getting the hell out of here."

"I'm not leaving you behind, Tommy."

"Yes, you are. I've got a plan," Tom said and pointed to the back of the room.

Looking back at his cousin, Wayne asked, "You sure you want to do this?"

"It's your only chance of survival, just leave me one of these lanterns."

Wiping a tear from his face with the back of his hand, Wayne said, "Your mother's gonna..."

"She isn't gonna say anything," Tom said. "Go now!"

Harley-Jane and Peaches hugged Tom, murmured sweet apologies in his ear, and fed their rifles, then filled their pockets with more bullets. Wayne strapped on his holster–his Peacemaker was on the left and Tom's Navy Colt was on his right.

"Ready?"

"Go!" Wayne yelled, flipping the pistols out of their holsters.

Harley-Jane kicked the door open, fired, and struck Hector in the chest, blowing him across the open hallway. Peaches came out swinging, knocking a cannibal to the ground with the stock of her rifle before mashing his throat with her boot. Wayne raised his pistols and walked out of the room, ready to fire, when a charred-black arm knocked them out of his hands. General Escobar kicked the door, grabbed Wayne by the front of his shirt, and tossed him down the hallway. Arms stretched out in front of him, he slid across the hallway and hit the open door.

"This is my world, you little bastard," Escobar snarled angrily, stomping toward him, "and you're just gonna have to live with it."

"No, thanks," Wayne said and kicked the door.

It hit Escobar in the face as Wayne got to his feet. He opened the door again–the tomahawk was embedded in the General's forehead, holding him against the door. He heard movement to his left as six more cannibals came pouring out of the other rooms. They wore nothing but animal furs and were baring their teeth in black, canine grins; they had pointed pale ears and jagged chins. *'Just sit down and get something to eat before the others get out here.'* echoed through Wayne's head. *That's what he meant*, he thought, *when he said that to Javier.*

He ran down the hall, his boots stomping hard across the floor. He retrieved his guns from the floor, flipped them on his fingers, and fired, cutting two more cannibals down.

"Let's get going," Wayne hollered, crossing the courtyard. "Cover me!"

He dragged one of the tables to the other end of the courtyard, waved the girls over to him, and helped them onto the wall. Peaches knelt on top of the wall, aimed her rifle, and fired, cutting down two more.

"Get the hell out of here!" Tom yelled, holding the door open.

From where he stood, Wayne could already see the color draining out of his cousin's face—blood ran freely down Tom's leg, pooling around his feet.

"Come on, let's go," Wayne said, pulling Harley-Jane over the wall. "Come on, Peaches."

He and Peaches jumped over, landed on their feet, and ran as fast as they could into the dark-choked desert. In the courtyard, Tom held the door open, letting the scent of blood draw his attackers close in around him. He backed up into the room, holding the lantern in both hands. Stumbling, he fell on top of a large wooden crate and raised his hands above his head. The pale-faced, pointy-eared cannibals closed in; the one closest to him grabbed his ankle and bit down, spraying blood across the floor.

"I'm coming home, Daddy," Tom said and tossed the lantern into the back of the room, amongst the crates marked **DYNAMITE**.

Running away, Wayne wiped another tear from his eye just as Casa Sustantivo lit up the night in a giant ball of red-orange flames.

A REAL TREAT

JIM BRONYAUR

All Ally wanted was a map. There should have been some in the trunk of the car—that's where her father had put them four years ago when she'd gotten her license and bought the car. They weren't there. There was a gallon of water, so old the label was faded, a small grey box with jumper cables and other items for an *'oh shit'* moment, including three blankets, a pair of winter gloves, and her favorite winter hat—the brown one with the yellow and orange stripes and the poof-like ball sewn on top—but no maps.

"Who would steal maps?" she asked herself slamming the trunk.

Through the back window and windshield she could see the outline of Bobby as he lay on the hood of the car. His hands were behind his head in a jock-like '*I rule the world*' fashion and his left foot tapped to some song that wasn't playing anywhere but in his mind.

"Bobby," she growled. "Son of a bitch!"

"Where's the map?" Chrissy asked, walking toward Ally. She'd needed to use the bathroom, and being stuck on what a broken post claimed was **ETERS HIGHWAY**, she knew holding it would do no good.

Ally thought a woman squatting in a patch of woods and doing her business was a little gross. It reminded her of when she was a kid and Bobby had told her that only boys could pee in the woods because a spider or snake might crawl up in a girl and lay eggs and then the girl would turn into a mother spider or snake and eat everyone. She hated spiders and snakes so she never peed in the woods just in case Bobby was right.

She hated him for that, among a thousand other things.

"Hey, you okay?"

Ally looked at Chrissy and smiled. "If we drove away with him on the hood, how long would he stay there? A minute, if that?"

Chrissy shook her head smiling.

"I'm serious. He took my maps. We're officially lost!"

"He took your maps? Why?"

"Ask him."

Chrissy looked at Bobby and frowned. She'd had a crush on Bobby since she met him ten years ago. She'd been ten and since Bobby was then twelve, there wasn't much of a chance at the marriage Chrissy had dreamed of. But the crush was still there, even though it somewhat faded, usually when Bobby talked.

"I'm serious—let's leave him here."

"Stop it," Chrissy said as she walked toward the front of the car. "Bobby?"

"Hey puss-face," Bobby said, smiling. Chrissy had a bout of acne in her first year of high school and since was called 'puss-face'.

"Don't call her that," Ally snapped, stepping up next to Chrissy. "Where're my maps?"

Bobby waved his hands, "Maps. Who needs maps?"

"We do!" Ally shouted. "We're lost!"

Bobby sat up and let his feet dangle off the side of the car and put his hands down, flexing his non muscles. "Come on, we're on a road trip—no maps. We get lost, oh well. Let's get un-lost–drive this road out. Who knows what we might find, right?"

"I wanted to be in Ohio by dark," Ally said. "We're supposed to be in Wisconsin by tomorrow night…before Uncle Jackie…"

"Kicks it?" Bobby asked with a mocking sneer.

"That's mean," Chrissy said.

"What? That our drunk, burn out of an uncle got into a car and crashed into a pole? That they're going to pull the plug on him? That after twenty-two years of living, he actually gives a shit about us?"

"Stop it," Ally said.

"What? Tell me I'm not right…"

"Just stop."

"Okay, okay," Bobby said, putting his hands up. "All I know is that I was in Philly with my friends and then you swing by with your friggin' maps telling me we have to get to Wisconsin."

"So you took the maps?" Ally asked.

"They're safe in a trash can on Market Street. Wanna go get 'em?" Bobby flashed an evil grin, filling Ally with rage. It was the same look he used to have when he'd twist the heads off her dolls or Godzilla-like attacked her tea parties.

"You know what, Bobby? You're an asshole! Mom wants us all out there and you have to find a way to mess it up."

Bobby pretended to cry.

Ally lunged at him.

Chrissy stepped in between the two siblings before any punches were thrown.

"Okay, everyone calm down, just calm down. Bobby, go take a walk, please."

Bobby slid off the car with a shrug. "Later," he said and walked away with a cocky strut.

"Ally, calm down for a second," Chrissy said.

Ally nodded–this was exactly why she insisted Chrissy come on the trip. She knew Bobby was going to be a pain. Not to mention Chrissy was like her sister. She had no father and her mother had a drinking problem that lingered so she spent her childhood between her aunt's and grandmother's. That was until she was fifteen and Ally's parents let her live in their base-ment.

"I'm fine. He just gets under my skin," Ally said, kicking the front tire– she half-expected it to explode to top off their luck.

"It's okay. We'll find the highway. We have to, or at least find a place to stop."

"I wish I hadn't listened to him before, you know, with the traffic and his shortcut idea."

Chrissy laughed. "Who cares?"

"I do!" Ally yelled. "What if Uncle Jackie dies..." She stopped and shook her head. "Who am I kidding? Bobby's right–that guy's a loser."

"Yeah, but isn't he rich?"

Ally nodded. "That's why everyone is probably going to see him–hoping they're in the will or something. God, I hate family."

Chrissy wished she could have felt that, but her family was borrowed.

"Okay, here's what we do," Chrissy said, grabbing Ally's shoulders. "We stick Bobby in the backseat–not the trunk–and just drive. There has to be something, right? A sign. A gas station. Anything!"

Ally nodded. "You're right. I'm getting hungry so hopefully we find something soon."

"Hey!" Bobby shouted. "Hey!"

Ally and Chrissy watched as he came charging back.

"I found something!" he yelled. "A sign–it's hidden by an overgrown tree."

"What's it say?" Chrissy asked.

"Etersville–five miles."

"Eters?" Ally asked.

"Well, we are on Eters Highway, right?" Chrissy asked.

"Yeah, I guess so," Ally said, "but I've never heard of it."

"Oh well!" Bobby shouted. "It's a place to stop and buy more precious maps." He laughed–his damn weasel laugh that pinched every nerve in Ally's body–and opened the car door and dove across the backseat. "I'm taking a snoozer; wake me when we're there."

"See?" Chrissy whispered. "Everything's okay. He'll be sleeping and we have a place to stop. Just a little detour, right?"

Ally nodded and looked down the road. It didn't seem possible a town could exist–everything was empty.

* * *

Etersville did exist–five miles or so from the covered sign was another sign pointing left. It was the kind of sign you wouldn't have noticed unless

48

you were looking for it. It was handmade, childlike almost; two pieces of wood nailed up as a cross, standing a few feet out of the ground.

Ally made the turn and the smooth Pennsylvania pavement became a rough dirt road. With each heavy bump, Bobby snorted and snored, but never woke up.

Just as she was getting ready to throw the car in reverse and go back to the pavement, the dirt road opened up a little and there were houses. Actual houses! They looked old and neglected–some even dilapidated. She took her foot off the gas pedal to coast into Etersville–the tires chewed on the rocks as an eerie silence came over the vehicle.

"This is creepy," she said. "We should go back."

"No, no, look, there's a store," Chrissy said, pointing.

There was a store, and a gas station with two gas pumps; one was missing the gas hose and nozzle; the other had the nozzle but was rusted; and there was a long light above the gas pumps blinking like it was fighting death.

Ally pulled onto the concrete slab and put the car in park–she felt her nerves bouncing but tried to keep cool.

"I'll go in to see if they have a map," Chrissy said.

"I'll go with you," Ally said, "just in case."

"What about Bobby?"

Ally turned to see that he was still asleep. "The hell with him. If he comes in, he'll probably just act like an ass and get us kicked out."

The two girls walked up to the store slowly, their eyes darting around. The windows were grimy–the large one on the left side had a large crack and a piece of cardboard was taped behind it. Chrissy opened the door and was greeted by the soft jingle of a bell and a golden colored cat sitting on the floor, tail moving left to right like the pendulum of a clock.

"Hey there, kitty," Chrissy said as she reached down to touch the cat.

"Don't," Ally whispered. "What if it's rabid?"

"No, ma'am, it's a cat," a voice called out.

Ally jumped and looked up to find a very plump woman sitting behind the counter. She was wearing a moo-moo dress, the kind that was an obnoxious pink with large orange dots on it. The woman was reading a book that was missing its cover and a small television was on, half static, half voices shouting in a different language.

"Pardon me?" Ally asked.

"You said, 'What if it's a rabbit?' It's not a rabbit. It's a cat."

Ally smiled. "Oh, I didn't mean rabbit. I meant…well, nothing."

"Hi, I'm Chrissy. This is Ally. We're sort of lost."

"Sort of? I mean there's only lost and not lost, right? What's sort of? 'Specially being in this town."

"Okay, we're lost. We were hoping you had a map."

"We'll pay for it," Ally added–she looked around the store and realized it was empty except for bent shelves, most of them rusted.

"What am I gonna do with money?" the fat lady asked laughing. She coughed, hacked up phlegm, and spit it on the floor. The phlegm came out in a large chunk…red, like blood, with something white in it–pearly white.

Ally stepped back, disgusted.

The cat meowed, scampered to the small pile, and began to eat.

"That's gross," Chrissy whispered.

"Nah," the large woman said, "just a little leftovers, is all."

The cat bit down on the white part and it let out a chilling, small crack. *Like a bone*, Ally thought.

"I don't have any maps anyway," the woman said. "Sorry. This really ain't the best part of town. What you need to do is head up north a bit–ten minutes, if that. Plenty o' help there."

"Maybe we should just have Bobby go for a walk and check," Ally whispered to Chrissy.

The fat woman put her book down and perked up. "Who's Bobby? He a boy?"

"Uh, yeah, he's my brother," Ally said.

The woman looked past Ally and Chrissy, licking her lips excitedly. "He in that car out there?"

"Yeah. Why?"

"Just askin'."

"This is weird," Chrissy said. "We should go."

"Come," the fat woman barked, "I'll draw up where to drive."

"Say, where's the next town at? Or even better, where's the highway?" Ally asked.

The woman coughed again but this time nothing sizable came up–just a few red specs.

Blood, Chrissy thought. *This lady is coughing up blood.*

"Here, look," the woman said as she reached down and pulled out pen and paper. "I'll draw where to go. There ain't no towns 'round here. And the highway?" The lady laughed, sending her venomous breath into Ally and Chrissy's eyes, burning them. "No highways here. You want a map? Go here. They'll get ya out."

After scribbling and chewing on her tongue for a few minutes, the fat lady handed Ally the map.

"Like I said, 'bout ten minutes," the woman said. "Just keep driving."

Ally and Chrissy's eyes met and they could read what the other was thinking—*get to the car, now.*

They thanked the woman who was smiling with a small glob of drool coming out of the right side of her mouth. Ally stared in disgust, her stomach turning. Chrissy grabbed Ally's arm and pulled her out the door.

"We're not going any deeper into this place," Ally said.

"We have to," Chrissy replied. "But we won't get out of the car if it looks like this."

Ally shook her head. "I don't like it. We should just get back to the ro..." She froze. "Where's Bobby?"

Before Chrissy could answer she looked in the backseat and saw it was empty. "Dammit, Bobby," she whispered.

"He's gone," Ally said. "He wouldn't leave, would he?"

"I don't know," Chrissy replied. "Maybe he woke up and saw us gone and came looking for us."

"But where?" Ally asked looking around. "Look at this place..."

Everything was old, crumbling, and abandoned.

"Hey, that thing the woman spit up...did that..." Ally sighed. "Never mind, it's stupid."

"Tell me," Chrissy said.

"I think it was a bone..."

"This is crazy," Chrissy said. "We have to get Bobby and get out of here. I don't like this place."

"What if something's...wrong?" Ally pleaded.

"Like what?" Chrissy yelled. "This is insane. Your dumb brother probably went walking up the path or something. You know him, always exploring, being the tough guy. Or who knows, maybe he's hiding right now waiting to jump out and scare us."

"Bobby!" Ally yelled. "Where are you?"

Both girls started to scream, but they stopped when they heard a loud smash behind them. They spun—their hair floating around them—hoping to see Bobby standing there with a shit-eating grin on his face. Instead, it was the plump woman, and she looked annoyed—her hands were red, and her lips were too.

Just sauce, Chrissy told herself.

That's...blood, Ally thought.

"What's the noise for?" the woman bellowed.

"Bobby's gone," Ally said without thinking.

The woman smiled a sly smile. "I'm sure he's fine."

"He was in the car when we came to talk to you," Chrissy said. "Did you see him get out, maybe while we were talking?"

"Didn't see a thing," the woman said and started to suck on each one of her fingers.

Hot sauce, Chrissy told herself.

Blood, Ally thought and her stomach turned again.

"Well…he's missing," Ally said.

"Ask Gertie and Margie for help," the woman said.

"Who the hell is that?" Chrissy asked.

The woman pointed and when Ally and Chrissy turned, sure enough, there were two women walking toward them. Both were old, but not too old. Fifties…late forties, who knew. Being in their early twenties, Ally and Chrissy thought everyone was old.

"Afternoon, dearies," one of the women said, wiggling her fingers. "I'm Margie." She had a thick rope attached to glasses around her neck, making her look like a cliché version of a librarian.

"And me? Well, I'm Gertie. Good old Gertie, the ladies call me." Gertie was tall and skinny. The first thought that came to both Ally and Chrissy's mind was witch.

"My brother's missing," Ally said–she knew she was making it sound like her brother was a six-year-old and not the adult he really was, but she didn't care.

"Oh, never missing. Not here," Margie said with a smile. "Was he in the back of your car there?"

"Yes!" Ally said.

"Perfect!" Gertie said. "You were looking for the highway, right?"

Ally nodded.

"That's him then," Gertie said to Margie.

Margie nodded. "He's with us."

"Where?" Chrissy asked.

"Up there in the back, where it's nice. Don't mind how this looks here. We prefer to be left alone."

"I'm sorry we bothered you," Ally said.

"Oh heavens, no!" Gertie said, clutching her chest. "Never! Not with Bobby…he was…well…he was a real treat!"

Gertie and Margie shared a snickering laugh.

Ally and Chrissy looked at each other—annoyed and frightened.

"Can you take us to him?" Ally asked. "We really need to get directions to the highway. My uncle is dying and we have to get to Wisconsin by..."

"Then a walkin' we shall go!" Margie yelled as she and Gertie turned and led the way.

Ally looked at Chrissy and shrugged her shoulders. Chrissy did the same and they followed.

"I'm going to kill him," Ally whispered to Chrissy.

Margie and Gertie laughed again.

The walk was silent other than the rocks and gravel under their shoes. Ally looked around and noticed that there weren't any animals—no birds flying anywhere, not even a squirrel.

"Why aren't there any animals?" she asked.

Margie and Gertie stopped and turned, their faces cast against the late day sun creating a dark glow. Gertie leaned in, her glasses hanging from her neck. "They say variety is the spice of life." She nodded, winked, and continued to walk.

"Plus, we don't often get treats like Bobby anymore," Margie added.

Ally opened her mouth to say something but Chrissy smacked her shoulder.

I know, Ally thought. *Just get there, get Bobby, and get the hell out of Etersville.*

Just as the fat woman said, about ten minutes into the walk the entire place changed. There was a small town hidden behind the run down one. The houses were small—cottage like—but in great shape; they were different colors with green front lawns. Each one seemed to have the same small concrete slab front porch with a single rocking chair—it was like something out of a vacation brochure.

"Wow, look at this," Chrissy said. "It's beautiful."

"Why, thank you," Margie said. "We like to keep ourselves hidden and in good shape."

"Indeed," Gertie added.

They stopped walking at the exact middle of the town; there was a grassy patch with two park benches and different color flowers surrounding it.

"Okay, where's Bobby?" Ally asked, wasting no time; the sun was starting to hide behind the trees and that meant dark was coming.

"Oh, right, Bobby," Margie said. "Let's go see if Agnes has him ready."

"Ready?" Chrissy asked.

"Gertie!" a voice yelled.

Everyone turned to see another woman standing on her porch. She looked eerily like a perfect mixture of Gertie and Margie and was holding something in her hand.

"Let's move," Gertie said hurriedly to Ally and Chrissy–it was the first time they'd heard the woman's voice laced with concern.

"How's the day?" the woman yelled from the porch.

"Guests, my dear," Margie shouted back. "Inside please."

The woman bit into the object she was holding, sending liquid squirting all over the porch. From the distance, Chrissy thought it was a piece of chicken, maybe a leg or thigh. Ally wasn't sure what to think–if it was chicken, it was really raw because the liquid that came out of it was blood.

The woman raised her arm and waved to Gertie and Margie using the hand holding the food. When the sunlight hit it, both Ally and Chrissy could see what it really was–a hand. A human hand with all five fingers, slightly charred, but still intact. The roundness of the thumb and the thin pieces of muscles of what used to be attached to a wrist, flapped as she waved.

"That's a hand!" Chrissy screamed.

Margie grabbed her shoulder and spun her around. "Oh, child, you must be hungry–seeing things is all."

Before Ally could say a word, Gertie locked her arm tight into Ally's and walked her away too. Ally struggled for a second and was able to look back. The woman on the porch was gone, along with the hand. At first she thought maybe they really had imagined it, being in a strange town and with Bobby missing. Then she saw the puddle of blood on the porch–it *was* real.

Bobby, she thought. *Where's Bobby?*

As the two ladies led the way, more people came to their porches. They were all women holding either something that looked like a body part or had blood on themselves.

Gertie had such a strong grip on Ally's arm there was no way she was getting away. And even if she did break away, what about Chrissy? Margie had her arm around Chrissy. What would happen if they both broke away? Where would they go? Ally looked back a few times and wasn't really sure where she was now. All the houses had blended together creating a mixture of colors that all seemed to touch each other. She couldn't believe it but she, Chrissy, and Bobby were actually lost while lost.

"How much farther?" Ally asked.

"Oh dear, we're close," Gertie said.

Another person opened their door–a little girl with blonde pig tails. She wore a red dress and had freckles on her pudgy cheeks–she was so perfect that she looked like a kid from a commercial. This at least made Ally and Chrissy smile for a second.

"Suzie-Ann, please go inside for now," Margie said.

The little girl ignored the request and stuck her hands in her pocket. She pulled out tiny balls, a little bigger than marbles. They looked kind of gooey and on one side had stringy things dangling from them.

"Margie, we should move faster," Gertie said—she was concerned and Chrissy couldn't keep her eyes off the little girl.

Ally, in the meantime, had an idea of what the 'marbles' were but didn't want to believe it. When the little girl began to juggle some of them, she saw how they were firm, but squishy if squeezed hard enough.

The little girl tried a fancier trick—she threw three of the objects in the air at once while still juggling two in her other hand. Margie and Gertie kept walking, dragging Ally and Chrissy with them. The trick failed and one of the objects hit the ground with a soft splat. It landed perfectly, a little turned, but it was obvious what it was—an eyeball. The nerves hanging off the back of it made it look like a balled up jellyfish.

"That's an eye!" Ally screamed. "An eye!"

Chrissy began to thrash and push away from Margie, screaming.

"Suzie-Ann!" Gertie yelled. "Now!"

The little girl bent over and picked up the eye and wiped it on her dress, leaving a smear mark. Then to Ally and Chrissy's horror, the little girl put the eyeball in her mouth and started to chew. They heard it pop before ooze started pouring from the little girl's mouth. She tucked it into her cheek making it look like she had a large piece of candy and tried to yell to Ally and Chrissy, "It's a treat! A good one!" Only it came out as, "Iz-a trea! A goo ne!"

Ally fought Margie's grip and screamed, "Where's Bobby? What's happening?"

"Oh look," Gertie said with excitement, "we're here! Oh, Agnes is going to be so happy to see you two."

"Now, wait here a moment," Margie said, pointing a long finger at Ally and Chrissy as her face went crooked and evil. "If you try and leave, you'll never find your way back and you won't have Bobby." Then she smiled and she and Gertie walked into a dark brown house with cheap wood paneling on the exterior. It was one floor and long, like a hall or something.

"I want to go home," Ally said as the door clicked shut. "I don't…"

"We have to get Bobby," Chrissy said.

"Why is he all the way up here?" Ally asked. "Why would he come up here?"

Chrissy shrugged her shoulders as her mind played the best and worst scenarios. The best would be that Bobby came crashing through the door with a map. The worst…

"Those were eyes that little girl was playing with," Ally said. "And that woman… she had a hand and was eating it!"

"I know!" Chrissy said. "I saw it too."

"How does a place like this exist?"

"It's hidden. Only dummies like us find it."

The door opened and Margie waved them in. "Bobby's waiting for you."

As Ally and Chrissy walked slowly through the door, they realized where they were–a dining hall. There were two long tables with benches all filled with women who had plates full of food in front of them. Once Ally and Chrissy were in the hall, the door shut behind them with a thunderous boom. Everyone looked up at the sound and started to applaud.

"Okay, okay," Margie said, waving her hands. "They don't even know what they did yet."

"What we did?" Chrissy asked.

"Where's Bobby?" Ally asked–her voice drained and her eyes were staring off into space, mind tired, hungry, and confused.

"We're a special community here," Gertie said. "One of a kind. Do you know why?"

Because you're freaks, Chrissy thought. Then she said, "Because it's all women?"

"Yes!" Margie cried out. "Only women!"

"Where's Bobby?" Ally asked again.

A few of the women at the tables began to laugh.

"Not only just women," Gertie continued. "We believe in a higher existence." Gertie smiled and everyone in the room did too. She then motioned toward one of the women. She stood up and they saw that she was tall and muscular.

Chrissy felt her heart race.

Ally was still looking around the room with her lips moving, silently saying, *Bobby?*

Gertie pointed to the door and the big woman who stood in front of it. "Here, we're a community," she continued. "But we aren't ashamed of our animal instincts either."

"What the hell does that mean?" Chrissy asked, trying her best to stay with it because she knew Ally was ready to collapse.

"Do you know how certain spiders and bugs mate?" Gertie asked.

"What?" Chrissy asked.

"See, they mate…but then as a sacrifice–or maybe revenge–they eat the male after they're done; there are bugs that attack the male and destroy him. Others actually eat the male for nourishment. And some, because it's how nature wants it to be, the males actually just fall over into the female's mouth as if to say, '*Here, eat me, it's my destiny…*' Well, that's us–that's what we do."

Ally looked around and her eyes began to focus. The plates of food weren't food at all. They were body parts: guts; fingers; toes; and rolled up skin. *Flesh all around.*

"You eat people," Ally whispered.

"Mostly men," Margie said in a correcting voice. "We keep nature's plan on the human level too."

"You eat men?" Chrissy asked. "For real?"

One of the women picked up a finger and tossed it through the air. Gertie threw her hand up and caught the finger. She opened her hand and held it out to Chrissy like it was a trophy.

The finger was slightly bent and had grill marks perfectly aligned up and down it.

Chrissy stepped back and covered her mouth. "It's real," she whispered.

"Of course it is," Gertie said.

"Fresh too," Margie added.

"Taste it," Gertie said stepped toward Chrissy. "Fingers are great. If cooked right, they get a nice crunch on the outside. You just chew through some of the skin and then pull it all off the bone. And if the knuckles are small enough, you can eat them too!"

Chrissy turned and wanted to run but the massive woman was blocking the door–her arms were crossed and between the mix of fat and muscle, each arm looked bigger than Chrissy.

"Don't run, child," Margie said. "This is nature."

"No, it's not," Chrissy shot back. "This is horrible! Terrible! You all should be… arrested or something."

Margie laughed and was soon joined by Gertie and most of the women in the room. The women cackled, howled, and bellowed, all like animals–like a bunch of hungry predators ready to eat.

The noise snapped Ally out of her trance. She looked at the finger in Gertie's hand and screamed. The shriek echoed off the low ceilings and walls, and everyone stopped laughing.

"Bobby!" she screamed.

"Ally, what's wrong?" Chrissy asked.

Ally pointed at the finger, but Chrissy didn't understand–it was a finger. She didn't see anything special or different about it.

"Look at the nail," Ally said, "it's halfway missing."

"So?" Chrissy whispered.

"A month ago Bobby was trying to dam up the creek behind our house and he dropped a rock on his finger. His finger exploded and his nail fell off…"

"Oh no," Chrissy said, "oh no…"

"Yes!" Margie yelled. "You've brought us our first real meal in weeks!"

"Thank you!" Gertie added.

The entire room began to clap and cheer, with some even standing.

"No, no, no," Ally repeated.

"Stop it!" Chrissy yelled. "Just stop!"

"What's wrong?" Margie asked as the room began to quiet down again. "We were going to give it to you tonight, as an honor."

"Give what to us?" Chrissy asked.

Gertie pointed to another woman and she left the room.

Ally began to cry, almost in hysterics.

Chrissy kept cool, scanning the room for exits–they needed to get out and get into the woods. From there, with a little luck, they needed to go downhill until they found the road. From there? Run like hell or find the sign for Etersville and get the car.

The woman kicked open the swinging door to the kitchen, carrying a covered silver tray. Her smile was stretched ear to ear and the rest of the women in the room followed the woman with their eyes–she carried the tray and put it on the end of the table.

"Ready?" Margie asked.

"No," Chrissy said.

"Oh, Bobby," Ally said staring at the finger still in Gertie's hand.

"This is for bringing Bobby to us," Margie said. "He'll feed us for a few days. Young, fresh…"

"And tender!" a woman shouted from the back.

"Yes, and tender. And for that, we give you the best part…"

Margie lifted the lid.

"Oh, it's so fresh!" Gertie said.

Chrissy screamed and stepped back. Ally toppled to the floor and she curled up into a ball, crying and whimpering like a hurt animal.

It was Bobby's head on a platter. From his eyebrows up had been removed and the skull bone was cut open to expose his brain. His eyes were open, but the eyeballs were gone, leaving hollow gaps. His mouth had been sewn shut loosely with black string and the bottom of the serving plate was filled with blood. One of the women at the table took her spoon and started scooping up the blood before dumping it back onto the exposed brain.

"Keeps it moist," she said nodding at Chrissy.

"Bobby," Chrissy whispered. "Bobby…"

"If you aren't going to eat it, we will," Margie said smiling.

"Don't be rude!" Gertie snapped. "It's their gift."

"Eat brains?" Chrissy asked. "How can I…"

"Bobby!" Ally screamed from the floor.

"Okay, that yelling has to stop," Margie said. "This is a happy feast."

Chrissy looked away from Bobby's head. A new game plan formulated in her head–Chrissy wasn't sure how she was able to think, but she did. Part of her mind told her it wasn't real, that it wasn't Bobby's head. It was a joke, a big joke. Bobby had hidden somewhere else and now was in the backseat of the car again where he belonged.

Of course that wasn't true, not a word or thought of it. But for Chrissy, it worked–she needed to get Ally and get out. No matter what happened…just leave. Walk out… Chrissy wiped her face with her sleeve, trying to clean up a little bit from the snot and tears.

"We're going to go," Chrissy said in a shaky voice. "My friend's uncle is sick and going to die. We…"

The entire room gasped.

"Uncle?" Margie asked. "Could you bring us another treat?"

The room started to bustle with muffled conversation at the idea.

"No–he's in Wisconsin," Chrissy said; the room echoed with a collective sigh. She instantly regretted it. She should have said yes. *They would have given me directions to the highway!* she screamed at herself. Kneeling down, she rubbed Ally's shoulders. "Come on, sweetie, we have to go."

"But…Bobby," she cried. "He's…dead…"

"We have to go."

"Stay for a while," Gertie said. "Everyone wants to meet you."

"No! The hell with all of you!" Chrissy screamed. "You…you freaks. Yeah, that's it! Freaks! You're all freaks, in your freak town, eating people."

Chrissy's eyes looked at Bobby's head again and she felt tears flood her eyes. "We're leaving. Leaving you freaks…"

She lifted Ally off the floor, keeping her back to Bobby's head. They slowly started to walk when Margie cleared her throat and the large woman moved away from the door.

Chrissy–with Ally hanging from her shoulders–moved through the doorway. "It's okay, we're going. Nothing to worry about."

"Where's Bobby?" Ally asked.

"He's at the car," Chrissy said. "We'll be fine."

The sun was gone–replaced with a dim moon and a few stars. Chrissy had no idea where she was going but every step away from the dining room, Bobby's severed head, and from the cannibal community was a step in the right direction.

"It's all okay, baby," Chrissy kept saying, but in her mind she kept imagining waking up in a motel somewhere in Ohio, sweating from the nightmare she had to be having. The night was quiet other than the scraping of Ally's shoes on the dirt and rocks as Chrissy pulled her along…

* * *

"Shame to see," Margie said to Gertie. "Shame, shame."

"Don't they understand how nature works?" Gertie replied.

"I guess not."

"But there's good news!" Gertie said. "We have dessert!"

The dining hall roared in hungry cheers.

Outside to Ally and Chrissy, it was only a murmur.

"Everyone gets one bite," Margie announced. "Don't fill up…yet."

"Why not?" a woman yelled.

"Because…what's second best to eating the male species?"

Everyone in the room looked at each other.

The muscular woman who'd blocked the door stepped forward and bellowed in her deep voice, "The meat of the same kind?"

"Yes!" Margie yelled. "And what would be better than a midnight hunt?"

Gertie smiled wide. "Ladies…we have two young girls out there–lost and distraught–and we have our first frost coming in two weeks so we could use the meat for winter…"

I LOVE YOU

KEVIN MILLIKIN

"I have something I need to tell you," Ann said, leaning across the dinner table as she spoke—she smelled of heavenly perfume, complimenting her already angelic perfection.

Tim smiled, nodding intently—every word she uttered was like manna from heaven upon his ears. He looked at her, mesmerized, as the twinkling candlelight reflected in her eyes, making her look otherworldly.

She's going to say it, he thought, his heart skipping every other beat. *She's going to tell me she loves me!* The thought alone excited him beyond all belief. He found himself struggling not to say the 'L' word first, fearful he could be reading too much from her body language, fearing that he would ruin the moment in his haste. But before his fantasy could come to life…she continued.

"Listen," she sighed, "there's someone else."

His heart stopped and his blood froze. "What?"

It was all he could will himself to say. It felt as if someone had reached across the table and stabbed him violently in the chest; the pain was immense.

She leaned back into the shadows, obscuring her face. "There's someone else." Her words no longer loved, no longer cared.

In the darkness, her eyes were black orbs, reflected harshly by the same candlelight that had just comforted him. She looked vicious, like a demon or a witch. *Yes,* he thought wildly, *like a witch!*

Never in his life had Tim felt so weak; he had never dealt with someone as heartless either. He struggled to find the right words, but the only ones that came to mind were *bitch* and *whore*. Vile thoughts and hateful actions flooded into his mind's eye as he looked at her. Sitting there, he struggled to keep his cool but he could already feel the tears beginning to dam behind his eyes.

"Why?" she hissed–her face pulled back into a snarl as she laughed harshly and pushed herself toward the front of the chair. "You really want to ask this *now*?"

Tim nodded–the lump in his throat not allowing him to speak.

"Yes," he demanded finally. He tried to sound stronger than he really was but found his words held no meaning as he sniffled back a tear. Who was he kidding? He knew he couldn't fool anyone, let alone her.

"Well, for one, you're selfish–want me to continue?" she spat, speaking to him like an ill-behaved child. Before he could reply she pushed her chair back from the table, her face wild, almost beast like. "You're jealous, self-centered, and pathetic." As Ann ranted on, she held up her fingers, counting them off as she spoke. Slowly, she cocked her head and smirked, "But, I'm sure you knew all of that... Am I right?"

He didn't reply. His eyes were aflame and burned through her. He found himself searching for the right words and he wanted desperately to cut her down just like she had him, but in the end he found none.

He felt something change inside of him, like water being forced through frozen pipes; his internal pressure rose, reaching its breaking point before bursting altogether. At that moment he knew just how much he hated the bitch for everything she'd said, and most of all, he hated her for being right. In the end he remained silent, knowing all too well that he would never be the same again.

Without speaking, without blinking, Tim just sat there with his eyes fixed upon her as he let his pure, unbridled hatred grow.

She blinked, cocking her head like a bird. For the first time he saw her for what she really was—a demon wanting nothing more than to tear his soul apart, to eat his heart and feast upon his well being,

"You just gonna sit there?" her words were vile and bitterly spoke.

Not this time, he thought. *I'm gonna do to you what you did to me.* As he uttered these words to himself Tim realized he'd been clutching his legs—his knuckles were white and his body trembled.

"You're not leaving me," he hissed through clenched teeth. His voice sounded distant, almost foreign, a far cry from whom he'd previously been.

"Where the fuck do you get off telling me what to do?" she retorted, sliding her chair away from the dinner table and standing. If she hadn't responded, he probably wouldn't have known he'd even spoken. "You know what? Never mind. I'm leaving. Good..."

"No!" Tim shouted, jumping to his feet. He knocked over his chair in the process and it fell backwards against the floor with a deafening crash. "I mean, no," he repeated lowering his voice as he spoke, desperate to regain his composure. "I'm sorry. I didn't mean it like that. Please, sit."

"Why?"

"Because..." he said, picking his chair up off of the floor, "because I want to talk about this."

As he pushed his chair back to the table, she told him, "There's nothing to talk about—it's over! Done!"

Tim sighed—he needed this to work.

"It's just because I want to know why...why it's over. What I did wrong, what you did. I just want closure, you know? That's all."

As he spoke, he picked his plate up off of the table. It was spaghetti, but to him, it now resembled nothing more than a pile of rapidly cooling and congealing shit.

"I'm sorry," he said, wobbling around the table with slow wounded steps. Walking across to her—she looked at him with wide, cautious eyes.

"I'm sorry," he repeated, taking her plate and stacking it on his, shooting spaghetti out of the sides like a squished bug. *Horrible people like you don't deserve the time I spent cooking this food,* he thought.

Ann relaxed a bit, realizing he meant her no harm.

"I'm sorry," he repeated yet again. "Sit. Please." His voice was quiet and hollow, like that of a wounded child's.

"Why are you sorry?" she asked, slowly sitting back down.

Tim stopped, looking down at the checkered carpeting that ran under his feet, remembering the time they'd first met–it was a year ago, almost to the day.

They'd been waiting to catch the light rail together–strangers of course–standing a few feet apart. Tim had been reading that day's Portland Mercury; Ann was busy fidgeting with her phone. They were heading from Beaverton back into Portland–each with a reason different from the other. That was when she'd turned to him and asked, "You're in one of my classes, right?" Her face was scrunched as she squinted against the sunlight.

"Sure," he'd said, unaware of the beauty she held until he looked away from his newspaper, and finally when he did, his heart fluttered and he smiled.

"My name's Ann," she'd said, her eyes twinkling, even behind her sun glasses.

"Tim," he'd replied, a humble mess of happiness.

They'd ridden the whole way back with one another, well...after Tim had missed his stop. The two of them exchanged numbers and went their separate ways. After they'd met, everyday life became a blur. Ann eventually revealed to him that she'd never actually had any classes with him and instead used it as an excuse to talk to him. She could only smile when he'd told her that he'd already known. When she'd asked why, Tim simply replied that he hadn't begun classes yet.

Neither of them were bothered by the other's white lie; Tim just figured that it'd be something cute he'd someday tell their children.

Tim wanted to stay, locked in the moment, lost in his memory, but the shattering of glass broke him from his spell as a sliver of pain shot though his arm and into his shoulder.

Ann had screamed bloody murder the moment Tim smashed the dishes across the back of her head, falling forward across the table in a hail of shattered glass and discarded pasta. His heart burned with hatred as he did it; he loved every bit of it.

"Stupid bitch," he spat, leaning over her faint body. She moaned as he pulled her backwards and a trickle of blood ran down her brow, between the bits of glass that stuck in her hair–her face was painted red with pasta sauce and blood. He watched her for a second, listening to her breathe; the simple rise and fall of her chest mesmerized him. He wanted to see her move, watch her flinch. He was afraid she might have been faking it–waiting for her chance to escape. After a few moments, he realized she was truly unconscious.

Even better, he thought as he dragged her to her feet, struggling between his lack of strength and her deadweight as he pulled her body toward the kitchen. He knew there was no going back now; he was a goner for what he'd done. He knew the second Ann came to she would have the cops on his ass, throwing him behind bars. That was unless he kept her where they would never find her and took her with him wherever he traveled–they would have to be together as one.

Tim had spent the vast majority of his adult life in school, getting an education for a Ph.D. he now knew he would no longer need. He had nothing else to do but take what he'd done and just go with it and see where it took him.

History is full of it, he told himself as he heaved her across the tiled kitchen floor, dropping her between the counter and the pantry door.

She moaned softly as she hit the floor, but for the most part she remained out cold. He stopped, watching, waiting for her to wake with a scream, but that time never came. He knew he would have to move fast–he was fearful she would wake up any minute.

People eating people... The taboo thought alone sent his heart fluttering with the excitement of the unknown.

Tim had grown up with a fascination with the macabre. From where, he didn't know, but figured all of it stemmed from a midnight showing of the movie *Night of the Living Dead* he'd seen as a child. The images of teeth gnawing flesh off of bones had both frightened and delighted him, and the fact that his parents forbid him from watching it, intrigued him even more.

His fascination only grew stronger as he grew older. In school he learned about the Aztec people and the violence they'd inflicted both upon their enemies as well as in the name of their gods. Around that time he'd also learned about the Karankawa tribe of Texas. From there, he set out on his own, reading about other people like Ed Gein, Albert Fish, John George Haigh, Issei Sagawa, and Jeffery Dahmer.

In college, he'd learned about the people of Island Carib, in the Caribbean where the word *cannibal* was derived from. During Tim's first year of medical school a man in Germany named Armin Meiwes had made the news. Meiwes had been arrested after he'd cut off and sautéed another man's penis and together, they'd shared the cooked appendage over a glass of wine before the man bled out.

Tim hadn't thought about it in a few years, but now it was all coming back to him. What he'd known and what he'd read about these cannibals flooded into his mind, making him giddy at the thought that he, too, could join their ranks.

Cannibal, he thought with a smile. The idea of such a thing, though often boring behind a text book, now held a much greater and richer meaning.

In fact, he enjoyed the idea so much he had to repeat it, this time aloud. "Cannibal," he said and smiled again, leaning over to pluck a piece of glass from the young woman's hair.

His smile broadened as he fought back the overwhelming urge to kiss the beautiful creature on the cheek–those soft, rosy cheeks full of life and…nourishment.

As the seconds ticked past, he began to feel a strange arousal rise within his nether regions, one he could neither acknowledge nor deny, only now it came to him differently than it had in the past–it now felt as though it was deeper and much more personal. The sensation it stirred within felt as if it had been handed down through the eons as a personal gift from the gods. The urge to taste Ann's life was strong in him, knowing that he could now go far beyond the figurative, emotional sense and devour her.

Kneeling over, he kissed her gently on the cheek and then forehead. Gentle and loving he kissed her, while his heart leapt wildly within his chest.

Even though you'll never know how much I love you, he thought, picturing the two of them alone amidst a starry night. *We can finally become one with each other.* It was the most romantic thing in the world to him. How could he say no? He stopped, sat up, and smiled to himself, realizing how corny his thoughts had been before shrugging and returning to his *romantic* kisses.

Ann stirred beneath him. Her sudden movement and moan caught him off guard; Tim let out a yelp as he fell backwards.

Her mind registered the sensations of her lips being caressed and she licked them as Tim moved back to her, his heart violently fluttering–the thought of her coming to only pushed him further.

He noticed a small puddle of blood slowly seeping through her golden hair, slicking the floor's already glossy surface. Slowly, cautiously, he inched across the floor back toward her. Leaning in, he kissed her again, the godly sensation he'd felt, slowly slipping away; he was hungry to regain the waning sensation.

Tim was addicted to the thought of devouring her body, if the thought of it was this strong, he couldn't fathom what the act itself would be like.

His kisses grew in intensity, eventually evolving into soft nibbles–the *love bites*, as Ann used to call them–grew more and more violent with every peck. He came in his pants as her blood filling his mouth when he latched onto her face like a distorted suckerfish. The pain was unbearable for Ann; through the darkness of her sleep she woke with a scream as if someone singed her with something red hot. Tim wasn't scared–he wanted the fight and he wanted blood. Just smelling it made him want to become a feral beast and the taste of copper sent him over the edge.

She struggled to pull away, but he fell atop her, becoming deadweight, and the more she struggled, the harder he bit.

"Stop it! Get the…" she screamed and struggled to make her voice heard as he held her down, "fuck off me!"

Ann began to cry, heaving forth heavy, thick tears that slid down her face; Tim felt them as he brushed against her.

He forced himself to release her because he was afraid he would lose the surge of control he felt over her unconscious body, but he did–relaxing his jaws slowly. Instantly, he knew it was a mistake.

She sprang forward, her hand held tightly against her face, struggling to stem the blood flow. Her hands glistened with the red blood that was gushing from the gash he'd created in the soft flesh of her face. Tim snapped his head back in a snarl–like a wolf howling at the moon–and her blood seeping from his mouth and staining his teeth.

"You fucking psycho!" she cried, her face a mixture of emotions, all overlaid with pure, unbridled horror.

He only smiled as the scent of blood and fear filling the air. "If your blood tastes this good," he said, wiping it from his chin before licking it off of his fingers, "I can't wait to taste your body."

He smiled, wanting desperately to get to the *meat* of the matter and as if she could sense what was coming, Ann sprang to her feet, shoving Tim aside as he jumped at her. He spun quickly on his heels as she passed; stepping forward he slipped in a puddle of her blood landing hard on the kitchen floor, stunned. However, he recovered quickly and jumped back to the chase.

She tried to put as much distance between herself and Tim as she could, but the pain was excruciating and slowed her down. As she ran past the dinner table, the sight of it filled her with dread. She regretted saying what she had, knowing now that she shouldn't have said it while they were alone, but the realization was short lived.

Suddenly the front door appeared as she rounded the corner–closer, closer. When out of nowhere Tim tackled her from behind and their colliding bodies sent her forward, throwing her forcefully against the wall. Her head snapped backward violently, giving her whiplash. She yelped as her world went black only to snap back to reality as Tim grabbed a handful of her hair, bashing her face into the wall.

"You bitch!" he screamed, bashing her face into the wall again and again, until her forehead bled and her nose popped.

"You think you can leave me? You think you can run?"

As Tim rambled, he continued to slam her face against the wall, shaking the condo's structure, splintering the plaster and splattering her blood across the off-white paint.

"I love you!" he cried. "I fucking love you, you stupid bitch!"

She didn't hear a thing he said, with every whack she slipped in and out of consciousness until all she saw was black. Tim continued on, long after she'd slipped into the darkness. Realizing what had happened, he stopped, dropping Ann's limp body to the floor.

Oh God, he thought as his heart sank in his chest, *did I kill her?* Growing more and more frantic, Tim felt for a pulse but found none.

"Fuck, fuck, fuck!" He cursed as he quickened his search, eventually he found one, it was faint, but again, it was better than nothing.

It'll do, he thought with some relief.

Tim wanted her alive; he didn't want his first time to be with nothing more than dead meat.

What a mess, he thought as he took a couple of steps back to survey the damage. Blood and gore splattered the walls and slicked the carpets as if someone had taken a gallon of red paint and flung it across the room.

Instantly, he began running all of the facts and figures through his mind, realizing it was going to be a pain just to repaint and recarpet, but in the long run it was all going to be worth it. First, he needed to get her into the bathtub.

He felt no remorse for what he'd done. The only negative emotion he was feeling was the dread of the manual labor he'd have to put into cleaning up the mess, knowing damn well he'd have to do it all himself. *Next time*, he thought, *I'll be more careful how I handle this part.*

Looping both arms under her armpits, he struggled to pull her across the floor toward the bathroom, leaving behind a thick trail of blood in the process. He'd never been strong, but was rather the runt of the litter; he was the youngest of all his brothers and the smallest to boot.

He moved as quickly as he could, fearful she'd come to again; he knew he didn't have long.

Suddenly, a loud, metallic ring brought him to a standstill. It echoed through the condo like the thunder of an angry god. Dropping Ann, he realized what it was—her phone!

Tim moved toward the sound, finding it originating from her purse underneath her side of the dinner table. Quickly, he snatched it up and dumped all of its contents atop the table, where he found her cell phone. It was simple and compact in a shiny, lime green casing. As he reached for it the ringing stopped. Carefully, he picked it up, holding it away from himself like a horrid, dirty little thing. Flipping it open, he was greeted by the simple message: **1 Missed Call**.

Suddenly the phone came alive again, breaking the silence with a startled jump. Tim scowled at the name on the tiny LCD screen that read 'Scott'.

He became enraged. He didn't know a Scott, nor had Ann ever mentioned him as one of her friends, but somewhere deep down he knew who Scott really was. He stared a moment longer at the phone he held in his shaking hands before he cried angrily and snapped it into two worthless pieces. He yelled out, heaving the broken pieces of plastic against the wall. He continued his tantrum, screaming out like a savage on the brink of war.

The broken pieces of plastic fell to the floor and he watched them, his chest heaving with his labored breaths, his eyes wide and unblinking as if he was waiting for the pieces to grow legs and scuttle away like some kind of robotic beetle.

"Fuck it," he said, "I'll kill him too!"

His mind raced, what threat does this Scott fellow serve? At least now with her phone broken, he had no worry of Ann coming to and phoning the police, and to make sure of it, he unplugged his phone cord from the wall as well.

Tim pushed all of the remaining thoughts and worries out of his head; it was time to get back to the matter at hand. He twitched eagerly, wanting desperately to slice her open.

As a medical student, he hadn't had the chance to deal with the dead in such a way yet, he had another year of studies before they'd even place the scalpel in his hand and that alone bugged the hell out of him.

Now I can see what it's like, he thought. The idea of playing in her guts excited him in a way he'd never imagine. He'd grown worried over the amount of blood she was losing, but he knew it was taking too long; he needed to get done.

"I'm gonna enjoy this," he snarled, pulling her into the bathroom. With all of the strength he could muster, he heaved her over the edge of the bathtub, letting her fall the rest of the way. He rearranged her to look as if she'd been taking a bath—her knees pulled to her chest, her arms across her chest.

"What should you be?" he asked, standing over her. "Maybe a soup." He stopped to ponder... *No, use with pasta*, he thought. *Look where spaghetti got me.* The thought of it brought on a chuckle, and the fact he was now laughing over what he intended to do with her body made him realize he'd gone absolutely mad and that thought alone made him laugh even more.

"Ah-ha! Soup it is!" he exclaimed as he remembered an old cookbook given to him when he was a child by his grandmother.

His grandmother had never worked a job due in part to her husband, his grandfather, who believed a woman's place was in the kitchen, raising the children, and providing the meals. She'd never complained, even though she'd never agreed with the hand she'd been dealt.

To Tim, his grandmother was a world class chef, at least in his young mind. She'd always made the greatest meals when he'd gone visiting for the summer—pastas and soups, pastries and desserts.

On one occasion, he'd asked her if he could someday be as good of a cook as she was, and a few days later she'd given him a little red cookbook and told him that in time, yes he could.

He found the dusty old book tucked away in a cabinet above the kitchen sink and tossed it onto the counter.

"Now, all I need is a knife," he muttered, ripping drawer after drawer open, looking for the perfect blade, with no luck.

He muttered a choice curse word or two to himself. He'd never become the cook his grandma told him he could be; he had no culinary skills. After all, he was a modern man—if his food wasn't premade, prepackaged, and ready to cook he had no interest in it.

He flung open the drawer containing all of his utensils—jackpot, he'd found all of his knives, but the sight and selection of them was overwhelming. Flinging the drawer off of its rollers, he threw it to the floor where it landed with a crash. The sound was enough to make him cringe. After shoving the cookbook under his arm, he picked up the drawer, collected what had fallen out, and hurriedly left the room.

He found Ann just how he'd left her, but she was now moaning painfully, tossing her head back and forth as if she was caught within a terrible nightmare, and maybe she was.

He gently set the book atop of the bathroom sink, though he carelessly dropped the drawer again, sending a thundering crash throughout the tiny room. Ann leaped up in the tub, startled by the crash, jumping forward; she fell into Tim's arms as he leaned over into the tub. He held her tightly as she struggled against him—her broken jaw and jagged teeth kept her mouth painfully shut, though she wanted to do nothing more than beg him for mercy.

Her panic sent Tim into a wild frenzy of laughter. It surprised him that he was able to take on the role of the madman so perfectly, in fact it fit him like a glove, one he never intended to take off ever again.

He whispered softly in her ear, telling her everything would be over soon and all the pain she felt now would be rendered moot by the time he was done with her. Tim reached behind himself, feeling for a small, lavender colored hand towel. "It won't take long," he said as he crumpled the towel into a tightly packed ball, "but I'm sure it'll hurt like hell."

Ann screamed as he pried her jaw open and shoved the towel deep inside her mouth until she choked. She tried to spit it out, but it was packed in too tightly, locked deep behind her broken teeth that cut into it like jagged pieces of a jigsaw puzzle.

When she screamed again, it was only a fraction of what it had once been, but still, she tried; her will for survival was strong and that alone was starting to annoy the hell out of him. She struggled against him, but her strength was fading quickly and because of that Tim was able to hold her back with one arm.

While he held her back, he reached behind himself, his fingers grazing along the side of the fallen drawer; slowly, he pulled it closer. Blindly, his fingers caressed the knife blades, feeling for the perfect one.

He found perfection in the serrated blade of a steak knife; it pricked his fingers as he felt his way down the blade toward the handle.

By the time Tim reached the knife's handle he was sure he was bleeding from the numerous cuts on his fingers made by the blade's pointed teeth, but none of that mattered—not now, anyway.

Ann's pupils grew large as tears ran down her face, washing the blood away. "No, please, no!" she cried through the towel, struggling against him.

Quickly, he brought the knife around—its blade slicing through the air, catching the soft overhead light in its steel surface, shining like a bolt of lightening. She screamed, but it was muffled and momentary. The steak knife entered her stomach quickly, tearing away little pieces of her flawless skin, piercing through her tightly toned abs like they where nothing more than wet paper.

Tim found no resistance as he pushed the knife deeper into her. Blood bubbled out from around the blade, gushing into the tub as it washed across his hand and somehow across his clothing.

She fell silent, a dribble of fresh blood seeped from between her lips and the towel. Ann's eyes were once again like they'd been when they hid beyond the candlelight– soft, kind, and bathed in a loving grace–and for the first time in a long time, it felt as if they belonged to the girl he'd fallen in love with.

Her lips quivered and her eyes growing glossy. Finally, she stopped struggling as though she'd forfeited her will to survive.

He pulled her closer to him and the knife, and as he did, he kissed her gently on the cheek.

"I love you," he whispered, brushing his lips against her ear.

She died in his arms. Slowly, he pulled the blade out of her body. She came with it as though it was an extension of her being. With his hand on her shoulder, he pushed her body back into the tub. In his deranged, lovesick mind the whole act of homicide had been justified, it was romantic and the staple point of their relationship.

He knew it was something he would never feel again, but like a heroin addict, he'd spend the rest of his life chasing the high.

Ann's dead body slumped backwards against the side of the tub. Dropping the knife, Tim quickly spun around. He had work to do–very dirty work as a matter of fact.

Rummaging through the drawer, he set about looking for the sharpest blade he could find. He found it in a small, four inch shearing knife along with a tiny pair of scissors he'd procured from beneath the bathroom sink; he set about snipping off her clothes.

First, he removed her blouse and then her pants. He felt somewhat guilty as he did it, not for the prior deed of murder, but for her lack of will. He knew he could have his way with her if he very well pleased and it was that, that tugged at him, showing him how real all of it really was.

He slowly looked her over, noting her stomach lacked any choice cuts. She lacked what she'd deemed an unhealthy lifestyle–the time she hadn't spent at work was spent at the gym. Gently touching the bleeding wound on her stomach, he knew what he needed to do.

He looked her over one last time–she truly was a goddess to him. Tracing his fingers along her thigh, he found what he wanted. It began just behind her knee, leading toward her firm buttocks.

Without hesitation, he pushed the knife into the tender, soft spot behind her knee–into the patella. He shuddered; it was eerie that the blade hadn't been met with much resistance.

Gently, he moved the knife left to right, slipping his fingers through the cut as he did, which allowed him to gain leverage as he carefully removed her skin from the muscle.

He moved carefully and slowly, fearing he'd rip her skin apart. He wanted this to be done neatly, even if the night's events hadn't gone accordingly so.

Tim did this all the way up to her buttocks and a large rectangle of loose skin slipped away revealing the tender meat below. After that, he took the knife and pushing down through the meat; he stopped only when he felt resistance from the bones.

Sliding his hand beneath all of it, he pushed along her femur, bring his hand to the bone. Pushing up from it, he slid his fingers across its surface, loosing the meat as he went–her bones were smooth like a polished stone, slick with gore. He did this all the way up her leg until he was able to set the large mound of dissected tissue aside.

Tim followed suit with the other leg as well, and after he carefully removed the meat from her thighs, he set it aside on a towel. After returning from the kitchen with a couple of large salad bowls and other containers he'd found in the cabinets, he took the knife and slit along her belly, spilling her intestines into the tub.

Carefully, he removed all he could, placing them in the plastic bowls, containers, and jars for later use. He looked back at her as he backed out of the bathroom; she lay there, looking up. Her head was cocked back at such a queer angle that she seemed to be looking to him; her eyes were glossy and her lips were parted with a bit of blood soaked towel hanging out, as if she was asking him: *Why?* As he walked out, he took one final look at the mess he'd made of her stomach; her belly was slit open from navel to ribs and her body had been peeled open and hallowed, all her organs gracefully removed.

He looked back to the stacks of plastic containers and jars–he planned to clean them and carefully label every single one for later use.

* * *

The pot of stew bubbled on the stove–popping and hissing over the flame. He'd already added the key ingredients, leaving the liquid a brackish brown–the color of rust. He was proud of himself as he carefully removed the pot from the heat and ladled himself a small bowl. Steam rose into the air like a puff of smoke and he smiled, leaning forward to inhale the aroma radiating from it; the smell was strong and rich like a good cup of morning coffee.

He loved Ann for giving herself up so he could live *his* life to the fullest and as he dipped his spoon into the bowl, his mouth began to water in wicked anticipation. Gently blowing upon the spoon and its contents, Tim pushed it into his mouth and the hot liquid spilled onto his tongue. The texture alone excited his taste buds as he slowly swallowed it, savoring the moment of the intense flavor. The taste, the texture–everything was foreign and still it contained a comforting sense of familiarity.

He smiled, pushing a small chunk of Ann's thigh onto his spoon before popping it in his mouth. His jaws clenched tight against it, spraying meaty juices into his mouth with every grind of his teeth against the fibrous tissue, and as he set the bowl down, he vowed to himself that this wouldn't be the last time.

Someday, maybe soon, he thought picking his bowl back up, placing his lips against the brim as he knocked it back, *I'll taste this sweet treat again.* He sucked down a hearty mouthful and some of the soup dribbled down his chin to be soaked up by the collar of his shirt.

"Oh God," he moaned, setting the empty bowl down on the counter, intoxicated with the magical elixir. Deep down, his stomach grew heavy and gently rumbled as if it approved of what he'd done.

He knew it was Ann–somehow she was there–somewhere inside him. The two of them were now bound together as one forever and ever. It was the greatest storybook ending anyone could ever ask for.

A quick knock came from the front door, accompanied by three more that followed in quick succession. Suddenly, the simmering of the pot seemed louder and the grumble in his stomach grew deafening as his heart plunged through the darkness.

Was it the police? His mind raced as he stood and went to the door, placing a panicked ear against it before the knocking continued. Again, one knock followed by three awkwardly placed knocks.

"Who is it?"

Through the door he heard the person awkwardly adjust themselves. *Had they too been listening?* he wondered. A pause followed–a long beat that Tim wanted no part in. "Who is it?" he repeated.

Finally, after a long pause, the voice replied, "Scott."

Tim could only smile.

VEND THE SKIN

ALAN SPENCER

The end of his left arm was a smooth pink nub–cauterized. No burn marks. No griddle lines. No scent of cooked flesh lingered in his bedroom. No blood. No pain.

Strange, Chuck Haggerty thought, waking in bed for no reason, snapping out of an unnatural coma-deep sleep, laying there drenched in a net of cool evening perspiration. The room seemed to eye him back and say, *I didn't see anything happen either.*

People talked about shock and how the body responded to heavy losses of blood and severe damage, and what he was experiencing now was a lack of reaction. He was normal, calm even, as he tried to understand how he was supposed to feel about his missing left hand.

Blinking once, he looked down at where his hand used to be. Blinking again, he stared at the wall. Blink yet again, he noted the intricate folds of his bed sheets and the shadowy grooves they created. Four times, and the end of the nub glistened in his view, as if perspiring. Five times, he lifted the blank nub and looked at it closely, seeing how the outer layers of skin looked like plastic–shiny and brand new. Six times, his mouth went dry when a horrible jolt of juiced-up electricity shot up his arm, as if the veins were suddenly hooked up to a nine-volt battery. He unleashed a guttural screech, letting the pent up energy out in one long note of discord and sheer terror.

Mrs. Jones in room 4 on the fifth floor–the one directly below Chuck's apartment–phoned the police. She'd been ripped from sleep by the horrible human emanation which pierced the silent night's air. Nine minutes after the call, a police unit arrived at his apartment. Ten minutes later, an ambulance arrived to cart a blank faced Chuck Haggerty to the emergency room.

*   *   *

The next morning Chuck awoke in a recovery room facing a detective who'd gone far in changing the stereotypical investigators' exterior. He wore a pair of blue jeans and a green v-neck shirt with his badge pinned to the short sleeve. He was young–maybe in his thirties–Chuck guessed. His face glowed youthfully–the overall appearance of someone still turned on by their job, and Chuck's case had the man aroused.

"I'm Detective Ryan Miller," he said, stepping closer to the bed before continuing his spiel. "Mr. Haggerty, are you able to answer some questions? Do you remember anything–anything at all–about what happened to you last night?"

It was a full two minutes before Chuck registered that, yes, he had been a victim of a crime, and yes, his left hand was missing—not that he could tell with the bulging bandages concealing the nub. The shock was removed by a heavy dose of pain killers, so heavy he could taste iron under his tongue and was experiencing a light floating sensation, as if he could sink into the mattress and doze off again; all he had to do was close his eyes and allow it to happen.

But Detective Miller dug his fingers deep into the meat of his good arm, demanding answers, removing the bullshit friendly banter tone from his speech. "I need to hear what you know if I'm going to protect you and everybody else out there," he growled–his breath reeked of coffee and a cigarette. The combination of the two was like sugar and tarmac. He spat out words of harsh encouragement, "You're the ninth man in the lower Boston area to wake up missing his hand. I give you three to six weeks before you get attacked again, or you could get lucky and they'll leave you alone completely. But who knows if they'll let you go. It's a hell of a gamble, pal. I've been on this case for three months and I've got no fucking leads. So if you saw a face, or a profile, or if the guy was carrying an axe–any detail like that, anything...just tell me something!"

Chuck couldn't remember much after the man's harsh grating words. The bed was just too comfortable and the drugs too strong to resist the wooing arms of slumber. He drifted into unconsciousness right before a series of doctors and nurses forced the worked-up detective out of the room—not that it would be the last time he'd see the man.

Chuck was lucky that missing his left hand didn't prevent him from performing his job at Guard Dog Security. During his normal routine he patrolled a four level office building—mostly spaces for well-to-do lawyers and businessmen. But for now, he used sick leave to recover from his horrible ordeal.

In the past two weeks he'd received many get well cards and kind words from friends and family who were still at a loss on how to help a man cope with having his left hand stolen. Nothing seemed to help though. He didn't know how to assuage the sensation that he was never safe in his home, and how when he closed his eyes—much to the help of a tall glass of whiskey and the impression of the 9mm underneath his pillow and the chair propped under his bedroom door that promised to make a clatter if disturbed—he knew his other hand could be taken next, or his foot, or anything else the stealer wanted. The selection was his or hers to make at their discretion.

What right did they have coming into my home and taking what wasn't theirs? he wondered.

But the question of his assailant's motives was what really haunted him, as did their methods. How did one steal a hand without shedding blood, and even Dr. Martinsen kept commenting, "It's impossible. What we have here is clean amputation, Mr. Haggerty. No infection. No blood loss. It's as if they wanted you unharmed, so-to-speak."

During his recovery, Chuck was visited by his ex-girlfriend, Rose Neeman. Standing there in his doorway, she looked over his nub, though he kept it covered in a white silk cloth in an attempt to mask his affliction that still drew eyes.

"You poor man," she whispered, taking in the loss of the appendage. "It's unbelievable. Unthinkable. Who would do such a thing to someone?"

"That's a damn good question," Chuck said in agreement. "I woke up and it was gone. The police found no evidence—no fingerprints or signs of forced entry. These people are good. Professionals."

"Professional limb takers?"

"That's a theory. The detective on my case believes there's a group of people doing it to many people across the United States. He said over the last few years there has been hundreds of cases of people waking up with some part of them missing. And that's not accounting for those who don't wake up at all or go missing forever."

"Jesus Christ, don't talk like that," she cried, placing her hand under his jaw lovingly—her caress could always tame the wild beast in him and subdue it with love. He missed her so much, but judging by the way she hadn't returned his calls or tried to hook up with him, it was over and she was better because of it. "I wanted to see for myself that you were okay. You look like you've had a rough go of it. You're not drinking, are you?"

"This house is as dry as a desert," he lied, and hoped she didn't spot the half empty fifth on his coffee table.

She wouldn't understand his drinking or the recuperation process. How else could he sleep? How was he supposed to stay calm knowing it was easy for people with the capability of limb snatching to just come in and take what they wished at any moment?

She'd been speaking and he forced himself to refocus on her. "Treat yourself well, okay? I have the numbers of some really nice gal friends..."

"No, I'm fine," he said, cutting her off with a lie. "I'm dating someone. She's really cute and likes westerns. Can you believe that? A girl who likes westerns like I do. She even loves Charles Bronson flicks. I can't lose."

He was spending a lot of time alone because he feared for his friends and family. They too could end up like him, or worse. He didn't answer his phone and didn't go to work. He had a healthy savings account that would pay for his rent and booze, so he was taking extended time off work; Guard Dog Security understood. Nobody would question his reasons for wanting some time to think things out. His boss, Artie Gregg, gave him the business card of an excellent therapist. "He gets to the bottom of things really quick. He doesn't milk the bank with unnecessary sessions."

Chuck never called the therapist.

A couple of questions kept him planted on his bed, with a door and a 9mm between him and the limb takers: (1) What would be the point in taking one hand? (2) It was so easy to do it, so why wouldn't they come back for more?

They'll be back and I'll be ready, he vowed to himself. *Take my other hand. Please. Go ahead. Just poke your head through that door, and I'll blow it the fuck off.*

Sitting on his bed, aiming the barrel of the 9mm at his bedroom door, he passed the days eating from bags of greasy potato chips and slugging back mouthfuls of warm bourbon, masking his restlessness with a false sense of ease. He was in control. The people who took his hand would arrive, and he'd get his revenge. He'd sleep again, finally. Maybe go out on a real date with a real woman, and she wouldn't even have to like westerns. All she had to do was appreciate a good time—when he could appreciate a good time too, one of these days.

It took an entire week before he could finally look at himself in the mirror again. His beard was metallic gray; he shaved it off, badly irritating the skin due to a poor shaving cream lather job, and because the mane was so thick.

His eyes bragged of the alcohol he'd ingested by tinting the whites yellow, bordering on jaundice. Had his liver stopped functioning? Had it formed a restraining order against him for the abuses he'd inflicted upon it?

He touched the skin of his face to see the way it folded like a stretched out piece of tissue paper; older skin was sensitive and could tear with the slightest touch. Yes, he was defiantly growing older. Weary. How much longer could he go on like this, being a sitting duck, a waiting amputee victim?

He pictured himself as an eighty-year-old man in a bed with life support hooked up to his body and the 9mm in his decrepit hand. He'd be so arthritic he wouldn't be able to lift the gun and fire it.

With a disgusted shake of his head, he dismissed the thought and returned to his bedroom.

Boredom was the norm of his existence. He spent most of his time walking in circles around his apartment, alert, though suffering a severe case of ennui. That's what made a good security guard, watching things under any circumstances, extreme or mundane—almost always mundane.

That's why it came as a shock to him when he awoke to something happening as opposed to being right on top of it as he'd planned to be.

It was already too late when he opened his eyes. There were two men in his apartment and his bedroom door was jacked open. The chair was on the floor, the top of it broken, snapped from the body. Why he hadn't awoken to the commotion was beyond him, but it was too late now.

The man standing at the foot of his bed was familiar, but he was wearing strange clothes; baggy, thuggish clothing, a gold chain around his neck, and a hat turned to the side. When the man spoke, he recognized him as Detective Miller.

Chuck tried to stand up, to shift from his position on the bed, but he couldn't move. He was paralyzed from drugs. He felt their unnatural anesthetic power taking hold of him, rooting to his very core. He was so drugged he could barely will the rise and fall of his chest as air filled and left his lungs.

Detective Miller approached him, his left fist bloody. "Are you okay, Mr. Haggerty?"

Chuck's tongue weighed a thousand pounds—it could have been stolen for all he knew. He cased his body with his eyes, but in doing so made himself dizzy. Everything went blurry and he blinked rapidly to try and regain his perspective.

"I know what they did to you, so stay calm; I've got everything under control. You see, this man on the floor, he smashed the door open and fired a tranquilizer dart into your neck. But I've been casing your apartment—keeping watch. I knew in my gut they'd come back. But it was still a gamble because I've done stakeouts outside of people's residences who were victims of these people before. I've failed all this time, but now...now I've got them by the balls. I've tagged the armored truck two blocks from this building, and I'm going to call it in..."

The detective stopped talking abruptly when, through the air duct right above his bed, a hermetic pop sounded, followed by a dart jutted out of Detective Miller's trachea.

He instantly collapsed and his eyes rolled into the back of his head. The grate was kicked out of the wall, landing right next to Chuck's left leg.

In seconds his head was encased in a burlap bag. More footsteps entered the room. Five pairs. Eight pairs. Ten pairs. Twelve pairs. They just kept coming and they worked in unison; precise, swift, and motivated.

He was being moved, though he couldn't feel it—he could only sense the movement. How were they carrying him out? Wouldn't anybody else notice his body being taken out of his own home?

He didn't know how late it was, but apparently it was too late for help—too late to protect himself from the people who'd stolen his left hand and had come back for the rest.

The first thing Chuck heard was the whiz of tires rolling on the inter-state—the noise had been his lullaby until his eyes shot open. He was propped in a passenger seat of a large vehicle—the armored truck Detective Miller was talking about. He still couldn't move. It was as if he was in a cocoon made of his own body, trapped under his own skin with his muscles having lost their ability to obey his nervous system.

The man sitting in the driver's seat noticed he was awake and started talking, "I'd be fired—probably switching places with you—if they knew I was letting you sit up front. It's a *long* drive, if you catch my drift, so I like the company. That other guy in your apartment looked too young to converse with, but you, you're my age. So let's talk. I think you can talk. I suggest you enjoy our time together, because once we get there, it's over for you. I won't sugar coat it."

Chuck couldn't roll his eyeballs to the left far enough to view the man, and it was almost pitch black in the cab—the only light was the soft glow from the dash. The roar of the engine seemed loud in the silence that stretched between the two men and its constant hum made Chuck's ears ache. He desperately wanted to express fear—the horror of knowing he was being taken somewhere to die, or worse, be dissected, taken apart for an unknown cause.

He could talk, but only clumsily and in short spans, "W-w-whudda ya do?"

"Now that's a loaded question. I'm like you, Chuck. I do a routine, bor-ing job. I drive people to and from one place to another. I'm constantly on the road. I'm e-mailed an address and I drive to it. People are there waiting to give me bodies—bodies like you, Chuck. And don't bother talking, because I know what you're going to ask me, so I'll just tell you. I like to talk, you see. I could drink a gallon of coffee and down a handful of uppers or sit on a wet towel like some truckers do, but talking keeps me wide-eyed and bushy-tailed. Bullshitting. Shooting the breeze, man, you betcha!

"So what do I do, huh? It's more like why do they do what they do, right? That's what you want to know. I'll tell you one mistake you made. They had a hell of a time getting into your place. They could see you were aiming that 9mm at your bedroom door, waiting to blast them to hell. But they had a job to do. You're on the list. That's how you ended up here with me.

"They don't mess around, Chuck. They know their business. They've been doing it for decades. Probably before I was born, when they were still a small business. Working out of the backs of small commercial boats on dockyards, or in the backs of tricked out ice cream trucks, or even those rigs that bring frozen dinners to homes. But now it's commercialized. Industrial. Marketable. But you'll never see what I'm talking about. I bet you're wondering why they came back for you after taking your hand. Know this, friend, they don't always come back. They take a piece the first time using their special cutting machine, like a heated up paper-cutter. Then they try that piece, first. If they like the flavor they go back for the rest, and apparently, they couldn't get enough of you, Mr. Haggerty. They must have raved over you to go through all the trouble of getting you here in this truck with me."

They hit a bump and Chuck felt the vibration rattle up his back, through his spine, and jostle his head; the feeling was coming back to his body in pins and needles sensations.

How far do we have yet to drive, he thought and wanted to ask the faceless driver. *Is there any chance, any chance in your soul, in your heart, that you would let me go?* But he knew the answers already. The man had done this before many times, and one more man with one more plea bargain wouldn't make a damn bit of difference.

He welcomed the feeling back into his body, praying he would be able to move before it was too late. To save himself, before they did what the man had warned him they would do—cut him up into pieces.

He pretended he couldn't talk, though it didn't deter the man from chatting about his son who'd gone to state through his high school football team, the Thunder Hawks. First time in fifteen years, he boasted. His son had scored two touch downs, being a wide receiver. Biggest yardage Wamego High School had ever seen.

"They dusted off the record books, and it's official," the driver bragged proudly. "Dusty, he's broken their record. My kid, and just think, his old man couldn't run a mile without having to have open heart surgery."

There were more details, but he instead listened to his body. He felt the cool air shooting through the air-conditioning vents touch his skin. He could twitch his toes. He willed his right arm to budge—the one with a fist— the only weapon on his person. But he couldn't move otherwise. He imagined pivoting in his seat, seizing the wheel, and driving them off the road. He'd punch the man in the throat, and if he had a chance, use his fingers to gouge out his eyes, maybe strangle him enough to immobilize him and make a daring run for anywhere.

Looking out into the darkness, the driver took the next exit and headed for a giant building that had the appearance of a beaten up, abandoned factory. The sign over the top read **_Anderson Goods Processing, Inc._** The parking lot was empty except for a line of rigs much like the one he was in—all semis and armored vehicles and 'tricked out' ice cream trucks—human transports.

Advancing through the security checkpoint, the driver spoke with a bored-faced attendant who let them through, saying in a bemused voice, "Go on in."

After they passed many closed off dock entrances, they came to a garage access that was wide open. Chuck couldn't see anyone inside, but the lights were on. Taking a wide right, the driver steered straight for the open access. Once they were inside, he reached into the glove compartment and hit a button that closed the heavy garage door behind them.

And that's when Chuck moved. Not wasting a single second, he drove his only fist toward the man's face, hitting him just under the ear and the crevice of his neck. The awkward blow was enough to send the man tumbling to his side, out the driver's door he'd just opened, and head-first onto the cement floor. Clumsily climbing out of the cab of the truck, Chuck arched over the man, waiting for him to call out for help, or to counterattack. But instead, he remained face down in a growing pool of blood, unconscious. He'd landed just right and had been knocked out, or worse, but Chuck honestly didn't care.

Still working out the numb kinks in his muscles, he hobbled to where the garage door opener remained clipped to the dashboard. He tried to open it to make a getaway, but it wouldn't open. There was a keypad of five numbers across the bottom. He pounded them, trying to guess the combination, and after many frustrating minutes of trial and error, he gave up.

There has to be another way out of this place, he thought. *I just have to look for it.*

The only audible sound in the building was the buzzing of the incandescent lights above him. Beside the entrance they'd used, there was a solid wall with one large door beside another garage port—both were closed. Creeping carefully, noting the security cameras that seemed to angle and follow his every step, he approached the door and was surprised it was unlocked. Poised to turn the knob, he sucked in a deep breath, knowing he could run right into the enemy. Easing the barrier open with caution, he lunging forward, ready to go out with a brutal fight. Nothing but a narrow, poorly lit passageway greeted him. The only light was at the end and so he followed it, having no other alternative but to keep on moving.

Boxes were stacked along the walls, with no labels marking them. He was curious and wanted to tear one open, but there wasn't time. For all he knew he could have security—or whoever occupied the factory at this late hour—stalking after him.

After walking for what felt like a city block, the passageway ended and he located a dull, amber light under the crack of a door—the only direction to move next.

Before braving the next obstacle, he smelled something in the air—a mix of caramel corn, roasting meats, and grease—as if from somewhere far off, vats of fries were being cooked. His stomach roiled as he realized what was happening and why they'd taken his hand. But such things were impossible. It couldn't happen. Maybe it was possible in the Middle East or some speck of a third world country where nobody could police morality and uphold standards of human liberty and freedom, but not here.

He ignored his intuition for one simple thing—survival. If he didn't go on, he wouldn't find the door that would lead him the hell out of the building.

Stepping through the next doorway, he entered a wide-open area that looked like an expansive work space.

He heard the prattle of two voices chatting about their wives and their wages, and he stayed low behind the machines that filled up the room. Amber lights emitted from glowing steal devices that reminded him of paper cutters, except they were the size of cars; the rest of the room was cast in a reddish haze as the red bulbs glowed like burning cherries.

"Hey, you hear that?"

Chuck stopped breathing, kept low under a conveyer belt line, and prayed they hadn't heard him.

"No, man, I don't hear shit. Now can we finish?"

He was safe for the moment. They had no knowledge of his presence. A button was audibly struck from a station, and the roar of many devices coming on at once filled the room. Steal shears slid against each other as they sliced through something. Gears pumped—un-oiled and screeching. Steam pumped and hissed out of an array of pipes. The dull roar of motors churned and conveyer belts buzzed and spun.

Directly across from him, Chuck saw a line of hooks swinging from a machine much like the ones at a dry cleaner's, except the hooks were loaded down with human arms instead of clothing—each limb had been severed at the elbow. He counted twenty, thirty, forty, fifty, and the line kept going. The arms entered a steel box, where at the edge, a thick syrup rained down, covering the appendages in a sweet coating—it had to be sweet, he could smell it and even taste it on his tongue. Continuing and reappearing as they came out of the other side of the machine, gleaming and oozing with the syrup, the hooks dropped down onto a conveyor belt covered in thick granules of sugar. The arms were rolled until they were adequately sweetened, then they entered an oven with fires blazing within. The arms cooked–sizzling and kicking out the sick meaty smell of what shouldn't be cooked.

He gaped in shock as more machines performed their duties. Down a steel slide, eye balls rolled, literally spit out from a tube to land on a metal sheet, before dispensers overhead drizzled icing on them. The steel sheet pivoted, and they were dumped down a long channel to land on yet another steel sheet and be covered in dry flour. After this coating they resembled donut holes and the belt continued, dropping them into vats of popping grease.

On another machine, intestines were stretched out and hammered by piston gears until the shit inside of them was spit out both ends. Then the empty casing was opened up at both ends by rods sending streams of water through them, finishing the cleansing process. The guts were then sucked up into a vacuum slot where God knows what else was done to them.

With morbid fascination he witnessed the unbelievable. He spotted human heads–all of them bald–being held in mechanical grips as wooden sticks were shoved up into their bases. The heads were then rolled in caramel and covered with nuts.

Chuck even spotted torsos without appendages, juicy and covered in unknown oils and marinades, turning in rotisserie ovens. The skin darkening as they were baked to a desired end. Other vats were popping with boiling stews of arms, legs, and innards, each kicking up a ripe bouillon tang.

Finally, his eyes paused on the conveyor where hands were laid out, palms up, as knives shot down and severed fingers. The fingers themselves were diverted down a different channel, once again for a special, unknown purpose. This was where his hand had ended up. Somebody had eaten it and liked it, and had wanted more of it.

"I thought I heard something... Hey you! What the fuck do you think you're doing in here?"

The two workers were heading right for him. They each wore dark brown jumpsuits with gas masks over their faces. Both men were covered in dark stains–either blood, sugar, grease, or all of it smattered together. One was reaching for a gun he'd tucked into a pocket of his jumpsuit, the other his walkie. The second barked the words, "Warning! Code 86. How do I proceed? How do I proceed?"

Chuck acted on instinct and kicked one dead center in the stomach. The worker stumbled backwards several feet, falling into the piles of hands being cut up. He ducked as the other worker tried to punch him in the mouth. He heard an awful, blood curdling scream as the first man's head was chopped into five different slivers.

"You bastard! Look what you've done! You killed Frank!"

Before the man could raise his gun, Chuck ran at him, ramming shoulder-first into his mid section, plowing him out of the way so he could dart off, ducking, weaving, jumping, and losing himself in the collection of machines.

"He's on the loose! Code 86! Code 86!" the man shouted into his walkie. Chuck could no longer hear him as a blasting alarm filled the work area and emergency lights flashed at every doorway.

He didn't know where to go next; there were dozens of doors and accesses. He spun in a circle, trying to choose, hearing the other doors open and slam, knowing they were on their way to address the 'Code 86' in progress.

More footsteps pounded after him, gaining on him. The emergency buzzers were suddenly silenced and he could hear dozens of people edging dangerously closer to his position.

"Where's the son-of-a-bitch?"

"He went that way!"

"No, that way!"

"Does anybody know where this guy is?"

"Split up. Everybody take a sector and we'll meet up. Emergency Protocol is in full effect, fellas. And don't be shy to use your guns, *it's business hours.*"

Forced to make his choice, Chuck selected the white-painted door a few feet from him, and when he charged through it, he quickly discovered it was not the way out.

He was instantly blinded by painfully bright lights and white-painted walls and ceilings. The entire room was overpowering to him after the dimness of the rest of the building. It wasn't a room, just another hallway. Scared, but also wanting to gain more distance from the men who were after him, he trekked on, finding nobody, but hearing voices and other sounds of people; banter, humming undertones, fingers tapping on glass, purses and pocketbooks opening, buttons being pressed, and women flirting with their men–some of them childish and acting like spoiled brats. "Please, Daddy, I want it. Can't I have it? I've been a good widdle girl."; "You've spent this much money on me, why not spend some more, huh? Aren't I worth it?"; "I'll cook this time like a good wife. I promise. Just give me what I want."

He kept rushing along the hall that turned out to be ongoing. A left would turn into another left. A right would lead to another right. He kept trying to find an end to it, and each time he failed. He kept reeling at sights he passed by, like the vending machines. Something so common and unimpressive turned into a macabre display. *Only a sadist engineer could drum up something like this,* he kept thinking, passing more of the machines–seemingly hundreds of them.

Gasping for breath, he almost crashed into one of the couples he'd overheard talking as he turned a corner and darted though a door. He couldn't turn back, already spotted, and even if he could whip around and run, he would be heading right for the people he was trying to evade.

The couple was a man and a woman. They were ritzy, with a mink coat and business suit–dressed like they were going to an opera. The man was in his sixties, while the woman was under half his age; it could've been the man's daughter for all he knew. She had jet black hair, wore magenta lipstick, and looked like a woman out of a fifty's speakeasy with a cigarette on the end of a plastic stick, unlit. Her hands were incased in silk gloves that ran up to her elbows, and a hat–something high end and foreign–sat on her head.

Chuck was about to spit out questions and ask for a way out, when the rich man said, "I need your opinion on something, friend. Would you humor me? My wife and I can't decide–it happens to all of us." With a broad smile he continued, "I'm sure it has happened to you too."

Chuck had no concept of what they were talking about, but he edged closer to them, thinking he could butter them up, act like one of them, and follow them to an exit.

After standing with them for ten painful seconds, the man pointed at the glass. "Which do you think is good for an anniversary dinner?"

The man was pointing at a vending machine with the complete human anatomy on display. One entire person could be purchase all at one time. The parts individually shrink-wrapped for optimal display. The dark-skinned male inside the machine was sectioned off piece-by-piece–even his genitals.

Next to the machine, rows and rows of hands were available to purchase individually, some plain, others roasted, or covered in coatings ranging from 'Toffee Crunch' and 'Tex Mex', to 'Honey BBQ' and 'Chocolate Lover's

Delight'. Glancing around, he noticed families with children. Some of them sharing a 'coated' hand treat while they shopped. He gagged as he took in the entire scene. It was like being inside a sick, twisted, horror movie.

He glanced at the other machines at random. The images of human parts jumped in his vision as if they were still alive in their casings. Tongues were designed as chewy suckers. Barbequed spines looking like meat snakes sold in foot long segments. Nerve endings sold individually wrapped as chewing gum. Gallbladders marinating in a honey bourbon sauce were offered in bite-sized snack packs. Wads of labial skin gleaming in pools of white icing–the label advertising the name, 'Cinnamon Love Cakes'. Testicles flavored with coconut and sugar rubs, justly named 'Sweet Balls'.

His gag reflex was working overtime, and he couldn't take anymore. His reaction exploded out of him in the form of slamming his fist into the male customer's nose. The bone cracked like one of those old pop guns, and blood gushed from both nostrils, covering his mouth and chin in bright red. The woman ogled the blood on her husband's face and licked her lips; enticed, her eyes grew two sizes larger than normal.

Before Chuck could slap the expression off her face, men from all angles charged in and tackled, cuffed, and restrained him.

The workers apologized to the man, each of them prattling their regrets and how this was a horrible inconvenience–asking how they could make it up to him.

"This is outrageous," the bleeding man spouted, receiving help back up to his feet by a pair of workers who'd removed their masks to reveal they were normal working class men. "I mean, I thought we were paying for quality, and that included competent security! He could've hurt my wife. This is so outrageous! I want to talk to the manager–someone who's in charge. For the amount of money I pay just to have access to this place, and then to be assaulted–it's insulting beyond words!"

Out of the throng of workers appeared a man in a silver suit and heavy rimmed glasses, sporting the overall look of a corporate CEO ready to swoop in and save the day. Chuck could hear the man assuage the victim as he wiped his face clean with a kerchief, though his nose was still running red.

"Come with me, Mr. and Mrs. Wellington. I have a perfect solution for our problem–my sincere apologies. An unexpected event has unfolded, and I'm sorry you were a victim of our incompetence. As I see it, we can remedy this by giving you carte blanche. Anything you want, but I do have a recommendation, and normally we charge more than two million dollars for this service because of the risk and the cost of the take-home kit, but for you, our valued customers, it's on the house..."

* * *

"I think he's awake..."

Chuck awoke slowly to a steady tapping noise. Wading through a thick fog of unconsciousness, he noticed his eyelids stuck together with sleep and he couldn't move, though it wasn't because he was drugged.

"It's time, honey."

The face of the woman from the warehouse stared in at him, and the man he'd punched was standing behind her, his nose encased in a bandage. He glared in at Chuck, delivering an eyeful of hatred...*and hunger.*

"Do you want to do the honors, honey?" he asked his wife.

"I think we both should," she replied sweetly with a broad smile.

Licking their lips and salivating, they stared in at his naked, hairless body. The couple pressed a button he couldn't see from his standpoint inside the box. Once they pushed it, long cylinder coils to his sides turned orange, throwing off intense heat; soon the chamber would be oven-hot.

From behind him, a steel rod pierced through his back and out through his stomach. It scraped his spine and severed many nerve endings before he could cough up blood and scream in mortal terror. And before he could register anything else, he was turned upside down like a rotisserie piece of meat. The heat in the chamber climbed so high that his eyes exploded in their sockets and his heart ceased to beat from shock and loss of blood.

The couple watched the dead, cooking piece of meat, and then the husband urged his wife aside after reading the console on the giant oven. "He's got another hour, honey. Let's go have a drink and relax a bit before dinner."

89

STALKERS BEWARE

REBECCA BESSER

Mitchell Peterson stood backstage with a knot of anticipation growing inside his chest as he listened to the crowd gather for the concert. It didn't matter how many times he and his band took the stage, it still excited him. Adrenaline would spike his system and he'd be a music making machine for hours on end. But the music wasn't the only thing that got him going, there were all the girls–groupies by the dozens who wanted a piece of him and everyone else on stage. Being wanted that badly took the high to a whole new level.

After lifting his guitar and sliding on the shoulder strap, he peeked out at the people who were settling into their seats, waiting anxiously for the band's appearance. He scanned the audience looking for just the right one and he saw her sitting in the second row off to the left of the stage.

The woman he'd spotted had long, curly, darkish blond hair that hung loose around her shoulders. She was wearing a white tank top with the band's name stretched taunt across her generous breasts and a pair of black jeans that fit her perfectly.

"You ready, man?" a gruff voice asked from behind him.

Mitch turned to see Dave, the drummer for the band. He smirked, "Ready as always."

The two men laughed. *Ready as always*, was their theme for music and women. Having traveled from gig to gig together for months, they'd become as close as brothers. Mitch sometimes felt closer to the people he traveled with than his own family. At least they understood the driving need to create, to keep moving, and to make something of himself and his name. They were all in this together and they understood him like no one else could, or would. Sometimes he thought people just didn't want to take the time to understand him, too busy with their own mundane matters.

The lights dimmed and the men looked at each other, grinning broadly, each making a fist and bumping their knuckles together before they charged out onto stage as they were announced.

"May I present to you, Wane of Existence!"

The screams and cheers of the crowd drowned out all other sound for almost an entire minute. Mitch closed his eyes and let his body absorb the sound and excitement of the crowd as he played the first cords of the opening song. He felt the music course through him, caressing his soul and setting it on fire. Feeling like he was free and weightless, he let it take him, carrying him beyond himself and what he could be to a place no one could touch him–he was in his zone.

Song after song, the concert went on. Mitch noted how the blond woman watched him and screamed out his name and how much she loved him. She would be an easy mark. Most of the groupie-stalkers were, or else he wouldn't be able to feed his appetite. This particular one had been at every show in the area for the last six months–he'd even seen her at one of their out of state concerts. Every time, she tried to get backstage to see him, telling security she was his girlfriend.

Before he knew it, they were done and backstage. Mitch was almost surprised to find that he was covered with sweat, but it was something he'd come to expect; he'd be so fixated on his music, he wouldn't notice anything else. Downing bottle after bottle of water to sate his thirst, he started to think about the blond and his hunger.

Mitch did his duty, signing autographs and talking to people who'd spent the extra money and bought back stage passes. But as he went through the motions, the blond was on his mind. He hoped she'd try to get backstage again tonight, because he had plans for her.

She didn't disappoint. He grinned broadly when he spotted her and her friend talking to stage security, trying to convince the men to let them come backstage.

Excusing himself, he headed over and picked up some of the conversation.

"I'm sorry, ladies," one of the security men said. "Like I already said, we can't let you back there without a pass."

Mitch put his hand on the man's shoulder and said, "It's all right—would you ladies like an autograph?"

The women smiled at Mitch, nodded eagerly, and pressed themselves up against him while he tried to scrawl his name on what they wanted signed. He felt a hand slide into his back, left pants pocket and ignored it, allowing a small piece of paper to be withdrawn. After signing autographs, he allowed them to get their pictures taken with him, using their cell phones.

As they were walking away, he watched them closely, noting how the blond withdrew something from her pocket and whispered to her friend, who looked shocked and amazed. His plan had worked like a charm, and now all he had to do was sit back and wait.

"What was that all about?" Dave asked—he'd noticed the exchange while he was talking to someone from the stage crew about when the equipment would need to be loaded and moved out.

"That crazy-blond-stalker-chick was here again," Mitch said, as they walked together to the green room. "I thought maybe if I gave her an autograph she'd finally leave me alone."

Dave laughed. "Like that's ever going to happen! She'll follow your sexy ass around until the day she dies!"

Mitch grinned and twisted the top off another bottle of water. He didn't say anything about his plan to his friend, there were some things that didn't need to be shared. But Dave was right, she would follow him around until the day she died, that he was absolutely sure of.

"Speaking of stalkers," Craig—another member of the band—said, "what happened to that redhead who was after you for eight months, Mitch? I haven't seen her forever."

Mitch took a swallow of water and shrugged his shoulders. "Don't know. Maybe she found someone else to be obsessed about. Maybe she got knocked up by some guy and has to stay home now. How should I know?"

Craig laughed. "Yeah, maybe!"

Dave winked at Mitch and looked at Craig. "You're just jealous because you don't have any crazy bitches tryin' to crawl between your sheets and follow you to the bathroom!"

Craig scowled. "Shut up, fucker! I've got plenty of chicks wanting me, I just don't pay attention to them because I love Beth, and you know it."

Dave and Mitch laughed.

"Sure," Dave said. "That's what it is…"

Mitch smiled. "It's okay, Craig, not everyone can be as handsome as me—I'm blessed."

They all laughed, knowing Mitch got the most female attention because he was the most outgoing and charismatic man in the group, which they were okay with. After all, Dave was married and Craig was engaged. Troy, the only other member of the band, was shy and hid from the fans more often than not.

"Maybe you should start a groupie/stalker harem," Craig teased. "Then you could have all kinds of fun."

Mitch shook his head and finished his water. "While that sounds like fun and all, I don't want to die of some weird disease. Have you seen some of those women? They're scary!"

Dave smiled. "Very true. There have been some really scary ones following you around. How come all the pretty or decent ones disappear after a while, but the nasty ones are always around?"

"Probably because the decent ones figure out after a while that I'm just human like everyone else," Mitch said. "And the nasty ones can't get anyone to love them, so they have to dream about me."

Troy walked into the green room and heard the last comment. "Something like that," he said. "I think we're about ready to get out of here… How long will it take you guys to get your shit? I want to go home."

With that, they gathered their personal belongings and made sure everything was taken care of and loaded. They'd hired a crew to handle the equipment for this tour, which was nice. They keenly remembered the days when they'd had to set up and tear down their own stuff.

Finally on the bus heading toward home, Mitch had some time to think about his plan. If things went as smoothly as they normally did, he would be a very happy man in a night or two. Glancing at Troy, who was sitting on the built in couch reading a book, he wondered if he would be up for a double again. Troy was the only one he trusted to participate in his dark activities. After a few moments of thought, he shook his head, letting go of the idea. He wanted to enjoy it alone this time. It was always...*sweeter* somehow when he took care of things himself.

* * *

It was three o'clock in the morning when Mitch unlocked the door to his small house. He stumbled inside, kicked the door shut, and locked it. With a heavy, tired sigh, he hung his keys on the hook by the door and dropped his bag to the floor. Trudging into the kitchen, he extracted a beer from the fridge and opened it. Tossing the cap in the trash, he picked up the handset of his phone to check his voice mail. He would have preferred to go straight to bed, but after missing an important message once when a friend had been taken to the hospital, he now checked his messages right away.

He almost started laughing when he heard he had forty-five messages, betting most of them were left by the blond, and he was right. She'd called multiple times, leaving messages that ranged from pathetic to obscene; he'd been right on when he'd picked her.

After hanging up the phone, still laughing to himself, he downed the rest of his beer and went to take a shower. The hot water relaxed him to the point he almost fell asleep standing up in the shower. He turned off the water, stumbled out of the bathtub, quickly toweled dry, trudged into his bedroom, flopped onto the bed and was instantly asleep.

* * *

When Mitch woke up it was last afternoon and his stomach was rumbling. Stretching, he got out of bed, pulled on underwear, baggy jeans, and a T-shirt while thinking about what he wanted to eat. He picked up the phone to order pizza and heard an insistent beep telling him he had more messages.

I must have been really tired, he thought—he normally woke up when the phone rang. Absently, he punched in his pass code while looking into the depths of his empty refrigerator, trying to find something to snack on until he could get some decent food.

It was the blond again. She'd left more obscene messages and they were giving him some wild ideas. With a sigh, he wrote down her number and deleted the messages. He dialed her number. After only two rings, she answered.

"Hello?" she practically purred in his ear.

"Hi, is Marcy there?" he asked in an offhand tone, knowing it was her without asking.

"This is her," she said and giggled. "Who's this?"

"I think you know who this is," he teased, grinning. "You're a very bad girl, leaving all those naughty messages."

She giggled again. "Did you like them?"

"Yes, I did," he said. "Why do you think I'm calling?"

In less than two minutes, he set up a time and got her address to pick her up for a date that evening and then was off the phone.

"Too easy," he mumbled to himself.

Mitch found some microwave popcorn in a cabinet and decided it would have to do. He didn't want to spoil his appetite, looking forward to a filling meal later. He carried the bag with him, munching on the buttery snack while he mentally went over everything he would need later that night, checking to make sure it was in place. Everything was where it should have been and was ready. It had been months since he'd had a woman over, but he was meticulous with his preparations, so he didn't have to do much.

*   *   *

Hours later, Mitch rang the door bell at the address he'd been given. Marcy answered the door looking lovely in a slutty sort of way. She wore entirely too much makeup, her skirt was a little too tight and short, and her shirt showed too much cleavage. It was all right with him, he wasn't taking her home to his parents, so he admired what she was so blatantly offering.

"Hi," she said, biting her bottom lip and looking him over.

"Hi, yourself," he said with an appreciative smile. "You ready?"

"Yup," she chirped, grabbed her purse, shut the door behind herself, and made sure she brushed up against him as she sauntered out to his car.

Mitch followed her slowly, watching and admiring the muscle tone of her legs and the firmness of her ass; he couldn't help but lick his lips in anticipation. Rushing forward, he opened the car door for her and was inwardly pleased to see her smile as she tucked her hair behind her ear while she climbed in. She was well on her way to trusting him, and he would need that trust later tonight if he was to get what he was after.

Walking briskly around the car, he slid in the driver's side and shut the door behind him. As he reached forward to turn the key in the ignition, she took a hold of his wrist and tugged it over until his hand was resting on her knee.

"What's your hurry?" she asked, leaning her head back against the head-rest and arching her back like a content kitten, showing off her breasts.

He gently squeezed her knee, massaging the soft, warm skin of her leg with his fingertips. "I thought you might be hungry."

"Oh, I'm hungry," she purred, "for you." Sitting forward, she leaned over and kissed him on the lips, slowly and gently. Pulling back, she blinked her big grayish blue eyes at him. "Do you want to feed me?"

Mitch grinned. "If that's what you want."

She giggled before kissing him again.

He knew what she wanted. It was the same thing all the others had wanted, so he gave it to her. Thrusting his free hand into her hair, he kissed her back, hard. She whimpered and wrapped her arms around his neck and tried to climb onto his lap, but he turned sideways to keep that from happening. She started to grope at him and claw at his clothes desperately and he had to force himself not to shove her away in disgust and tell her to get the hell out of his car, but that wouldn't get him what *he* wanted. Slowly, he pulled back and forced a smile.

"I'll give you that later," Mitch said, kissing her again. "Right now, we're going to go have dinner."

She whimpered and stuck her bottom lip out in a pout, but nodded. Sitting back in the passenger seat, she tried to adjust her ridiculously short shirt and look semi-decent.

Starting the car, Mitch looked in his mirrors to make sure nothing was coming and caught the look of steel in his own eyes–he was seething inside. He couldn't believe that most women didn't have any self respect and thought the only way they could hold a man's interest was to throw their bodies at them. Shaking himself mentally, he refocused on what he was doing and the woman beside him, reminding himself of later and what was to come. These thoughts easily brought a natural smile back to his face.

They made light, polite conversation as they traversed to the restaurant he'd chosen for dinner. It was out of the way and small, but they had good food. The meal seemed to fly by with Marcy constantly talking about all the stuff she thought musicians were interested in, just like all the others had.

While it pleased him they were so interested in what he'd accomplished, he thought the absolute obsession and brainwashing–leaving no room for their own thoughts–was incredibly sad. Plus, they had no idea who he really was and only seemed interested in the surface stuff they *thought* he was. By the time the meal was over he was almost thoroughly depressed by his ultimate loneliness and disgusted by her hero worship attitude.

After they were both back in the car, he decided to move things along a little faster than he normally would have.

"I was going to take you to a movie, but I'm still a bit tired after the long tour," he said with a crooked grin. "Why don't we go back to my place and watch something there?"

Marcy's eyes brightened and she was completely pathetic in her eagerness to please. "Oh, that sounds great! Really!"

He drove them back to his house, knowing there would be no movie, and he was right. As soon as they walked through the door, she practically threw herself at him. In no time flat she had her skirt off, showing off her red, see-through thong as she slipped off her shoes.

"How about I just put you to bed? Since you're so tired and all..." she said, wrapping her arms around his neck and standing on her tip toes to kiss him.

"Mmm," he murmured as he slid his hands down her back and cupped her bare ass, "that sounds like a great idea." She squealed as he squatted down slightly and gripped the backs of her legs behind her knees, lifting her and wrapping her legs around his waist. "But first, let's take a shower."

"Yes, babe," she breathed into his ear as she nibbled his earlobe, "anything you want."

In a frenzy of tearing off clothes and trying not to fall down, they made their way down the hall and into the bathroom. Soon they were naked under the hot spray of the shower, enjoying each other vigorously.

"Tell me when you're coming," he growled against her slick, wet neck as he thrust into her.

She whimpered and begged him to fuck her, and he did. Her breath was coming in short, deep pants and he knew she was almost there. Reaching down to the handle bar above the soap dish, he yanked the circular tube hard and it popped out of its hold smoothly, just as she started crying out that she was having an orgasm. Lifting the tube above his head, he thrust his erection deep into her as hard as he could, becoming more excited by the moment, knowing what was about to happen and anticipating it with all of his being. He watched her face as her body shook with sexual pleasure, and at just the right moment, he stabbed the tube downward, sinking the blade attached to the handle deep into the side of her throat. Her eyes flew open as she cried out sharply for the last time. Ripping the knife back out, he buried his face in her neck, sucking and licking at the blood he'd spilt as he too came with intense pleasure.

After the rush of his climax eased slowly from his quivering body, Mitch became acutely aware of the spray of the shower falling over him and the limp, dead body of Marcy in his arms. With a smile, he laid her down on the floor of the shower and quickly washed himself off while she bled out. Soap suds and blood swirled together as they both raced down the drain and out of the tub. He'd learned long ago that making the kill in the shower was the best way. He liked it because he didn't end up with as much of a mess.

Turning off the shower, he carefully stepped out of the tub and toweled dry before opening the cabinet under the sink and extracting a large, folded sheet of clear plastic and a rolled up package of chef knives. He proceeded to unfold and lay the plastic on the floor–kneeling on it–and then he opened the roll of knives, looking over their pristine steel thoughtfully. Choosing a blade, he leaned into the tub and made a long, deep cut in Marcy's throat, pleased to see only a slight trickle of blood ooze from the new wound.

Having butchered women many time before, it took him only an hour and a half to get all the useful meat from Marcy's corpse. Leaving the meat in the tub, he lifted out her skeleton and laid it on the plastic sheet. Wiping the blood from his body on the damp towel he'd used to dry himself earlier, he looked down at what was left of his most recent dedicated stalker with a twisted grin on his face. She'd been incredibly easy and it wasn't as late at night as he'd anticipated when he'd done his planning. Meaning he also had time to dispose of her bones before bed. He hated leaving them lying around any longer than he had to. Living in the country and being sur-rounded by acres of forest, he had a lot of privacy, but he didn't want to take it for granted, just in case.

Stepping over the pile of death in his bathroom, he headed down the hall and to his bedroom, where he donned a pair of sweat pants and an old, black T-shirt. Slipping on a pair of old, mud splattered sneakers, he headed back to the bathroom, now ready to take out the trash. The thought of the word 'trash' at this point always made him laugh, because in his opinion he was taking out the trash of womankind. They were slutty, easy, and severely lacking in the self respect and character that any human person should have. In some ways he viewed them as nothing more than animals–bitches in heat that he took care of and put out of their misery.

Dragging the tarp and shuffling backwards, even though it didn't weigh very much, Mitch made his way out the back door–pausing briefly to flip a switch that flooded his back yard with light–and continued across the porch, down the steps, and toward the wood pile. Once there, he yanked his axe out of the stump he used for splitting wood and got to work severing the bony limbs from the once life-filled woman. After he had them cut down into smaller, manageable pieces, he started up his gas powered wood chipper and struck the head of the axe back into the stump. Slowly, he fed the bones into the grinding part of the machine and watched them come out the other end in small, mulch-like chips. The noise was incredibly loud in the quiet evening, and the bright flood lights mounted on the back of the house would have made everything crystal clear had anyone been able to see back there, but he'd put up a privacy fence shortly after moving in. At the time it was to keep the neighbors' dogs out of his yard, but when he'd started giving in to his dark urges, it had come in quite handy. He also knew the neighbors wouldn't think anything of the noise. He worked strange hours, and with band practice and concerts his schedule was erratic at the best of times. He'd often mulched fallen limbs late in the evening, even took the time to take care of fallen branches for his closest neighbors–almost half of a mile away–who were an elderly couple, both in their late eighties.

After all the bones were taken care of, he sent through a couple of four inch diameter limbs to clean out any meat or bits of bone that might have worked into the gears–they did their job well. Soon he was done mulching and he shut off the machine. The silence that surrounded him was almost eerie after the loud noise of the mulcher, but he delighted in it. He loved peace and quiet as much as he loved the noise and energy of being on stage.

He hummed one of the songs he was currently working on while he shoveled the bone/mulch mixture onto a larger heap of mulch sitting off to the side. Once they were added, he shoveled some of the old mulch over the new, knowing the bugs would eat whatever flesh was still there, and that the heat of the pile would dry the bone out faster.

Yawning and stretching, standing the shovel back against the fence from where he'd gotten it, he dragged the bloody plastic sheet over to the hose reel and unwound the hose. He lazily sprayed it off as if the red streaks were nothing more than paint. Once it was mostly clean, he went inside and retrieved a gallon of bleach. He dumped some on the tarp, sat the gallon jug on the steps so he wouldn't forget to take it back in when he went inside, and sprayed the plastic down again. When he was done, he hung the plastic over the rail of his porch and set a rock on each end to keep it from blowing away.

"Well, that didn't take long," he muttered to himself as he picked up the bleach and headed back inside. He took it with him and set it on the bathroom floor, knowing he would need it after he finished butchering and bagging the meat in the tub.

As he stepped into the kitchen, ready to open the fridge door and grab a beer, he almost jumped out of his skin when the phone rang, startling him. He snatched up the handset and pressed 'talk'.

"Hello..." he said, glancing at the clock on his microwave that said it was only a little after nine o'clock. "Oh, hi, Craig. No, I wasn't busy..."

He listened and laughed. "You know I was just thinking the same thing. Why don't we have the cookout here? I'll even provide the steaks!" He grinned, thinking of all the fresh meat he had in his bathtub. "Awesome! Saturday it is. Tell Dave it's his turn to bring the beer!" With another laugh, he hung up, shaking his head.

Mitch got the beer he wanted, grabbed a couple of boxes of gallon and quart freezer bags from a cabinet, and headed back to the bathroom. Setting everything down, he opened the beer and downed it; tossing the bottle in the trash can he looked over the dark red masses of meat before him. Turning on the water in the tub, he picked up piece after piece, rinsing and then slicing them into the cuts he wanted before putting them into freezer bags. Before he knew it the meat was gone and he'd finished off one box of the quart bags and more than half of a box of gallon bags.

He set the steaks for the cookout aside so they wouldn't get mixed in with everything else. Gathering as much as he could in one armload, he headed out to his small garage to deposit the meat in his chest style deep freezer. He returned to the bathroom and did the same with the rest and put the steaks in the fridge in the house.

After washing out the tub and cleaning his knives with bleach, he took another quick shower. As he pulled on a pair of boxer shorts, his stomach rumbled and he remembered he hadn't eaten much for supper because he'd been disgusted by the woman and because he was looking forward to eating her later.

Wearing a grin as he walked to the kitchen, he opened the fridge, took out a bag which held one 'Marcy steak' and another beer. He put them on the counter and grabbed a pair of tongs from a hook above the stove. Just the thought of a grilled steak had his mouth watering and his stomach growling louder in its eagerness. He was glad he'd purchased a gas grill when he'd moved in. He'd had a charcoal grill before and really liked the flavor they gave food, but the gas grill didn't take hours to heat up, so he'd decided to try it and was pleased with the ease of grilling it gave him. Collecting his food, beverage, utensil, and some seasoning, he once again headed out the back door, this time, not leaving the porch.

In minutes the grill was hot enough to start cooking. Opening the plastic bag, he used the tongs to fish out the raw, red meat. He half-laid it on top of the bag and sprinkled both sides with seasoning before he placed it on the hot grill; it sizzled and spit as the heat attacked the bloody liquid dripping from it. He shut the lid and let the heat do its job while he enjoyed his beer—standing on his porch in nothing but boxers, taking in the peaceful night. A couple minutes passed before he opened the grill and flipped the steak—his stomach growling again as the aroma of it cooking rose into the air to tease him. Licking his lips he reluctantly closed the grill again and took the bloody bag into the house and retrieved a plate; by the time he returned the steak was done to his liking. He turned off the grill and plated his prize with the tongs and went back inside.

After acquiring a steak knife, fork, and another beer from the kitchen when he put the tongs in the sink, he settled into his recliner to enjoy his meat. He cut into it slowly, watching the natural juices seep out and onto his plate. Raising the fork to his lips with the first bite impaled on its prongs, he paused for a moment, building anticipation for his tongue as he breathed in the intoxicating aroma of grilled human flesh. Placing the little chunk of meat in his mouth, he closed his lips over the fork, sliding the morsel off with his teeth as the flavor exploded on his tongue and he moaned in ecstasy. He savored each and every bite with his eyes closed as he lovingly chewed each piece before swallowing it. He ate more than half of the steak before taking a drink of his beer because he didn't want it to interrupt the circus of delight his mouth was experiencing.

Before he knew it, his steak was gone and his stomach was full, but he was still disappointed his enjoyment had to end. Putting his dishes in the sink, he made his way to bed, tired and sated from his meal.

Climbing into bed, he smiled, thinking about Saturday and the steaks waiting in the fridge. That thought alone kept him smiling even after he'd fallen asleep.

* * *

Saturday arrived and so did the band and their families. Mitch stood on his porch, proudly manning his grill while he watched the children playing in his yard, and the adults sitting or standing around talking; everyone wore happy smiles as they enjoyed themselves.

"Those steaks sure do smell good!" Dave said, coming up behind him and punching him lightly on the shoulder. "I wish you would tell me where you get your meat so I could go to the same butcher! Nothing I buy ever tastes the same."

Mitch laughed. "I would tell you, but then I'd have to kill ya!"

Dave laughed. "Fine, keep your secrets! You'll just have to cook for me more often that way, and I won't complain about that!"

"No," Mitch said, "I don't suppose you would. Hey, the meat's done–you want to get everyone rounded up so we can eat?"

"Sure thing, man," Dave said, heading down the steps and into Mitch's back yard to do just that.

Mitch removed all the meat from the grill–steaks for the adults and burgers for the kids–and put it on a large platter. He turned off the grill and headed down the steps himself, to the picnic tables setting off to the left side of his yard.

"Here you go!" he said, setting the plate in the middle of the table. "Enjoy!"

Everyone dug in and soon the heaping mound of meat was reduced to a few pieces to be saved for later.

"Hey, Mitch," Craig called from the far end of the table, "too bad you didn't invite that little blond who has been stalking you, then you would have had a date for this party!"

Mitch laughed, eating the last bite of his steak. "Oh, she's here in spirit, I'm sure."

Craig laughed, and as Mitch looked around the table he saw that Troy had a smirk on his face. He winked at Mitch and shoved another bite of steak into his mouth.

She was there all right, and she was now a part of all of them...

DELIGHTFUL FILLETS

CHARLES DAY

Trevor knew he was being followed the moment he left the bar because an extremely large figure cast a dark shadow against the brick and mortar building, coming down the alley and picking up its pace as he ran as fast as he could between the two buildings, until he approached a dented, old dumpster. He quickly slid between the rusty steel and the damp brick wall, letting out short bursts of breath almost silently, hoping he wouldn't be heard as he crouched down, frightened for his life. With only a dim, yellow light from a lamp post high above to provide him with light, he watched his adversary creep up slowly toward his hiding place—the shadow coming to a stop against the brick wall. It then seemed to slide to the ground, a sure sign that the stranger had moved closer to the dumpster. He peeked out slightly, trying to remain hidden but it was no use—he'd been found.

He gasped for air, kicking and screaming as a large figure came around the rusty, steel garbage collector and grabbed a hold of his blue, denim jacket with two large, gloved hands, forcing him into a headlock. Trevor tried to scream again, but a large cloth was pressed against his nose and mouth. The scent of a chemical substance crawled into his burning nostrils and he began to feel dizzy, like the time he'd been given sweet air by his dentist, only this didn't feel like the buzz he'd enjoyed while staring at the good-looking dental assistant. He attempted one last time to break free, but his abductor–who had a firm hold on his neck–was stronger, and he held Trevor tight until he lost the battle, succumbing to the chemical he'd inhaled.

The large man carried the unconscious Trevor over his shoulder and walked out of the dark alley toward his black van; he opened one of the two doors in the back and tossed the limp body onto the carpeted floor. He pulled out his pocket knife and reached for Trevor's arm, slicing a chunk of flesh off his bicep; he took the bleeding piece of raw meat and placed it in his mouth, grinding his jaws and teeth as he began to chew.

"Mmm, tastes like chicken," he said aloud and laughed as he slammed the door shut. He looked around to make sure no one was in the area, placed the chemically saturated cloth in his back pocket after wiping the blood off of his mouth, and jumped into the driver's seat of the van, slowly driving off while looking at the moon filled night ahead.

*   *   *

It was your typical November morning–cold and breezy with brown, crispy leaves already off the semi-naked trees, scattered on the ground, reminding everyone that winter would soon follow. Gabriel stepped on the leaves and enjoyed the crunching sound underfoot as he approached a light pole full of rusty staples and nails. There, hung a new sign, similar to others he'd seen around town recently, announcing that another young man in his twenties had gone missing; he made a total of three from the neighborhood over the last couple of months. In fact, one missing young man's mug shot was posted on the back of the milk carton he'd purchased last week. The missing man on the sign was from the neighborhood and liked to hang out at the local bar every weekend with his buddies, drinking beer and having a good time. Gabriel remembered seeing him on occasion when he'd stop in for a drink or two and had known him fairly well; he'd had long hair and was always wearing a black shirt with different rock bands displayed in colorful letters and graphics on the front, usually covered slightly by his blue, denim jacket. *Why are these young, single men suddenly disappearing?* he wondered to himself. *It doesn't make any sense.* He'd purposely moved with his wife Cindy to Sandersville, PA to get away from the crime and murders they'd been surrounded by back in NY, and now this–young men going missing.

He looked away from the sign and walked up to the local deli to get what he'd originally come out for this early fall morning. He heard the crunching of leaves under his shoes as he made his way to the brick building and he felt the forced, hot air from the heating ducts above hit the top of his head and then his cold, red checks, warming him up almost instantly as he entered the establishment. His nose filled with the aroma of fresh bacon, eggs, and golden hash browns sizzling together on the heated grill. Although he would have loved to order a breakfast sandwich right there and then, he'd only come in to pick up some rolls, a large cup of coffee, and the sliced ham and cheese combo special that was on sale every weekend. He joined the rest of the town folk–three to be exact–waiting in line to be served by the two clerks in white aprons.

"Morning, Gabe, how are things treating ya?" Pete from the local hardware store greeted him with a smile while standing ahead of him in the line. He was a tall, friendly fellow–green bean thin with a country feel to him because of his flannel shirt, overalls, and straw hat.

"Couldn't be better, Pete, how's the family?" Gabriel replied.

Pete stared at him and waited a few seconds before replying, "They're fine. How's the wife?"

"Good as can be," he said and decided since Pete had grown in this small town, if anyone knew what to make of the recent disappearances, he certainly would. "What's with all the single men going missing? Have they decided to move out of town without telling their families?"

"You know…my whole life living here, I've never seen anything like it," Pete said with a sigh, looking at the floor and scratching his unshaven chin with his dirty hand, going silent again for a few seconds as if he were lost in his own thoughts. Without warning, he looked up from the floor, smiled and continued, "It's just been these last couple of months. All of a sudden three young men go missing and their families are wondering why their loved ones would just up and leave–something's not right."

Gabriel's eyebrows bent and wrinkles appeared in his forehead as he frowned thoughtfully. "That's what I'm thinking. Maybe we have a serial killer in our midst, like what's his name...Jeffery Dahmer, taking our young men?"

The line moved forward and it was Pete's turn to order. While waiting his turn, Gabriel thought hard about what the owner of the hardware store had said. From behind him, another customer walked in, bringing the cold breeze from outside with him as the bells hanging above the door started to jingle like a set of Christmas bells; he noticed it was the new neighbor who'd moved in last summer.

"Hi ya, Gabe! In for some fresh rolls are ya?" Rocco asked, taking off his baseball hat to reveal his shiny, bald head. He was a heavy set man and Gabe could tell he liked to eat by the large gut he carried. Nonetheless, he did his best to hide it well, using his large sweater and beige khaki pants to cover it up.

"You guessed right. I'm going to make my wife breakfast. How about you? Picking up some breakfast as well?"

"Just some coffee and a pastry–need to watch my weight," Rocco replied, staring down at Gabe, who was at least a foot shorter. He pointed ahead with his large, pudgy fingers, giving Gabriel a signal, telling him he was up next. "Time to place your order, buddy–looks like you're next."

Gabriel stepped up to the counter and asked the deli worker in a white apron to slice him some fresh ham and cheese. He watched as the meat slicer was turned on–the large blade spinning fast as thin slices of ham fell down on top of each other. A mound of fresh meat soon piled up and was wrapped and placed on top of the deli counter, followed by a small packet of freshly sliced cheese.

"Here you go, Gabe, anything else?" the man with clear gloves asked, pushing his order to the edge of the counter.

"A few of those fresh rolls behind you, Mac, and a large black coffee," Gabriel said with a smile and watched as Mac place the rolls in a brown paper bag, and poured some dark liquid into a cup.

"You're all done," Mac said, adding the bag and cup to the rest of Gabe's order. "Mary Joe will ring you up. Next!"

Gabriel took his order and moved out of the line so Rocco could place his. He said goodbye to his neighbor, paid for his items, and walked home; he was still thinking about the three missing men as he came to his driveway. He looked over at his new neighbors' house and saw– from the second floor window–the image of someone who seemed to back away and out of sight purposely, replacing the white curtains. He thought it strange, but figured it was Rocco's partner, Dirk. He knew they were a gay couple and he didn't mind, feeling that an individual's sexual preference was their own business, and as long as they didn't try to make a pass at him, he was okay. Nonetheless, he did think they were kind of weird and reclusive.

He entered his house to be greeted by his wife, Cindy. He admired the way she looked right then, wearing a pair of blue jeans that seemed to be painted on her legs and ass because they were so tight. They complimented her soft, white wool sweater that unfortunately hid her beautiful, large breasts; her long, blond hair gently ran down beside each of them. He felt his love juices begin to flow, giving him an instant erection as he walked straight up to his sexy wife, set the brown bag of rolls, cup, and deli meat on the small table to his right in the foyer, and gave her a gentle hug.

He spoke first, letting his true intentions be known. "Hey, honey, you in the mood? You look all sexy in those tight blue jeans." She was about the same height as he was, so he knew she was aware of his intentions the moment he took a hold of her ass—squeezing her left cheek—and pulled her tight against him. Within only a few minutes of foreplay, they were on the living room couch ripping each other's clothes off.

The television was on when he walked in; Cindy had been watching the morning news. They both lifted their sweaty heads from underneath a blanket when the newscaster started talking about the most recent missing person in their town.

"Seems we have another man missing up in the hills of Sandersville, PA. Apparently, the family contacted the police to report their twenty-one-year-old son was at a party on the 1st of November and never came home. As the days pass, the police are searching the town, but nothing has yet been found. Sandersville has now seen their third missing person's case in the last two months. I spoke with the mayor of the town and he said they'd never had a single case like this before. All of a sudden, it's like someone decided to pick their town for abductions and he's determined to find the culprit. We'll be back with more..."

"I told you, Cindy, something's not right. When the first young man went missing, I figured maybe he took off with his girlfriend and decided to hook up in another town, but after the third, no fucking way. Somebody evil is behind this."

"Gabe, stop it, you're creeping me out. I don't want to think about the possibility of some serial killer walking around town, preying on our young men."

They went back to cuddling with Gabriel doing his best to keep her mind occupied with better things.

* * *

Later that evening the sun retreated and a smothering of darkness enveloped the town of Sandersville.

Sam and Tommy drank a few beers before they decided to call it a night and walked out of Dooley's Pub and Brewery.

Tommy stumbled out first, swinging his right arm up and around Sam for support. "So long there O' Dooley, hope you have some beer left when we come back." He looked up at his best bud–his only real friend since High School–and started to sing, "La, la, la...lala, we don't need no stinking badges, right, Sam?" He groggily remembered all the good times they'd had, including the ones they'd shared since graduating.

Sam liked Tommy just the same, so carrying him to the truck wasn't an issue, and Tommy knew this, so he held on tight, continuing to sing a few notes as they stumbled closer to his friend's neon blue Ford pickup; he watched the headlights come on as Sam hit the automatic start button on his key ring. It was dark in the parking lot–darker than other nights they'd left Dooley's–and Tommy looked up, noticing the light toward the back of the parking lot was out. *Strange*, he thought, *it was working just fine last night.*

He continued to lean hard on his buddy's right shoulder, eventually causing them both to stumble and fall in the gravel parking lot. Tommy felt the small, jagged pebbles push into his blue jeans, poking at his flesh and bone. The uneven pressure of the individual stones irritated his knees and made him uncomfortable, so he leaned harder on Sam for support, until he was pulled away, sending Tommy back down into the gravel face first. Two black work boots quickly advanced toward his face and then, without any warning–before he could look up and see who was attached to the boots– one of them came straight at him, hitting him in the nose and mouth, knocking out a few teeth and causing the cartilage in his nose to explode. A stream of warm, salty blood spilled from his face and lips.

Tommy felt the pain in his jaw radiate through his head as he brought his hand up to his face where it was quickly filled with flowing blood. He spit a few teeth into the gravel with a string of blood and mucus. His vision blurred but he could still see the boots walking away, barely, and he could hear the crunching of gravel, which seemed to become more distant. Suddenly, he heard the slamming of a car door or perhaps it was the tailgate of his buddy's pickup–he couldn't be certain. Nonetheless, he certainly knew his face had been busted up something awful; the excruciating pain from his dislocated jaw shot up into his head, forcing a severe migraine to pulsate through his brain as if someone had grabbed a hold of his gray matter and begun to squeeze it hard.

Where the fuck is Sam? he wondered. One minute he was leaning on him for added support, and a few seconds later they were sprawled out in the parking lot of Dooley's Pub. *What the hell was that all about, and who was wearing those boots?* As the questions stirred in his sore brain, he felt as if he'd become airborne, heading straight for the stars, instead, he realized, he'd just been lifted off the ground by a tall, heavy set man with huge, black gloved hands and black work boots.

Tommy saw the ground moving as he watched those boots walk after being thrown over the man's shoulder. Shortly after, he was tossed into the back of a pickup truck, landing next to his buddy Sam.

Oh God, he thought, as his intuition came back to him and the pieces began to fit together, *we're being abducted!* The posters of missing men—all single—came flashing through his aching brain. He was single. Sure he'd had a few girls here and there, but no serious relationships, and Sam, to his left—who was out cold on the floor of the pickup truck bed with blood oozing down the side of his cheek from a busted lip—he'd always been single.

The engine roared and the pickup started to move. Tommy felt the shaking from the wheels as they ran over the loose gravel and a few small potholes. They were both lying in the bed of a pickup, being tossed around as if they were in one of those bouncing, blow up, play sets, except this was cold steel, making it even worse for the pain he was already experiencing.

Sam remained unconscious as his limp body bounced closer to Tommy each time the pickup made a hard left or right, and then it came to a complete stop, sending Tommy's head into the large, attached steel toolbox unexpectedly. He shook his head to clear away the stars he was seeing directly in front of his eyes and looked straight up at the real stars scattered in the cloudless, late night sky. The cool air helped the blood around his lips and nose coagulate, like post nasal drip not wiped away for a while, crusting up on the skin.

He heard the tailgate slam down before he felt his legs being grabbed as if two vice grips locked onto his ankles and tightened one click short of crushing his small bones, and then he felt himself being pulled out. He hit his head again—against the edge of the tailgate—before being slammed down to the dirt with that same large, black boot directly in front of him.

It was so close he could smell the sweaty leather, because this time the boot had stepped on his chest, pressing down to keep him from crawling under the truck, or a rock, or any damn place for that matter.

His back started to ache, while at the same time his chest felt like it was about to crack open wide under the pressure of this fat man's weight, and it was at this point he started to get really scared for his life, because he knew it was probably going to end.

A man's voice–the abductor's–growled down at him. "You little prick, don't you fucking move or I'll gut you right here."

His vision was blurry, but he could see the large man looking down at him with a sausage sized finger pointing right in his face.

"Don't hurt me... What…what did I do? Why me?" he asked.

His abductor didn't answer, instead he removed his boot from Tommy's chest–the weight relieved so he could breathe again.

Tommy watched as the stranger threw his buddy Sam over his shoulder before taking a hold of his leg again dragging him like a piece of meat, across the ground.

After a few bumps and bruises to his backside and head while being dragged, he found himself inside a room. He was then lifted over the man's shoulder, yet again, and was still too weak to do anything about it.

Was he drugged? He felt like he had to be, otherwise he would have kicked the man in the balls by now and made a run for it.

He wanted to act as his mind cleared a bit more, but his aching body didn't seem to be up to the task and he felt as if he was in a slight state of paralysis. He looked around helplessly as he was placed on a cold, metal exam table in a dimly lit area surrounded by the smell of rubbing alcohol. A cold feeling of dread began to pour over him as he looked to his right while he was being strapped down; the abductor already had Sam secured to another exam table.

Tommy took notice of everything with his clearing eyes–his buzz had worn off a long time ago, giving way to fear. The chill from the cold metal made him shiver; he knew the situation wasn't good and that he had to get away now or else he'd probably be dead before sunrise.

"Oh, my God! What's going on? Where are we?"

Tommy heard the voice and thought about how to respond to the questions: *We're about to be slaughtered by the serial killer who's been taking young, single men, Sam, because we were in the wrong fucking place at the right time for him.* Had he voiced his thoughts? He wasn't sure. Nevertheless, Sam began crying.

Tommy watched the large man leave the room and come back in with a white apron on and long black rubber gloves that reached up to his elbows. He was holding a large power tool with a long, thin cutting blade.

He watched in horror as the man started slicing pieces of flesh from Sam's cheek while his friend screamed in terrified pain.

The man turned and stared straight into Tommy's eyes as he took a chunk of cheek flesh and put it in his mouth and chewed. He felt some acidic bile force its way up his throat as the man smiled, continuing to chew on the piece of his friends face. The sight was unbelievable and so horrible that it caused him to faint.

*   *   *

Gabriel had woken up early, with the sun peeking through his window, gently smacking him on the face and causing his eyelids to flutter open. He'd quickly dressed and made his way downstairs for breakfast. While finishing his meal with a hot, steamy cup of coffee, he decided he'd rake up the leaves in the backyard. He stood up from the kitchen table and looked out his back window while stretching. He'd taken care of the front yard yesterday, picking up hundreds of crispy, brown and yellow leaves that had covered his dying grass; at least eight full, large, black bags were sitting out front waiting for the garbage collectors. He put on his jacket and headed out the front door to collect some empty bags and his rake from the garage, and went around to his backyard.

He started raking by his old, rickety wooden gate; it was worn down from years of nature's elements. A good pile of leaves had already been blown up against the fence he shared with his new neighbors, and as he started raking he could hear the rustling of leaves and whispers of a conversation from the opposite side. He became curious, so he peeked through the narrow opening between two wood planks and caught a glimpse of his neighbors; he watched them fussing over an area toward the back of their yard. The tall, heavy set man was digging with a shovel; the short, slender one was dragging something in what looked to be the same type of black bags he had in his back pocket, and it was full. From the way he was grunting and sweating, Gabe knew it was loaded down with something heavier than leaves. Finally, the bag reached the hole in the back of the yard and was shoved in.

Gabriel couldn't resist the temptation to watch–what his neighbors were up to was too interesting. *Why would they bury that large black bag in their backyard?* he wondered. He knew it was none of his business, but he also felt that perhaps they were burying something that was toxic, and it could leak into the drinking water–his drinking water.

The fat man started pushing the dirt back in, over the bag. He glanced toward the fence and Gabriel felt his blood rush to his head. Had he been caught snooping? Now startled, he moved away from the narrow slit in the fence and started raking again, but he could hear rustling and crunching of dead leaves getting closer, closer.

"Hey, buddy, can I help you?" the fat man asked as he stopped what he was doing and started walking toward the fence.

"Nope, everything's okay. Just raking some of these leaves up." But that wasn't all–he'd just witness his neighbors burying something in their backyard. He looked up to see the fat man peeking over the top of the fence at him.

"I hear ya. Good day for bagging leaves, *neighbor*, isn't that right?" It was Rocco, the man he'd been in line with at the deli yesterday.

Gabriel responded as he resumed his raking, "Sure is. I'm hoping to have them all bagged before late afternoon, and you?" He'd hope to hear his neighbor's explanation for what he'd just witnessed in their backyard. *Were they hiding something?* he wondered silently. Again, he knew it was none of his business, and he wished he hadn't poked his nose where it didn't belong. This wasn't the first time in his life he'd been caught snooping and he really hoped Rocco hadn't seen him.

"I saw you peeking through the gap we have between the wood of the fence here, probably wondering what we're doing..."

He'd been caught and now he felt stupid, like a snooping idiot.

Gabriel thought fast, "No, actually I was just raking and looked over as I was passing the gap. I was about to call over to you guys and say hello but…" He wanted to finish but Rocco interrupted him.

"We had a large snake, a python actually. She died on us the other night so we're burying her in the back."

He watched Rocco grin. It seemed a bit...devious; one that wanted to hide the truth but at the same time dared you to challenge what had been said. He wasn't sure why, but he'd never been in their house so he guessed it was possible he was telling the truth. "Sorry for your loss."

"Yep, no problem, you have a good day now, you hear." And that was it. He smiled and his bald head dropped back down behind the fence and out of sight as he walked away.

Gabriel heard him mumbling something to his partner soon after. He continued raking leaves, filling up a few bags before tying them shut and walking them to the driveway to sit with the others. That's when he saw the other man–the small one, who lived with Rocco–on the front lawn. He waved at Gabriel as he placed more bags on the edge of his lawn where it met the street.

"Hi there, neighbor," the small man called as he began to walk over to Gabriel.

They'd met shortly after the couple had moved in last year, but he couldn't think of the man's name right that second; he racked his brain and thought hard, *Dan...Derrick...Dirk, yes, that was it, Dirk.*

"Hey, Dirk, sorry about your loss."

"My loss? Oh, you must be referring to our dog. Yeah, it's terrible."

Gabriel tried to keep a straight face, but it was a strain. "So sorry–my condolences." He gestured toward his house and half turned, letting Dirk know with his body language that he had to getting going. "If there's anything I can help you with, please let me know, okay?" He reached out to shake hands and was shocked at such a firm grip from such a small and frail looking man.

He made his way back into his garage calmly, but was fuming inside.

Fucking liars, the both of them, he thought as he hit the button, sending the white garage door down.

*   *   *

"He thought we'd lost a pet snake, you idiot, but then you had to go and tell him our pet dog died. What are you, stupid?" Rocco yelled, slapping Dirk in the back of the head as he passed him on his way into the kitchen.

Dirk rubbed his head where his boyfriend had just struck him. "But, you should have told me you used the word snake, Roc, not *pet*. When have you *ever* liked snakes?"

Rocco reached into the fridge and pulled out a brown bag. He placed it on the counter and took out something wrapped in white paper. After unfolding the paper to reveal three thick slices of what looked like fresh ham, he reached up and retrieved a twelve inch non-stick skillet from a brass hanging rack and set it on the stove burner with a bang, letting Dirk know he was still annoyed.

"You see where this is going, right?" Rocco asked. "He's going to start questioning what we're doing." He looked over at Dirk and pointed to the fridge and said, "I need the butter, please." Turning on the burner he intended on using, he adjusted the dial to high to get the pan nice and hot before turning it back to medium. He put in a lump of butter from the container Dirk handed him and tossed all three slices of fresh meat into the pan. It sizzled as the butter popped, spraying droplets all over the stove top. He reached for a bottle of spices and gently sprinkled enough on the meat to give it some kick. The smell of frying meat, garlic, and other sweet smelling spices started to fill their nostrils and excite their appetites.

Dirk approached. "You're cooking one of those for me, right?"

Rocco turned and looked at him. "This is mine. If you want your own piece, go downstairs and slice a fresh one from the meat we have stored down there." He noticed his partner was still staring so he cut a medium/well slice right from the pan as it cooked, pierced it with his fork, and held it up to Dirk's mouth. "Here, taste it. What do you think?"

Dirk took the hot, juicy piece of meat into his mouth and began to chew. "Wow, Rocco, taste just like chicken."

They both laughed.

*　*　*

Gabriel knew they'd lied to him. Why would they come up with a different story about their pet dying if they weren't? A snake... A dog... Who was telling the truth?

The mystery of the truth only fueled his already mounting curiosity; he had to know what they'd buried in their backyard. Shit, they were his next door neighbors and if they were up to no good, he refused to allow it next to his abode.

Thoughts of a possible abductor and the missing men became a part of the equation in his mind. Had they just buried some young guy they'd captured and killed?

It was plausible, and if that was the case, he would let the authorities know right away. But he needed some kind of proof first and he knew where to get it, if his suspicions were true.

His strong curiosity had always been commented on by his parents.

You're always sticking your nose in where it doesn't belong, Gabe. It's going to get you in trouble one day, his mother had told him on numerous occasions while he was growing up.

You know, curiosity killed the cat, son. Best to keep yours out of other people's business, his father had scolded him on one occasion when he'd thought a few boys down the road had stolen some pumpkins off their neighbors' porch.

It turned out, however, that it was the owners who'd taken the pumpkins in to make pumpkin pies; he'd felt like an idiot for that one.

The owners laughed, but the boys he'd accused gave him a serious beating on the bus the next day, and he never forgot it.

Others said he had too big of an imagination, but this time, somehow, he just knew his neighbors were up to no good.

* * *

"Cindy, I'm going out for a walk—I'll be back in a while," Gabriel told his wife after they'd finished supper, and jogged upstairs to get a few things from their bedroom, including his camera. It was already dark outside and it was a good time to go check on things; the neighbors in question had gone out. He'd watched them from the bedroom window, which faced the side of their house, where he had a clear view of the driveway. They'd both come out; Rocco had taken the drive's side and Dirk the passengers'. He watched their headlights turn on and the reverse lights follow as they pulled out rather fast.

His wife's voice shouted up to him from downstairs, "Gabe, come here, you're not going to believe this!"

"I'll be right down," he hollered back, grabbing his Swiss Army Knife and tucking it into his boot, just in case. It didn't take long before he was ready, again his curiosity getting the better of him; he had to see what his wife wanted. After rushing down the stairs, he walked into the living room and saw her sprawled out on the couch, half naked, with her bare breasts showing under a pink blanket. He thought she looked sexy, but figured she wouldn't be in the mood. He sat down beside her, lifting her legs up and placing them over his lap. Her soft and silky legs felt good as he massaged them while looking over at the TV. He started getting an erection, until a sudden rush of blood escaped his penis and instead shot right up to his head.

"Is that Dirk—our neighbor—in the chef's uniform?"

"I knew you'd be surprised. Our neighbor is a famous Chef on the Gourmet Network," Cindy said and smiled, digging her bare feet in between her husband's legs, close to his crotch, to warm up her toes. However, it didn't faze him at all as he watched Dirk flip a large, thin slice of seasoned, raw meat in a fillet pan. It sizzled as he turned and twisted the pepper grinder. "The more pepper, the stronger the taste," he heard Dirk say to the audience that was clapping and applauding. He stood up, gently placing his wife's silky legs back on the black leather couch and walked closer to the TV. ***Rocco's Delightful Fillets***, was blazon across the top of the screen, and there he was in the background in a multicolored apron—Dirk's partner Rocco. He was at the meat grinder, running some meat through and encasing it in sausage skins.

The camera had moved in to get a close up of the large man's hands as he gently pulled at the casing and allowing the sausage meat to pour in. He quickly twisted it like you would a bag of garbage and then spoke to the audience, "This, my friends, is the best sausage you'll ever taste! Throw it on the grill at 350 degrees, for about twenty minutes on each side and enjoy." He raised his fingers to his mouth, clasped all five digits together, and gave them a kiss as they left his lips and opened. "Perfecto!"

The camera panned back to Dirk, who had his meat brown and crusty around the edges. He took it out of the frying pan, placed it on a wooden cutting board, and sliced right through the center while little bubbles of red juice and steam poured across the sides of his large knife. "Rare, simply the best I say. For those of you watching, place your order over the phone or online at roccosdelightfulfillets.com, and with every order you'll receive a free meat carving knife, but that's…"

Gabriel turned the TV off; he couldn't take anymore. These guys were famous—liars and possibly killers. They owned a meat company and had a live slot on TV, showing how to best cook their meat products, yet they were hiding something in their backyard. He began to think maybe this was their cover up. Nice neighbors and famous cooks with an evil side. That didn't sound right to him, but he needed to get into their backyard and dig up the garbage bag to see what was inside. An eerie feeling came over him and he shivered as a chill raced up his spine at the thoughts he was having. He began to wonder if they'd chopped up their dog—or snake—and used the flesh as their products and/or ate it themselves! It seemed too fantastical and horrific to be true, but deep down he *knew* it was.

"Cindy, I'll be back. I'm going out back to the shed for a second, before I go for a walk."

"Yeah, okay. Can you take out the recyclables?"

"You got it," he said as he went out back without the bag of newspapers.

Gabriel made his way to the shed, turned on the light for a quick second, grabbed his shovel, and walked back out. He looked toward his colonial home—at all the windows—and saw no evidence of his wife peeking or pulling the curtains out of the way to see what he was doing; now was his chance. He ran over to the fence and hopped over. He had nothing to fear since they were out and their alleged dog or pet snake was dead and buried, or cut up in their stew.

He approached the spot; the dirt was still fresh from the recent digging, giving of the musty smell of earthy soil. Thrusting his shovel down, he watched the rusty, metal spade disappear into the soft dirt. He came up with a load of soil, and another, until he found the bag. He pulled it out of the ground and using his pen flashlight to provide light so he could see, he opened it up to find nothing but bones and rancid flesh–possibly tendons and muscles.

"Holy shit, these are human bones," he whispered through trembling lips and started to feel sick. Bile rose up into his throat and he swallowed it back down. A crackling of leaves and the snap of a twig made him turn around only to be slammed in the face by a large object, sending him to the ground, out cold.

*   *   *

Gabriel awoke strapped to an exam table in a moldy smelling basement. It was dark and his head was throbbing, and from what he could feel, he had a possibly broken nose. Thick crusts of blood had coagulated around his nose and upper lip from his injuries, lending strength to his suspicion that his nose was indeed broken. Wiggling and straining, he tried to break free of the restraints that had a secure hold on him.

A man's voice–gentle and soft–whimpered out of the darkness, "Help…me…please…" The faint sound enticed Gabe to turn his head in the direction of the plea. After a few moments his eyes adjusted to the low light and he was able to get a dim view of another man on an exam table not too far from him.

"Hello? Where the hell are we?" Gabriel asked, but he didn't receive a response. Suddenly a faint light turned on–enough for him to confirm that he was indeed in a basement–and he could see that the guy next to him was a bloody mess. Chunks of flesh were missing from his cheeks and arms, and he looked like he was hooked up to some kind of a transfusion unit, because blood seemed to be flowing through the plastic tubes and into the man's wrists from the machine on the opposite side of the man's table.

"Who did this to you?" Gabriel asked with fear lacing his voice.

"They're coming, man. The fat one–he's eating me slowly. He cuts off pieces of me and chews it while I watch. The little one–he keeps asking the fat one to kill me, so he can slice me up."

"What the fuck? Are you kidding me?" Gabriel asked, horrified by what this poor young man had just told him. "These guys are my neighbors. How the hell…" That's when it hit him and everything came together; the lies about the pets; their TV commercial about meat; the missing persons; the fillets; and the best tasting meat in town. His neighbors were fucking cannibals! He couldn't believe he'd been living next door to people who were feeding off human flesh, even though the thought had crossed his mind when he'd thought about the missing young men. But what made matters even worse was that they were cooking, packaging, and selling it to make a profit on their sick addiction. Finally, his curiosity had proved to be useful. Now he needed to find a way out of this, get the police, and save the dying man from being eaten alive slowly.

Gabriel knew he *had* to break free. He heard an engine pull up to the house outside, beyond some high basement windows to his right. He couldn't see out because they'd been painted black and he knew why. The bastards were doing their best not to get caught. *Bones and tendons and muscles... They're taking what meat they want and disposing of all the unneeded parts and burying them in the backyard. These men are sick,* he thought. "My wife... I have to get to my wife," he said aloud.

He heard the engine stop and two car doors slam shut; Dirk and Rocco were back again, and he needed to break free more than ever.

They must have come home while I was snooping in the garbage bag earlier, he thought, *and knocked me out cold, tied me up, and went back out.*

Although he heard them, he couldn't see them; the only windows that were down were facing directly into their backyard. Through the fence and all of the trees, no one would hear him if he screamed. The neighbors to the right were elderly and had probably fallen asleep with their TV on, and his wife, she was too far away and wouldn't be able hear him if he screamed for help.

He heard footsteps above–two pairs of them–muffled, but shuffling around nonetheless.

"Please, don't let them eat any more of me. They're just keeping me alive to feed on me; they want to keep me from rotting, so I'll last longer. The little one threatened to throw me in their freezer if I kept talking."

Gabriel knew something had to be done, and then he remembered the Swiss Army Knife tucked inside his boot.

"Don't you worry, we're getting out of here, so help me God! Keep an eye out the best you can."

Dirk went to the fridge and Rocco headed to the bathroom after throwing his car keys on the kitchen counter. He figured he'd wait until Rocco came back from taking a tinkle, before asking him what they were going to do next. His partner eventually returned, zipping his pants as he entered the kitchen once again.

"Rocco, we go on live first thing in the morning and it's already past eleven, and to top off the mounting stress, we have a much bigger problem waiting downstairs," Dirk said, pacing back and forth.

Rocco turned and looked at him with evil in his eyes. "Yeah, so what are you getting at? It's not my fault you made our neighbor suspicious."

Dirk stared straight at him, waving his arms while still pacing. "But this is the same reason we had to leave the last town we were in! We eventually had the folks next door onto us, and then shortly after we ground them up, the heat came on. We almost got caught that time, Rocco!"

"All right, I'm thinking, I'm thinking," Rocco said with exasperation.

They both left the kitchen, worried about what to do now that they had their neighbor downstairs–whom Rocco had knocked out with a frying pan. After securing Gabriel to a table downstairs, they'd gone back to the hardware store for some items they were going to need tonight, including fresh blades for their cutting tools.

The demand for Rocco's Delightful Fillets was huge. Online orders had been pouring in ever since they were able to secure a small slot on the Gourmet Network, but Dirk was worried and had been growing more so over the last year, especially since they'd almost been nabbed in their last town. They'd managed to kidnap ten single men and take them to their meat processing lab–the basement of their last home–before grinding up whatever meat they could into Rocco burgers, or slicing off thick pieces and letting them marinate for days in a tank that made it look like raw steak.

It wasn't that they were running low on supplies or anything–they always managed to keep inventory above demand–because they were using raw steer and pork meats as well. What made things complicated was that they'd taken a fancy to the taste of human flesh a while back, and the ground up meat was especially delicious. Many of the customers wrote back and commented on the website, saying Rocco's burgers were simply the best tasting meat patties ever. And if Dirk or Rocco wanted to feed their own hunger, they would go out and kidnap a single male, drug him, bring him back home to their basement, and slowly eat him alive.

They'd moved to the living room, still discussing what to do; Rocco took a while to respond to a question Dirk was waiting for an answer to. "So, what do we do now? Are we going to grind him and our last catch up, and then pack our bags for a new town? Because you know sooner or later his wife is going to be knocking on the door with the police, Rocco, you messed up again."

"Fuck you! If it weren't for me, your business would be dead! I'm the one who goes out and gets you meat to satisfy *your* sick fetish! *You* made me into a cannibal, so we're both in the same boat."

"Yes, okay, but we need to act fast. Let's grind them both up and start looking for another place, Rocco. We need to get out of here! We aren't going to have time to stick around..."

Meanwhile, downstairs in the basement, Gabriel managed to cut through one of his leather straps, but before he had a chance to get to the other one, the basement door opened and the pounding of heavy foot steps could be heard coming down the stairs—it *had* to be Rocco.

He laid back and kept still, acting like he was still out cold. The man on the other table—Tommy—on the other hand was awake and shaking, but he was so drugged up he couldn't scream.

Rocco came down the steps alone. He walked straight over to the large, mobile, industrial meat grinder, barely glancing at the two strapped down bodies. The front, circular opening was large enough to insert a human body into, and he was preparing to send his two latest victims in, head first. Deep inside were large blades that did a great job of cutting through flesh and bone. In the past, Rocco and Dirk cut off as much flesh as they could before sending it through and disposed of the bones, but right now they needed to move out of town. There was no time to spare, so he would have to send them through, clothing and all.

The large brute turned on the switch and let the machine run. It was so loud that it could be heard by Dirk who'd stayed upstairs, finishing his menu for next day's episode on the Gourmet Network. Rocco came up close to the meat grinder's entrance and could see the blades spinning at such a fast rate of speed that they were no more than a blur—a sure sign the machine was warmed up and ready to take in its next unfortunate victim. He turned around to get Tommy, only to be greeted by the face of his angry neighbor, who quickly thrust his pocket knife into Rocco's throat.

Gabriel twisted the blade around in Rocco's Adam's Apple and pushed him backward so that his large, bald head was in perfect range of the opening in the grinder. Rocco had both hands to his bloody throat, gasping with an expression of pure terror on his face. Gabriel grabbed him by the balls and shoulder, turned him around, and forced his head into the grinder. The blades sliced away his skull, brain, face, ears, and chopped his neck in two as he let out one final scream. But Gabe didn't stop, he pushed Rocco in further, until he finally let go when Rocco's ankles and feet were sucked into the machine. He looked down–now realizing he'd been soaked in the sick man's blood–and stood silently for a second, staring down at all the pieces of clothing, flesh, bone, and the blood that had been scattered all over the floor. Suddenly, the light to the basement came on and a voice called from the top of the stairs–Dirk.

"Rocco, is everything okay down there?" Dirk shouted, coming down the steps, unable to hear anything except for the grinder mashing up something large.

Gabriel tried to snap out of the horror of what had just transpired–the sight of all the blood and the grinding of bones that could still be heard inside the machine. He finally snapped out of it and darted behind the stairs, watching the small man walk down the steps. When he saw his chance, he reached out and grabbed a hold of Dirk's ankles, causing the man to fall head first down the remaining steps and his face to slam against the cement floor.

He quickly came around the stairs and straddled Dirk, gripping his hair, smashing his already bloodied face against the cement until he went limp. Then he picked him up and carried him to meat grinder. Its engine was still cranking, but it wasn't as noisy since Rocco was now in the small barrel at the bottom, nothing more than red mush.

Dirk struggled weakly when he saw that he was being carried to the grinder, trying his best to break free, but it was no use.

"How do you like it, you little fuck? It's time to feel what your victims felt!"

"No, please, I'll do anything, please, don't become like us!" he cried out, hoping for forgiveness.

Gabriel ignored his pleas and shoved his feet into the large hole. The blades instantly tore into his white canvas shoes, cutting into his feet and drawing his legs in after.

Dirk struggled and screamed, digging his fingernails into Gabriel's arms, but it did no good; the force of the blades kept pulling him in further.

Gabe watched the fear grow on the small man's face as he was pulled in above the waist and felt the strength leave his tattered body before he finally succumbed to the machine and its whirling, razor sharp blades. At last, his head exploded as it entered the machine, ending the small man completely.

He stood and watched the blades continue to turn, swirling flesh and bone until it cleared and dropped with a *plop* into the barrel below. He was in shock at what had transpired; the blood; the horror; and the near death experience. Completely drenched in blood, he turned around and saw Tommy staring at him. He'd witnessed everything and had thrown up whatever contents had been left in his stomach.

"Oh, thank God, you saved us! Thank God! Please get me to a hospital–the pain...it's unbearable," Tommy pleaded.

Gabriel could tell by the sound of his voice that Tommy felt relieved he wouldn't be on someone's dinner plate–glad to have been rescued just in the nick of time.

Tommy struggled weakly against his straps as Gabriel came near. "Oh, thank God, please get these straps off–they hurt." He watched Gabriel walked toward him, slowly, looking down at the floor. He saw the pocket knife in his hand come up close to the straps, ready to cut him free, and his heart soared with the renewed hope of life. But instead of relief and freedom, he felt a sharp jolt of pain shoot straight up to his brain and he screamed.

Gabriel cut a huge chunk of flesh from Tommy's shaking arm. He held it up and stared at the piece of fresh meat, dripping blood. He put it to his open mouth and bit down. "Sorry, man," he said as he began to chew, "but I'm so curious to see why these guys were obsessed with human meat."

Tommy screamed in horror as Gabriel took another slice while still chewing on his first.

Yes, he'd always been curious type.

I told you, Gabe, he heard his father say in the back of his tortured mind, *your curiosity is going to get the best of you one day, you'll see.*

Tommy screamed again and again as chunk after chunk was cut from his bleeding arm...and eaten.

THE SCREAMING

MARK M. JOHNSON

Deep, icy blue rings around bottomless black pits dilated with twisted desire, as Dominic's cold analyzing eyes traversed longingly over the young woman's naked body.

She is exceptionally beautiful, he thought to himself. *Her immaculate face, framed by shoulder length golden brown hair, makes her the visage of an earthbound angel. Her lips, so full and deep red against her pale angelic skin, are made for kissing.*

She wore no makeup that he could see—there was no need for it. He caressed her cheek before his eager fingers casually wandered down her flawless neck, gingerly cupping one of her stunning breasts. He paused there for a moment before moving south across the flat expanse of her taught belly, to what his examination had just proved to be undiscovered country.

He had a thing for virgins, or at least he liked to tell that to his unwilling guests, and much to his joy this beautiful young flower was unplucked. Virgins were clean, unsoiled, the purest of all potential subjects. He wondered to whom she'd intended to give this precious gift. Nevertheless, it didn't matter because she was his and by the end of the night, *he* planned on being the driving force of her unholy deflowering.

She was strapped down to a specially made table with a black, lightly padded vinyl covering the top, with her legs tied—spread eagle. Her deep brown puppy-dog eyes lay closed in a chemically induced slumber. He remembered how taken he'd been when he'd first gazed into those eyes that were so deep and inviting. Never so certain was he that discarding his intended target and choosing the lovely vision that graced his table now had been the right decision. A chance encounter? Was she merely a victim of random circumstance? *No*, he mused wistfully, *there's something else afoot here. Destiny!*

"You were born for me," he whispered lovingly into her ear. Reluctantly, he turned away from his sleeping beauty to check the time. "Won't be long now."

When he looked back, he saw her eyelids fluttering and leaned in close so his smile would be the first thing she saw when she awoke. The sleeping angel slowly opened her eyes, moaned softly, and blinked away the chemical sleep.

Dominic's eyes widened and his breathing deepened as his anticipation grew. With a silly grin on his face, he said, "Wakey, wakey, lover," in a goofy, high-pitched voice.

"What?" she yawned and frowned with dawning confusion.

"It's party time, love, and you're the entertainment!" he shouted as he danced back from the table throwing his hands up in the air and spinning in slow circles so she could see his obvious attraction to her, as he was just as under dressed as she was.

When Rose saw the man's nakedness, and the erection between his legs as he danced away from her, she panicked, tried to sit up, and realized she was bound to the table and just as naked.

"Oh fuck...oh God," she whimpered, trying to pull herself free from the restraints that held her.

He stopped dancing and put his hands up on his hips, taking on a stance and expression of shock and disappointment.

"Oh *my* goodness," he voiced in his best replication of a southern nanny's scolding disapproval. "Such *language* from the precious mouth of an angel! I expected so much better from you, child."

"Oh Christ...oh God no! Oh please God, no!" she sobbed, continuing to test her restraints.

"Oh my lawd, *Jesus*," Dominic shouted with the accusing rant of a southern Baptist preacher, "We got us a blasphemer in the house. You have taken our Lord's name in vain. We have got to *cleanse* your soul, my precious child!" He bounced forward and placed his hands over Rose's forehead covering her terrified eyes.

"Demons come out!" he screamed passionately, pulling his hands away into the air, then repeating the gesture. "Demons come out!" he hollered even louder.

She screamed right along with him as he continued to perform the mock exorcism.

"Demons come out!" He screamed like a lunatic, shaking his fists in the air violently, spraying spittle over them both.

"No, no," Rose chanted in breathless sobs; thoroughly terrified, she shook her head violently. Squeezing her eyes shut, she repeated the word 'no' like a mantra to ward off the insanity.

Dominic passively watched her performance of wishful denial with a bemused grin and leaned in close.

"Yes, yes, yes, yes, yes, yes!" he retorted, screaming into her face with ever-increasing volume until he drowned out her sobbing voice.

She ceased chanting and stared, horrified, into his fevered eyes. Her naked chest heaved with panicked exertion and his eyes drifted down for a moment, taking in the splendor of her perfection before returning his gaze to her watery, shocked eyes.

"That's better," he cooed in a calming voice. "How are we going to get to know each other, if you're screaming in hysterics?"

"Know-each-other?" she babbled, struggling to catch her breath. "Oh God, please help m...me." She closed her eyes tightly and cried softly. "I'm not here," she wished desperately. "Not happening... Please, oh God, *please*."

Dominic expelled a long exaggerated sigh. "Now baby," he cooed, resting his elbows on the table next to her head. "God has nothing to do with this. I assure you, you're definitely here, and there's nothing He can do to help you." Resting his face between his hands, he gazed lovingly into her eyes as she slowly opened them and returned his gaze with confused trepidation.

"Why are you doing this to me?" Rose whimpered softly as her anguished face twisted into a grimace of terror-fueled emotion.

He mulled it over for a moment, his eyes wandering off as if deep in contemplation, then they returned and refocused on hers.

"Because I can," he stated matter-of-factly, shrugging his shoulders and rolling his eyes comically, "because I am; because I want to; because I need to; because the voices told me to." Dominic suddenly changed his voice into an imitation of a famous actor/Governor and growled in a thick Austrian accent, "Because you've been targeted for termination." He grinned and dropped the heavily accented monotone. "Take your pick. *This is* your reality. The sooner you accept that, the sooner we can move forward."

"Move, forward? Move forward to what?" she stammered, her voice cracking.

He smiled back in pure merriment, "Why to your torture, rape, murder, and dismemberment of course, silly girl."

Looking into the sparkling blue eyes of the lunatic, Rose was unsure of what she should have seen lurking inside of them. Lust for the kill? Insanity? Or maybe, just pure undiluted evil. What she saw instead was joy, unmistakable joy, amusement, and elation. As she came to this realization a righteous anger rose up inside her, momentarily eclipsing her terror, reveling in its comforting heat, she let it spill.

"You sick *fucker!*" she screamed, twisting in her restraints. Her face grimaced as she bucked on the table as hard as she could. She saw her frenzy was having no effect on her captor and ceased her fit. In fact, he seemed even more amused than before.

Dominic watched with charmed interest as his unwilling guest fought against her restraints. Seeing her stop and look up at him again, he observed her take in a deep breath, filling her lungs to capacity. Knowing what was coming next, he casually reached up–grinning in anticipation–and covered his ears. The young woman's high-pitched scream could have shattered an eardrum had she done it directly in his ear.

She paused only long enough to take in another deep breath, and then let loose with a louder scream that could have shattered crystal. Holding his hand up in front of him as if he held a microphone, Dominic stepped forward and launched into an almost perfect impression of Howard Cosell, a famous sports newscaster from days long gone by.

"*Ladies* and *gentlemen*, we have a *fighter* in the house tonight! Mr. Dominic, can you tell us what you think of this new development?"

Quickly shifting over a step to his right, he pretended to interview himself.

"Well, I'll tell you this, Howard, I am *very* happy to finally see a little fire in this young gal. I was getting worried there, but it looks like she's going to be a blast to work with!"

Shifting over again to the left, he again transformed into the long dead television sports reporter.

"Yes, Mr. Dominic, I would have to agree. It does *indeed* look like this ones going to be a lot more interesting than we originally anticipated. Can you tell us how you're feeling about this, miss?"

Walking over to Rose, still channeling Howard, Dominic held out the invisible microphone for her to speak into.

She ceased her struggling and stared up in wide-eyed shock as her kidnapper impersonated Howard Cosell's unique enunciation almost flawlessly. As he held out the nonexistent microphone to her, she was, at first, completely speechless.

"You're insane," she sobbed. "Oh my *God*... You're fucking crazy!"

"Well, ladies and gentlemen," he continued with his Cosell spiel. "I have to say that I *am* disappointed. I'd hoped for something a little, well, a little *more*, from this fiery little lady. What do you think, Mr. Dominic?"

He again shifted position and became himself.

"Well, Howie baby, I'd have to agree. After that earlier performance, I thought my guest might have something a little harder to say. Like you know, 'Fuck you, mother fucker!' or some such badass shit like that. Not..." He kicked his voice up to a higher, overly feminine tone, "You're insane! Oh my God... You're fucking crazyyyyyyyyyy!"

Switching back to Cosell he continued, "Well, that's all for now, and that's Mr. Cosell to you, sir."

Becoming himself yet again, he took on an expression of annoyed offence. "Yeah, well fuck you, Mr. *Cosell*." Turning, he smiled wide and put a hand up to stifle a light fit of giggles.

Rose watched Dominic perform in fascinated horror, taking in another deep breath, she began to kick and scream again.

"Yeah, baby!" Dominic cried. "Now that's what I wanna hear–look at how hard I'm getting!" He stood back–holding his erection in his left hand while his right hand waved up in the air—and began leaping around the room in circles, mimicking the riding of a bucking bronco. "Yeehaw," he screamed in a cowboy's western drawl, "I'm gonna break that wild pony!" Stopping in the middle of the room, he looked back at the stricken, shocked expression on his captive's face. His cheeks budged out, his eyes misted over with merriment, and he struggled to hold it in, spitting through his pursed lips before completely losing his composure. Falling back on his ass to the floor, he succumbed to a riotous fit of uncontrollable laughter.

As he rolled around on the floor consumed by laughter at his own antics, Rose closed her bloodshot eyes and wept softly, continuing to struggle weakly against her restraints. He slowly regained control of himself, stood, and wiped away tears before placing his hands on his hips and sauntering over to the naked young woman.

"Oh my gawd *damn*, woman, if only you could have seen the look on your face." He stood over Rose, looking down at her affectionately, "Priceless. Okay. I think it's time for a little getting to know each other better. Don't you think?"

Rose refused to acknowledge his presence—she kept her eyes closed and continued crying softly.

"Hello? Anyone home?" he asked and snapped his fingers in front of her face with no result. He let out a long exaggerated sigh of feigned frustration, turned to his right as if talking to someone else that wasn't there, and spoke, "Well, maybe if I bit off her nose... Do you think that might get her attention?" Looking back to his left, he answered himself, "Well, that might get her attention, but she wouldn't be very happy about it. Would you, Rosie?"

At the mention of her name, her eyes snapped open and she looked into Dominic's surprisingly soft, concerned eyes.

"How do you know my name?" she asked pointedly, as if she were not completely naked and strapped to a table like some kind of lab animal.

Grinning, he reached over to an adjacent table and picked something up—her Michigan State ID. He held it up for her to see, answering her question mockingly, "Forgot you were carrying this?"

"Rose Leanna Snowden. Age, nineteen, soon to be twenty in a few days, I see. Height, five-eight. Brown eyes. Sex? Yes, please!" Dominic laughed as he read off the little laminated card. "But it doesn't say stunningly beautiful, self assured, strong willed, yet soft and warmly feminine. Go figure, huh?" He sighed heavily and shook his head. "What kind of parents would let their beautiful, young daughter come down to Cancun for spring break?" Turning, he returned the card to the adjacent table and then leaned in close bringing his eyes level with hers. "Tell me, Rosie, how many times have guys asked you if it hurt when you fell from heaven?" he asked flirtatiously, gazing deep into her eyes.

Stunned again at his bizarre behavior, she shouted, "You're hitting on me?" Her voice took on an angry, sobbing tone as she continued, "You stripped me naked and strapped me down to a fucking *table!*" She screamed the last word and began to twist on the table, pulling on the restraints, still trying to free herself.

He shrugged his shoulders in mock confusion, "I just thought it was a good way to start up the whole getting to know each other thing."

She stopped struggling and looked at him with utter contempt, "You sick, rotten, *motherfucker!*" she screamed through her fear. "Go to fucking hell, you crazy ass, shit for brains *cocksucker!*" She threw herself from side to side violently and screamed as loud as her tired lungs could manage, "Somebody help me!"

He shook his head in mild disappointment, "Rosie, Rosie, Rosie, obviously you haven't totally grasped the nature of your current situation, so let me enlighten you." He stepped back and extended his arms out from his sides, palms up. "We're at a private resort, on a remote island off the coast of Mexico. There is no one around to hear your calls for help.

Even if by some unlikely chance someone were walking by this building at this very moment, they wouldn't be able to hear you because this is a sound proofed room. So, your screaming isn't going to accomplish anything except wear you out and make your throat raw and sore." He held out his hands in offering, "What do you say we dispense with all the struggling and screaming and have a little light, *civil*, conversation?"

Rose looked at him hard for a few seconds, and then turning her head on the table–she surveyed the room from end to end. At her feet, she could see a half-open door under a large flat screen television mounted on the wall and a wraparound mahogany bar to the right of the door. The bar was beautiful, worthy of any pub, hole in the wall, or classic bar she'd ever seen. Not that she'd seen many in her short, almost twenty years of life. The backlit, mirrored shelves behind the bar where fully stocked with what looked like every kind of liquor there was to be had.

To her right, she saw the same off-white featureless linoleum wall covering that dominating the rest of the room. At the top of the wall, along the ceiling, there was a row of eight, three by four foot dark shuttered windows. Along the wall below the windows, a mirror backed oak shelf ran the whole length and was about four feet from the floor, decorated with what looked like random objects. Among the items on the shelf were: a gold bracelet displayed on a holding rack; a pair of diamond earrings displayed in a similar fashion; a pair of dark red high-heeled shoes; and many more female related items.

As she looked at the objects arranged for display on the shelf, it suddenly dawned on her that she was looking at a trophy shelf. Turning away in fear and disgust, she looked to her left. There she could see a stainless steel morgue autopsy table about ten feet away. Beyond that, stood another table with numerous shelves and drawers, and strange tools on hooks attached to the wall. Behind her head was another door, this one at the end of a short hallway, and it was locked up tight, at least that's what it said on the security panel in big red letters: **SECURE.**

After checking the room, she looked fiercely back at Dominic. "Fuck you!" she spat with venomous, bitter hatred dripping from her voice, although the obvious fear in her leaking eyes betrayed her true feelings.

He sighed, "Okay, okay, I guess I'll start then." Slowly, like a stalking cat, he began to circle her, trailing his hand along the table's edge. "My name is Dominic Whittington. Do you recognize the name, hmm?"

Rose turned away, refusing to respond.

"Okay, maybe you do, maybe you don't. I thought you might because I've been out and about with a few of the younger members of the rich and famous in years past. Not to mention the fact that I'm on the FBI's ten most wanted list. Hello, don't you watch the news? I was in the headlines, babe." He sighed. "Unfortunately, the fickle media moved on and lost interest in me after less than a month." He grunted. "A month, after all that hysteria and the worldwide man hunt, I go from front page news to updates on the back pages. It's almost a crime in itself." He grinned in arrogant satisfaction. "Their man hunt obviously failed, but they had my face on every TV station on the tube." He looked down at her and smirked. "But not this face—this is brand new." He smacked his cheeks and giggled. "Beautiful work, don't you think? Cost a fortune. A few subtle changes to the nose and cheek bones, and taa-daa, I'm a whole new person." He chuckled. "The guy their looking for is a ghost now, and they'll be chasing him forever. So, what do you have to say, Rosie, anything?" He waited, but she offered no response, so he shrugged and gazed down into her eyes.

She stared hard up at his face, *Dominic Whittington*. A glimmer of memory flickered on the edge of her mind. She remembered something... *A year or two ago, something on TV... Something about a cop killer who kidnapped and murdered young women, in Texas maybe?* She looked away, suddenly more afraid than she'd been before, if that were even possible.

He searched her face for a moment, then strolled away from her and over to one of the eight, black leather upholstered high-backed bar stools that sat in front of the bar. He took hold of one and dragged it back to her table's side. Turning away, he walked back to the bar and stepped behind it.

"My dear, Rosie," he called out in a perfectly enunciated British accent. "Would you like a drink whilst we talk of times old and new?" Again, she refused to respond. "Suit yourself. I'm in the mood for a Captain and Coke," he finished in his normal voice. He hummed and whistled as he mixed his drink then ambled back, settled down on the bar stool, and rested his bare feet up on the table next to Rose's left hip.

"Now I could blabber on about all my likes and dislikes," he started up the conversation where he'd left off. "But I think it's your turn. Have you any interesting 'how I came to spring break in Cancun to lose my virginity to Jeff' stories?" Putting one hand behind his head, he smiled mischievously.

Her eyes widened in shocked surprise and he laughed aloud. "How could you?" she stammered.

He held up his hands in bemusement, "I'm educated, I'll have you know—six years of medical school under my belt, and you've been here for quite some time."

She frowned, and then the implications of what he'd said came into focus. "You, *examined* me?" she asked with a look of malignant disgust.

He grinned as if it was a secret they both held in the strictest of confidence. "Well, of course I did, you don't think I would engage in relations with a potential disease carrier do you? Now, come on, I had time to run a few important tests, and my conclusions are, you're a perfectly clean, pure as the driven mountain snow, virgin. The first to ever grace this room with your presence. Congratulations." He leaned back in the bar stool looking satisfied with himself.

She let her head fall back onto the table, staring up at the ceiling panels rather than looking upon the bastard tormenting her. "Why?" she asked in a trembling voice. "With your money and looks you could have any woman, anyone you wanted, you could have even had..." She stopped talking abruptly as the thought came to mind.

He sat up a little straighter; reaching out his hand, he gently caressed her ankle. "I could have even had...who? You mean you might have given me the time of day had I approached you in the bar? Shit, I know you would have, you would've given me the time, date, and your panty size. Don't you think I already know that?" Dominic stood up suddenly and began to pace the floor in agitated aggravation, spilling his drink as he waved his hands through the air. "That's why I waited outside, killed your Jeffy-Jeff, and took you by force."

"Jeff's...dead?" she stammered.

"Bah," he snorted, waving his hand dismissively. "Trivialities."

"Oh...*Jeffery*," she whimpered; fresh tears fell as she mourned her boyfriend.

"That's it? That's the whole reason to your question, *why*? I could have any woman in the world you say." He gestured wildly as he continued to pace. "I *have* had every woman in the world I wanted." To punctuate his point, he threw his nearly empty drink glass against the far wall where it shattered. "Shit," he paused, "I'm going to have to clean that up later. Damn." He sighed and then resumed his pacing and continued his rant. "I've fucked models, super models, young up-and-coming movie stars, mature movie stars, hot as hell little rich bitches, more college sluts than you can shake a dildo at! Shit, I even ass-fucked a well-known pop star." Dominic laughed aloud at the memory. "Oh boy, did I surprise her! I flipped her over for some doggy-style action, slapped a little ass-tro glide on and just slipped it in the back door!" He slapped his knee and doubled over laughing. "'But I poop from there,' she said. Oh-my-God!" He jumped up and down, laughing hard enough to wrest tears from his eyes. After a few minutes he regained control of himself. Taking on a more serious tone, he continued his rant, "And that's just it right there—I grew tired of it all, it wasn't enough, never was. You see, I have a...shall we say, unusual taste, for virgins. I've found after much experimentation that only their pure female flesh suits my palate, but even I have standards. I'm not a pedophile. I never touch anything under eighteen. Have to stay legal, right?" He grinned mischievously.

He stopped pacing, stood right next to her, smirking, "Do you have any idea how hard it is to find nineteen-year-old virgins? I even stooped to paying for them. I've had virgins from all four corners of the earth—cost a bloody fortune too." He grinned. "Pun, intended." Reaching out with his left hand, Dominic gently caressed Rose's inner thigh and smiled when he felt her cringe and try to pull away. "But even then it wasn't enough. They wouldn't let me do what I really wanted, what I *needed*—to taste their flesh. That's when I decided I was going to have to snatch some guests that I could do with as I pleased."

Rose whimpered, struggling to close her legs as his hand drifted slowly higher.

"But not yet!" he shouted as he snatched his hand back and stepped away from her side. "I have something I want you to see–a little movie I made of my most recent conquest. You might call it, something relevant to your future," he whispered under his breath as he walked away.

Her breath came in gasps as she sobbed. She watched the monster–who looked like an attractive twenty something man–walk over and kneel out of sight behind the bar. After a few seconds, he reappeared carrying a large touch screen remote control in his left hand.

"Okay, Rosie, it's movie time!" Dominic announced as he returned to the bar stool next to Rosie's table. Taking hold of the seat back, he turned it to face the TV screen and parked himself on it. "Tonight we have, *The Death Of A Slut*, staring Rhiannon Lea Reinke and Dominic Whittington!" he shouted in the obnoxiously loud baritone timbre of a boxing announcer. "Let's get ready to ruuuuuuuuuuuumble!"

As he manipulated the remote, the large flat screen TV came to life. Its blue-green light played across her face, reflecting in her eyes the still image of a naked Dominic standing over another young victim strapped down to the very table on which Rose found herself. The young woman had very light blond hair, and although it looked as if she were naked, a Native American blanket covered her from her neck to her knees.

"I film all of my adventures on a hard drive," he stated proudly. "If you haven't noticed already, I have cameras placed everywhere in this room to catch every conceivable angle." Looking away from the screen, he gestured toward the upper corners of the room, his hand waving in slow circles over his head absentmindedly.

She looked up and saw them–little cameras everywhere–all about the size of a roll of breath mints; they were painted the same color as the surrounding walls and were nearly invisible.

She looked back into the monster's eyes with her own dripping abhorrence, "So what do you do, whack off to these little, sick snuff films after you're done? You fucking pathetic, freak, loser, *asshole*!" she shouted with steel in her trembling voice.

Dominic's mouth fell open in surprise and his eyes glittered with bemusement.

"If you weren't such a filthy rich fucking freak with that silver spoon shoved up your ass, I might almost feel sorry for you," she snarled, holding his gaze.

His eyes narrowed–lips pressed together tightly–and he glared at her like a crouching jungle cat ready to pounce. Her brave, but feigned, defiance slowly wilted under his silent, withering stare. The bitter hatred in her eyes melted away second by silent second into naked fear, and still he said nothing. Gradually a smile began to bloom on his face–slowly trickling across his mirthless, thin lips until his perfect teeth began to show.

"Yes," he hissed under his breath–his eyes widening, gazing into her soul.

She looked back and saw a rising darkness; she saw death reaching out from the black pit of his soul and in silent terror, she turned away from them.

"What did you see in my eyes, Rosie? Can you tell me?" he asked in a harsh whisper.

She said nothing and kept her head turned away as tears leaked from under her shut eyelids.

"Did you see your death in there?"

With that, she turned her head suddenly and again looked up at him, her eyes weary and moist. Her face scrunched up, her lips trembled, and teetering on the edge of sanity, she clenched her jaw and forced herself to calm.

He watched her coldly, with the intense interest of a scientist studying a lab animal.

She began to gasp heavily, her chest heaving with the effort to get herself under control. Losing the battle, she burst into fresh bouts of sobbing.

He continued to watch with a curious tilt of his head, and his hard expression softened. "Okay, okay, calm yourself," he murmured soothingly. "There'll be time enough for all that later–right now its movie time." Up on the flat screen, the home movie began to play.

"Please," the young woman on the TV pleaded tearfully, "I'll do whatever you want, anything, you don't have to do this, please!"

Dominic looked down at her heatedly, his eyes burning with a fire extinguishable only by her blood. He grinned savagely at his prisoner, "Rhiannon," he shouted sarcastically, "did you really think that I was going to fuck that used hole of yours?"

Speechless and confused emotions flashed across the woman's face as if she was channel surfing through multiple expressions of horror and confusion.

He leaned forward, his face inches from hers and screamed in her face, "You fucking little whore," as he ripped away the blanket covering her naked body. "Did you think I was going to stick my cock into that used up fuck-hole of yours, you fucking slut?" He leapt up onto the table on his hands and knees, hovering over her as she screamed. "I only fuck virgins, and you're far from that."

Rhiannon squeezed her eyes shut struggling to turn her head.

He grasped her face roughly and turned it to face him. "Look at me!" he demanded. "Open your eyes and look at me, you fucking tramp, or I'll cut your fucking eyelids off!"

Her terrified eyes opened. "P...p...please," she stuttered.

"How many?" he asked in a severe whisper. "How many dicks?"

Her eyes darted back and forth in confusion. "Three," she offered in a desperate sob.

"Liar!" he screamed, slapping her across the face.

"Oh, God," she screamed.

"For every lie, I take something precious." He glanced down at her body, considering. Darting down, he clamped his mouth over Rhiannon's left nipple. His cheeks collapsed inward as he sucked the flesh up into his mouth, then his neck muscles tensed as he bit down while twisting his head.

Rhiannon screamed sharply, thrashing underneath him. With one last twist, he ripped the tender flesh away spraying blood across her body and his face; her screams intensified as she bucked under him.

He smiled at her, blood running down his face and neck as he opened his mouth and displayed the bloody nipple on the end of his tongue, waggling it against his bloody teeth.

"Oh...G...God," she shrieked, still trying to twist away.

Dominic made a show of chewing the bloody flesh in his mouth, then swallowed and smiled showing his teeth stained with her blood. "Mmm, yummy." He licked the blood from his lips, slowly savoring the taste. Then, he gazed down at the ragged, bloody hole where the young woman's nipple had been. "Oh, that has got to sting a bit," he laughed. Blood was running freely from the wound, gathering in a puddle under her body and dripping to the floor.

She gasped and sobbed, writhing weakly beneath him.

"How many?" he asked again. She gasped for breath while looking back at him–her face splattered with her own blood, eyes wide in distress. "How many," he repeated louder, "or shall I take the other one?"

"Fifteen!" she blurted out in panic and tumbled into weary sobs.

"Fifteen," he repeated, "that sounds about right. That's a whole lot of dicks–definitely not the road less traveled. I can't go sticking my favorite body part where so many have gone before, now can I?"

"Oh, God, please," she begged piteously.

"He can't help you dear, at least not until I'm finished with you," Dominic laughed whimsically. He picked up something just out of the camera's view, from a table tray to his left.

Rose whimpered when she saw the glittering sparkle of a long knife blade on the TV as his hand came back into the picture.

"Oh, please," Rhiannon gasped, her face twisting in horror as she glimpsed the blade in his left hand.

Dominic grinned down at her savagely with a crazed gleam in his eyes.

"You may be a filthy, used up whore, Rhiannon," he said as he waved the knife back and forth before her terrified eyes, "but even a slut as played out as you still has uses. I've checked you out thoroughly. You're surprisingly unsoiled by disease, which makes you useful...as meat."

She stared fixedly at the blade with new horror dawning in her eyes, and realizing what he was implying, Rhiannon thrashed and shrieked under him.

"You're going to feel a little pressure," he giggled as he drew the knife down along her trembling jaw, across her throat just below the chin, and then down to the breast he'd savaged with his teeth. Placing his hand over the bloody breast, he plunged the knife in and began to saw along the base.

Rhiannon shrieked uncontrollably, bucking and thrashing beneath him as he severed the breast from her body.

"Filet of tit," he giggled and licked his lips as he carefully placed the bloody meat on the table next to him, "puts filet mignon to shame."

Rhiannon shrieked one last time and then her eyes rolled up into her head as she passed out from the pain.

He looked up at her unconscious face and sighed. "One down," he laughed as he moved to her other breast and removed it with a practiced hand. He placed the second breast on the meat table and then gazed down at Rhiannon's face. "No, that's no good," he sighed. "You have to be awake for this." He raised his hand and brought it down against her face, once, then again. "Wake the fuck up, babe! It's not over yet!"

Her eyes blinked open, then widened as the pain registered and she screamed frantically, throwing her head from left to right. Dominic slammed his right hand down–palm open on her forehead–stopping her eyes dead center with his. He grinned, brought the knife up to her throat, and slowly dragged the tip across the flesh beneath her chin.

Rhiannon's eyes misted over as she looked away from Dominic's fevered gaze. She focused on the ceiling and saw through it to something only she could see. "Daddy," she whispered, crying softly in resignation.

Dominic paused for a moment in confusion, "Daddy?" he repeated. "He can't help you either," he hissed, thrusting the blade up into her throat with violent precision.

His cut pierced her thyroid cartilage and penetrated her trachea; he twisted the blade and cut through her throat until metal grated against bone. Withdrawing the blade, he tossed it aside hastily. Leaning down over her jerking body, he looked deep into her eyes and sighed with fascination as the life faded from them. Rhiannon's body stiffened in spasms, twitched violently, then slowly relaxed, giving in to the inevitable.

"Thank you," he whispered into the dying girl's ear. "Thank you." The close up image of Rhiannon's dead, glazed over eyes froze on the screen.

"How's that for *'must see'* TV?" Dominic asked with a laugh—his voice brimming with hilarity.

Rose heaved, gagged, and turned her head sideways, vomiting explosively onto the floor. She sobbed and gagged, spewing another stream of vomit as her bladder let loose.

"God damn it, Rosie! Look at this mess!" he shouted as he jumped up and circled around her. "And you've soiled yourself."

Her bloodshot eyes bled sorrowful tears for the young woman frozen on the television. Her desolate tears fell for the now long ago murdered Rhiannon, for those who had gone before her under the hand of this monster, for her own life, and all those poor souls yet to come. For her twisted kidnapper she had no words. She refused to glance his way as he labored to clean up her vomit and urine, instead closing her eyes and weeping for the murdered girl in silence.

"Right," Dominic piped up in his British voice as he finished the clean up, "I need a piss, too. I can't go shagging with a full bladder, now can I?" He, without another word, walked through the half-open door beyond Rose's feet, leaving it open behind him and turning left; he disappeared from view.

As soon as he was out of sight, she tested her bonds again, pulling and twisting on them, searching for weakness. Again she surveyed the room intensely, looking for something, anything to help her. The bonds that held her to the table were infallible, and there was nothing to sever them; he knew what he was doing. She came to the bitter conclusion that for her there would be no miraculous escape, no dramatic rescue at the last second. She knew what was coming, and if the video she'd just seen was any indication, it would be horrible beyond her worst nightmares.

Escape was impossible. Acceptance stole over her mind like creeping death and she turned away from it, gazing inward.

"You have to be strong, Rose." She heard her father's voice and felt the cool winter breeze on her face. He'd taken her out onto the ORV trails around Houghton Lake on his snowmobile. *"I found a new spot,"* he'd told her. *"You have to see this, Rose."* The memories came back to her as vividly as if they were happening that very moment...

They cut off a main trail onto a smaller, less used one and motored through a thick birch forest; the snowmobile's engine was incredibly loud in the silent winter woods. The bare limbs of the trees nearly blotted out the grey winter sky and their rough white trunks crowded in so close together that her father had to navigate slowly through them. After a while of weaving through the twisting trail, the birch trees fell away leading them into a winter green forest of pine. The trail angled sharply upwards and the machine's engine strained to make the climb. *"This is it!"* her father called out. She loosened her hold on his waist as the trail leveled and opened into a clearing at the top of a hill. He cut the rumbling engine and the winter forest's silence fell over them. There were no insects buzzing and chirping, no frogs croaking for mates, nothing but the gentle whisper of old man winter's frigid breath blowing through the trees. *"Look at that view,"* he said, gesturing off to their left. The hill overlooked a pristine conifer-forested valley, the flowing water of the Muskegon River cut through the valley like a coiling black snake. The white of the snow-covered forest made the black of the unfrozen river and the green of the pine trees brighter–more vibrant, more alive.

The memories of that day came back to her as vividly as if they were happening that very moment.

"It's beautiful," Rose said. "It's how the world is supposed be everywhere."

"Yes, it is," her father said as he dismounted the snowmobile. He unstrapped and removed his helmet, and then turned and lowered himself down to his knees in front of Rose. His breath plumed out in drifting clouds of vapor as he lifted his eyes to hers. "I have to tell you something, Rose."

She stopped breathing for a second and looked away from the stunning vista and into her father's wary eye. She'd known this was coming–all the whispered conversations between her parents in the past few months; her mother wiping away tears when Rose walked in, denying that anything was wrong; and the hushed arguments she could almost overhear. She took a breath and puffed out, "You're getting a divorce, you and Mom?"

He smiled sadly, his eyes watered and he blinked back the tears threatening to fall, "No, sweetie." He dropped his gaze to the snow at their feet and took a long shuddering breath before raising his eyes to hers again. "I have cancer."

She frowned as confusion and understanding raced through her mind; she looked deep into the hazel green of his eyes, searching. "They can fix you right? The doctors?" she asked–the desperation in her voice bleeding tears.

His lips flattened together, his eyes hardened, and he shook his head– the movement almost to slight to see. "No, baby, they can't."

The weight of his words settled over her chest, crushing her heart. Tears fell from her eyes and left little drops of sparkling ice on her scarf as they froze in the cold air. "You can't die, Daddy, please!" She thrust herself forward and threw her arms around his neck, sobbing. "You can't leave."

He hugged her back and his voice cracked. "You..." he sobbed softly, "you have to be strong, Rose." He slowly, but firmly, pushed her back, holding her shoulders tightly. She averted her gaze, wiping cold tears from her ruddy cheeks with her gloved hands, sniffling. "Rose," he said and lifted her chin, "you have to be strong. Your mother needs you and you need her– you have to be strong together."

She pulled the heavy gloves from her hands, tossed them to the snow-covered ground, and lifted her trembling hands to her father's face. "I love you, Daddy," she sobbed.

"I love you, too, baby."

The seven-year-old memory faded. She drew a shuddering breath and let it out with a whimpering sigh just as the lunatic walked back into the room. To think that she'd lived her whole life–with all its struggles and sadness, all the happy times and her achievements–only to die as the plaything of a madman. It angered her to the core of her soul–the unfairness, the insanity of it all. *I'll try to be strong*, Daddy, she thought. *I'll try.*

"Everything to your satisfaction I hope?" Dominic asked contemptu-ously, smiling down at her. Rose looked up in momentary confusion, and then turned away. "I have to say, that while I did enjoy your little struggle, I'd hoped you would have tried, well, just a bit harder, you know what I mean? You know, like really putting some desperation into it, maybe trying to break your own hands to pull them free or something." He sighed heavily. "Yes, I was watching your pitiful little struggling on a monitor in the bathroom," he uttered impatiently. "Remember," he waved his hand over his head, "you're on very candid, or shall we say, twisted camera."

He laughed lightly at his joke, and then in the next instant his smile morphed into a harsh sneer. "Shall we converse a bit more or are you ready for playtime?"

If Rose had heard his ultimatum, she gave no reaction.

"You see, I really hate the silent treatment, if you persist, I'll be forced to persuade you to talk to me. You really don't..."

"I won't give you what you want," she interrupted with a smooth, steady voice that betrayed none of the terror she was feeling.

His eyebrows rose in delighted surprise, stepping forward he placed his hand over her left breast and began rubbing his forefinger lightly over the nipple.

"And what is it that you think I want? That you assume you can refuse to give?" Her breathing quickened involuntarily at his unwanted touch. "What is it that you will not give? That I cannot take?" He leaned in closer as if to receive a whispered secret, raising his eyebrows again as he looked into her shifting, frightened eyes, waiting.

"We're done talking," she uttered in a calm, deadpan voice without meeting his gaze. "Just get it over with. I'm done playing your sick game." Her cold intonation faltered slightly at the last word.

Dominic paused for a few moments silently contemplating her words. "Very well then," he sighed.

His gently teasing fingers on her left nipple began to pinch. While his face remained passive, his fingers savagely pinched and twisted hard enough to draw blood from the very pores of her tender skin. Tendons clenched in her neck and her back arced slightly as fresh tears welled up in her tired eyes and ran down the side of her face, but she did not cry out.

"Interesting," he whispered releasing her nipple. "This is going to be very interesting indeed." Walking around her, he took hold of a small wheeled cart and pulled it over.

Glancing over nervously, Rose saw many sharp and shiny stainless steel instruments, many of which she did not recognize. She held her silence bravely as he walked around to the end of the table by her feet, and climbed up onto it.

She looked up into his eyes as he hovered over her knees, "Someday it'll be your turn," she shakily said.

"What's this?" he asked, with renewed interest as he climbed up higher and straddled her waist, planted his hands on her shoulders, gazing back into her eyes only a few inches from her face.

"When you fucking die–and you will eventually–I'm hoping for sooner myself..." she said, trying to sound fearless and succeeding just a little.

"Yes, please continue," he prompted with intense interest.

"...you're going straight to Hell. No stops, no detours, no doubts–you're going down on the express elevator."

He nodded his head thoughtfully. "If I believed in that shit, sure, I would have to agree."

"When you get there, we'll be waiting for you." Somewhere in the tired wasteland of her eyes something burned with indignation.

"We? Who's we, darling?" he asked with a laugh. "Please, enlighten me!"

"All of us. All the people you've hurt, all the lives you've taken–the young women you've tortured and killed–we'll be there waiting for you, and when you arrive *you* will be the one tied down to a fucking table and we'll be the ones doing the *biting*!" As she finished, her voice faltered again and she started to sob, but she bravely choked it down and looked firmly back into his eyes.

He smiled, and sitting back, he brought his hands together and ap-plauded enthusiastically. "Bravo, bravo," he shouted in his British accent. "I say, well said, luv. Well said indeed!"

"And you're right, I have to admit," he stated, returning to plain old Dominic's voice. "But I think if there were a Hell, my punishment, my…torment would be far worse than even I could imagine." He shook his head sadly. "But there is no Hell, my love, and there is no justice in this universe outside of man's law and punishment." Taking in a long deep breath he continued, "And right now, there's only you, me, and this room...and it's playtime."

"God damn you to Hell!" she shouted back. "God damn you to Hell!" Her voice trembled but she continued on, defiantly reciting the damnation repeatedly.

"I've always wanted to eat a virgin," he said, and licking his teeth with anticipation, he descended.

At first, there was only the horribly tender sensation of his lips and tongue, and she fought against the appealing tingles. She valiantly repeated her damnation of him until he began to use his teeth. After that, for Rose, there were no more words, only the sharp cascading pain and the screaming.

* * *

The sensuously hot water cascaded over Dominic's body—a sensation of a million lover's warm caresses, washing away the blood, cleansing him of the vestiges of his unspeakable sin. He opened his mouth and let the steamy flow spirit away the coppery flavor of his lover's life. Recalling Rose's defiant spirit, he beamed warmly as he revolved languidly beneath the hot shower's spray. How rewarding it had been when he'd finally broken her, epic really, how she'd begged. She'd lasted far longer than all of his previous conquests and proved to be quite entertaining.

He leaned away from the shower stream briefly and placed his hand under a small spout mounted in the shower-room wall, sensing his hand the dispenser deposited a copious amount of scented body-wash into his palm. Sliding back under the hot water, he spread the silky liquid through his hair and down his tightly muscled frame.

A pity, he mused as the scent of the soap drifted up and enshrouded him. His belly was full of her and yet his heart was heavy. He missed her. He actually missed her!

This realization stunned him. He'd long thought himself incapable of such trivial emotional attachments. Couldn't be, shouldn't be, however, as he explored his dark twisted mind he found it to be true; he was sorry she was gone.

"Well, I'll be damned," Dominic murmured as he ambled out of the shower, ignoring the steam-covered monitor mounted on the wall over the sink that showed his playroom in all its gory detail, and snatched up a towel. Behind him, the sensors in the shower shut off the temperature-controlled water and extinguished the soft blue light. Channeling the old vaudevillian comic, Groucho Marx, he chuckled, "'Truer words were never spoken.' Well, who's life *is it,* anyway?" he asked the empty hall as he tossed the soiled towel into the laundry chute and walked through the door into his bedroom; the question gave him pause.

In his room, clear plastic gear that would cover him head-to-toe awaited on a shelf inside a specially built hidden closet. He dressed in his dismembering outfit slower than usual as he mulled over his question. Rose's life had been, however briefly, his life, to give or take at his whim; he'd chosen to take it. For the first time in Dominic's life, he found himself second-guessing a kill, and there were more first times waiting in the wings of his evening yet to come. He sighed deeply. It would have been far too complicated to keep her for any length of time.

"Ah, bien," Dominic lamented in a Frenchman's elegant intonation. "C'est la vie, et la mort." He lifted his fingers to his lips, kissed them tenderly and flung them away gently into the air. "Au revoir, mon amour." A tear almost welled up in his eye. "Enough!" he grunted. "Good God, man!" he shouted to the lonely room, mimicking the voice of a Federation Starship medical officer named 'Bones'. "I'm a cold-blooded killer, Jim, not a sniveling wench!" Snatching up his cap and gloves, he stalked out of the room and down the hallway that led back to his rumpus room.

Dominic pulled the cap over his head as he hurried through the doorway from the hall and into the blood splattered room beyond, stumbling slightly as he stopped dead in his tracks.

"What?" he asked the vacant room. There should have been a bloody, ravaged, yet still strangely attractive body awaiting dismemberment on the stainless steel autopsy table—a table that now stood empty. He'd placed her limp, lifeless body there after he'd finished her; there were still many choice cuts to preserve for later meals. *Now she was…gone?* "Where?"

A sudden flash of light in the corner of his left eye answered the question. He lunged violently to the right, attempting to avoid the rapidly descending blade.

He succeeded only in changing the point of entry. Instead of plunging deeply into his neck, the large carving knife glanced off his left shoulder joint, cut through the heavy plastic gown he wore, and sliced across the shoulder meat a few inches from his throat.

Blood flowed abundantly from the deep gash as he fell, rolled, and leapt back to his feet as nimbly as an accosted cat. He hardly noticed the pain or the blood that flowed down his chest and splattered onto the floor, mingling with the blood of his victim.

"Rosie! You're still alive?" he shouted as he beheld the macabre bloody vision that stood swaying just a few feet away. "You're still alive," he scolded, waggling his finger and grinned widely. "I *must* be slipping."

Dressed only in her own blood, Rose stood only a few steps away, brandishing a massive, pointed blade in her right hand. Miraculously still alive, she swayed as if she were drunk on near-death. *Or on board a gently rolling ship's deck,* he thought, smiling brighter still.

"You've really no idea how happy I am to see you, luv!" he cooed to her in his best British imitation.

She didn't have the breath to reply; her breathing came in abrupt gasps, her chest rising and falling like the hammering pistons of a high performance race car running in the red. Her body displayed the marks of Dominic's twisted passion. Deep, ragged bite wounds screamed unbearable suffering from between her legs, her inner thighs, breasts, and the wound on her neck—the one that should have killed her. It still *looked* like a killing bite.

Did I not bite deep enough? he wondered to himself.

Rose's bloodstained eyes shifted and she took a hesitant sliding step toward Dominic.

"That's it, luv," he whispered passionately, still imitating a Brit, "let's 'ave at it!" Crouching slightly, he began to slide to her left, circling, his eyes locked on her bloody, hateful gaze. Suddenly feigning to the right, he dashed to the left and caught her blood-slicked wrist easily. "Too easy, luv," he chuffed. Twisting her arm viciously, he forced her hand open and her weapon clattered to the bloody floor.

He lifted his chin and gazed into the red tinged eyes of his delightfully unexpected and vanquished foe, their noses almost touching. Her eyes found his and he saw not defeat and bitter despair, but blazing triumphant resolve. "Huh?" he asked, cocking his head slightly as if disbelieving his own eyes. Then, he felt a sharp sting glide across the side of his throat as the scalpel hidden in Rose's left hand cut deep.

Dominic screamed.

Thrusting her away, he staggered back, his hands coming up in a vain attempt to stem the tide of his life pumping out.

Rose stumbled and fell roughly to the floor—her body smacking wetly, knocking what little breath she had left from her in a huff.

"Ssshhhhhiiiit," Dominic cried. "Fucking bitch! God damn it, Rosie!" His powerfully toned legs wobbled beneath him. Ignoring the pain, he dug his slippery fingers into the wound, searching for the spurting artery without success.

No time! his mind screamed. *Need a blade... Widen the incision... Find the bleeder!* He spun away and staggered toward his equipment table, his smooth confident swagger all but gone as his blood splattered on the floor behind him. His feet betrayed him, slipping on the smeared red liquid that covered the tile.

The equipment table seemed a hundred miles away; his vision swam and the floor reached up, cracking him in the face like a cricket bat.

"Ah," he sighed. With his blood flowing out, he managed with considerable effort to roll limply over onto his back. His hand fell away and the blood pumped undeterred onto the floor around him, and he became weaker with every beat of his stilling black heart.

His head lapsed over onto its side as rushing death sapped his strength away, and he caught sight of Rose staring at him from the floor across the room. "Checkmate," he hissed.

Her crimson-stained gaze burned. "We'll be waiting..." she sighed, and then her vibrant eyes went vacant like a pinched candlewick.

For the first time in his entire monstrous life, and unfortunately only for a few fleeting seconds, real, honest fear colored Dominic eyes.

Then, as if reaching out from her un-dug grave, Rose's valiant defiance pinched his candlewick as well.

THE TROJAN FARM ANIMALS

GARY WEDLUND

King Herodotus looked out at five thousand men who reeked of yesterday's fish. Their throngs of tents sat among streaming smoke, dotting the Sacamander plains. Dawn stretched Troy's shadow over the shore upon which rotted six hundred Macedonian ships. They sat bow up and were beached by the low tide. Some sails–white and blue–fluttered, furled and roped to a few of the main masts, though most seasoned captains had stowed their sails months ago.

"Hail, King Herodotus the Manly. Hath the Hittites stirred this cursed morn?" General Alexander the Small lisped while approaching the dim shape of his king.

Herodontus startled in his chair while under a blanket and beneath the shadow of his pavilion's awning. He stood. The king was already dressed in a bronze breastplate and a pleated skirt sporting a wet spot he hoped didn't show.

He slid his sword into his scabbard and plucked several lice out of his beard. "They're right where they've been the last two hundred and forty-four mornings–hiding behind the walls of Troy. Sometimes I wonder how Menelaus managed to sack this city in the first place. I suspect siege is useless. With all the hanging gardens, they can probably feed themselves indefinitely on the vines alone."

"Yes, this is not working," Young Cyrus, High Prince and General of the Spartan Legion said as he was walking past. "Some say inspiration alone was the key that allowed our ancestors to breach these gates, not famine."

"Come join us." Under his breath Herodontus added, "You arrogant Spartan bastard."

Cyrus came closer, banging his sword hilt on his shield–he bore a smug smile on his handsome face. "Hail Herodotus."

"This inspiration, you referenced; that would be the infamous Helen, I presume," Alexander the Small said and flipped his hand at the wrist as if dismissing the subject.

"Yes, Helen, one and the same. The whole army had her, and had her, and had her, and thus wanted her back."

Alexander shook his head. "Since we've perfected culture and learned Greek man is the higheth form, we've not had use for women beyond making new men, such as my son Alexander the Average." He picked up a rag and rubbed it across Herodontus's breastplate, spending an unusually long time polishing the bronze nipples.

"Here, here," Herodontus said while he waited for Alexander to finish polishing. He scratched his nuts and fidgeted his iron crown so it aligned with different knots from the ones worn raw by the headgear yesterday.

"While on the subject, Alexander, tell me again why you delivered your wife to the Hitite swine," Cyrus asked, before sticking his tongue in his cheek.

"Who?" Alexander looked up from the brass nipples.

"Zenthe, your large-bosomed wife; I miss her."

Cyrus asked this question every day. His desire for the company of women was considered very unmanly. Deep down, Herodontus wished custom allowed him to also say he preferred Zenthe to slave boys without admitting to a desire for the sordid act of heterosexuality outside the duty of impregnation.

"Oh yes, her—poor dear. I forgot abouth Zenthe," Alexander swept the air with the back of his hand, "entirely. I did think she'd inspire our army like Helen did—rally us, so to speak. She seemed to knowth nearly everybody. Some have asked."

"Not even a word of her?" Cyrus sounded desperate.

"A better question is how he managed to convince his wife to go in there and become a captive." Herodontus joined Cyrus in staring at Alexander.

"That was easy," Alexander the Small said and smiled. "I thuggested the shopping was to die for."

Cyrus squinted at him, seemingly a little angry after hearing he'd deliberately gotten rid of her.

"Well, it's true. I bought this purple thash from a merchant two years back, ohhh, you would not beee-lieve. I told her, Zenthe, sweetie, you must keep an eye out for..."

"Oh, cease your pathetic lisping, Alexander," Cyrus said. "Sometimes I forget your father is Alexander the Insignificant and expect reason from your mouth."

They started down the muddy path that led to the road before the gates of Troy, and soon arrived at the perfect spot for observing the main gate, which was marked by twenty thousand arrows just beyond their feet. Their yellow fletching beautified the landscape, reminding Herodontus of the wildflowers that sprang up on many feral fields near Macedonia. Several more sprouted as they stood watching the heathen Trojans clamor along the ramparts.

Cyrus banged his sword on his shield, making King Herodontus glad they'd nearly run out of wine and thus been forced to wake up without hangovers.

The mighty gates of Troy groaned open. Out popped Aophus, Herodontus's ambassador, who scampered toward them like he had a half cubit of rope tied between his ankles.

"Hail, King Herodontus," Aophus bellowed and bowed several times.

"What news arises from King Amuwanda–does he yield?" Herodontus asked.

"Did you see Zenthe, and did she ask about me?" Cyrus barged between his king and the ambassador, but then backed away when Aophus shook his head no. The ambassador looked at his king, too, and kept shaking his head.

"Drat!" Herodontus banged his own breastplate. "Didn't you tell him my offer to only pillage for a day and take a few thousand useless women as slaves?"

Cyrus nodded eagerly upon the words women and slaves.

"Our king's offer is very generous." Alexander shrugged as if saying he had no idea why they'd turned them down.

"Not a budge. Seems they have ample food–and distract themselves from hunger by flaunting their weak culture through publically lusting for the female form. Though they grow scarce of meat, their stores and gardens suffice," Aophus said. The wind shifted and an arrow landed between Aophus and Herodontus; they stepped a little farther from the ramparts. "But I've been thinking... Remember our Trojan horse?"

"There's not a chance it will work twice, especially after several centuries," Herodontus said. "They're on to us, and no doubt have long memories of that last bit of trickery. Besides, after two sieges, we've depleted these plains of woodland."

"I have an idea," Cyrus said. "We'll entice them into a narrow pass where a hundred Spartans can stand with interlocking shields and lay their entire army to waste at the sacrifice of a hundred mortal souls that will be instantly ushered to Zeus's mansions. A thousand virgins will lounge in each warrior's sleeping chamber." He ran toward the gate, yelled, "Huh!" then retreated from under a hail of arrows. Upon returning, he put his hands on his knees, bending over and gagging for breath.

"Excellent display of courage, young Cyrus," Alexander the Small said and patted the Spartan on his skirted ass.

"Quite the picture of Greek manliness, indeed." Herodontus actually thought running under the arrows for nothing but pride was the mark of an absolute idiot. "Yet I fear his tactic implies some other war. Here before us is the puzzle of these mighty walls."

Aophus paced before his king, then paused as if he'd come up with an idea. Herodontus knew his ambassador (who'd spent more than two hundred days negotiating within the walls of Troy) never came up with ideas on the spot. He mulled things over, almost always at an excruciating pace. Thus, the king's ears peaked.

"The horse was good, but thirty men are risky. Imagine those thirty men silent for most of a night while the enemy danced and sang, not to mention the abundant orgies and drink." Aophus gazed at the three with eyes honed in the art of persuasion.

"Yeth, all those wonderful Greek bodies, muscles pressed together…" Alexander the Small said, "unable to move…teasing and close, butts to groins, hands searching for purchase, ears listening to the sounds of orgasms and, oh goodness…dancing music. Gods help me boys, I can just imagine. Wooo!" He fanned himself. "I'm so sorry, you muth give me a second!" He sat on the sand and put his head down between his legs in order to suppress an urge to faint, Herodontus guessed.

Aophus started to roll his eyes, but caught himself. "Very manly of our Alexander."

"Here, here."

"Yes, that, what you said."

A crew of Hitite slaves started dumping buckets of the night's honey-dew over the part of the ramparts that abutted a ditch running alongside the main road from the gate. "Well, anyway," Aophus continued, as the sewage trickled near and they all instinctively moved aside. "We have an abundance of bronze breastplates and several good smiths. I propose we make three bronze idols to Athena this time."

"Three?" Herodontus asked.

"Yes, one for each of our mighty leaders. After all, the brace holding the gate can't be more than twenty stone. We shall need only two or three-heroic Greek specimens of perfect manliness to lift it."

"Bronze horses? Are not the legs on horses long and spindly? It may be beyond the skill of our craftsmen," Cyrus said.

Herodontus knew the man thought little of trickery, preferring suicidal slogging, usually shield to shield. Such was typical of Spartans, who were the last tribe of Greeks to learn language, and he suspected the first likely to go extinct.

Aophus put his hand on his chin, as if thinking. "We'll make simpler animals then. A pig, a goose, and a heifer, I propose."

Alexander the Small got up and volunteered, "I wanth to be the heifer."

"Don't you think a heifer is unmanly? We're Greek after all!" Cyrus yelled this so loud he drew five arrows–all of them twenty paces short.

"Good thinking," Aophus agreed. "A bull then. But, the bull will be largest, befitting only our king. The pig better fits your shape, Alexander."

"A pig?"

"We must be practical," Herodontus said, sealing the deal.

* * *

Three days later, the army attacked the mighty walls with poles and ladders, and many shields aimed up, catching the arrows that filled the sky; drumming and screams owned the air. Two giant catapults lofted flaming captured Hittites over the ramparts. The men of Troy tossed rocks and boiling oil down on the few Greeks who managed to make it close enough to try to scale the stone.

A large tent sat near the gate road where Cyrus squeezed into his bronze goose that was laid on its side and opened like two halves of an egg that connected by a pair of top hinges. "Can you believe I'm missing all the fun? And this…this is just ridiculous." He moaned as he kinked his knees over one support bar and his belly over another. This bent him in three—a jackknifed fetal position within the teardrop shape of the goose.

Alexander the Small crawled into his own half shell—there was more space and a wedge at the pig's back feet, allowing his feet and toes to fill in the haunches. A half cubit wedge of bronze separated the man's heels from his protruding ass that filled the bulbous hams. He lifted his head up to the side and laughed at Cyrus. "That goose head ith way too big, and it hath no neck. You look like a duck."

"You're a swine, Alexander. Why am I listening?" Cyrus asked. "Now somebody tell me why we have to do this while naked?"

"Aophus has been over this," Herodontus scolded as he leaned into the bull, lying on its side and open on the carpet. "There is little room and it might get hot. Besides, skin on bronze makes no sound, or at least not like our hard leather and buckles. He promises he'll have our sandals, skirts, and armor when the job nears completion and we are released."

Herodontus wiggled into his bronze example of livestock. He was glad he was king because the bull had ample room for him to put his arms most of the way down the forelegs and his legs all the way down the back ones. Other than pointed toes and a slight bend near the knees, the position didn't seem all that unnatural for a Greek. Still, being bent over was fairly embarrassing while in the bull, making him glad Aophus had volunteered to button them up before the guards came in to right the bronze idols.

Outside the tent, horns and drums signaled retreat, as planned. It was already high tide, and most of the tents had been struck, so within the half hour the entire Greek army planned to sail beyond sight of land, leaving the three bronze statues on their broad, wheeled platforms. Aophus had even thought to apply a chain to a hook riveted to the chest of each animal, enticing the Trojan dogs to latch on and pull them into their den.

Aophus came in and looked down at the three. "All set?"

"Of course, you fool. You know we've measured for this to the last finger of tolerance," Cyrus said.

Aophus took the criticism without comment and leaned over, setting the bottom leather seals in place before lifting the heavy left half of the goose and dropping it over the man. This sealed Cyrus's body in nice and tight. He aligned the two iron pegs to matching tabs and holes near the bottom, and sealed the goose shut with raps on the pegs from a hammer.

"A bit tight, don't you think?" Herodontus asked.

"If they break it loose, we're all discovered. Remember, I'm going to play the part of the abandoned Greek. They'll likely murder me and keep you three for ransom if this goes afoul. Not to worry, I'll bury the hammer out here, come get it, then pound the pins right out when you're nicely done."

"Sorry about calling you a fool, Aophus," Cyrus said. "Actually, good thinking. If this works, my sword shall be the first to cleave the head of the Hitite king." Cyrus's Adam's Apple bobbed, showing some nervousness. His head poked out of the neck hole and his butt hung out the back because both the head and ass had not yet been secured. The heads and asses screwed on later with a quarter turn. They helped to secure the halves, and once in place, allowed the men good air and a means of relieving themselves before the final minute of pulling the tent away.

Alexander the Small was shelled next. From where his head hung out of the pig's neck he had a glorious view of the goose's circular asshole, yielding a fine view of Cyrus's asshole, bringing a smile to the larger man's face.

Finally, Herodontus felt the left side of his body enclose as the other half of his bull dropped. While the ambassador pounded the pegs, Herodontus looked around, feeling odd with only his head exposed and the cool air on his backside. Aophus called two burly guards in to help right the three offerings to Athena. The wheels were well spaced astride heavy, metal bases, making each animal exceptionally balanced when upright.

"The ships are leaving now—we must hurry." Aophus nodded toward the two guards, who snapped their heels together and saluted with forearms across their bodies. They departed in haste, soon plucking the tent pegs.

Aophus unplugged a little stopper from the tops of each animal. "I'll leave these small holes open for air and secure them before the first sign of the gate opening, but the heads and tails need screwed tight before those two take away the tent and we're discovered." With that, the large buttocks were turned into place, and the heads were also set.

Herodontus had to hold his head to the side while the funnel piece for the mouth rotated along his cheek. Once secured, the funnel fit perfectly in his mouth, allowing him access through the animal's mouth to plenty of air. The piece was bound in hide, keeping the metal from irritating the king's teeth. There was only a palm's width of extra space within the bull's head, but as the king's head tired, he found it falling and the narrow end of the funnel sank nearly to the back of his mouth.

"All set to go," Aophus said.

Herodontus couldn't see much through the knife-width slits cut for the bull's eyes, but he did notice the sky when the tent was pulled away and there came a great roar of delight from the walls of Troy–a few minutes later the gates groan open. A rumble of approaching feet shook the earth. Almost instantly, hands patted and banged on the bronze bull. Men came around, cheering, boasting, and laughing.

"Make way, make way for the king!" someone called in the Hittites' sloven tongue.

Herodontus heard the crowd of enemy soldiers hush.

Aophus' hand must have been right over the bull's back because Herodontus almost felt an echoing pat and then the words, "All give homage to King Amuwanda, great leader of the Hittites. I fear I have been abandoned by the cowardly Greeks. They charged me only with this last service, that I should present these sacred offerings to the Goddess Athena, in honor of Amuwanda's great victory."

"Well said, Aophus. I hold you harmless. Be it written: We shall take these figures and set them in the court while we feast upon the blessings of Zeus and fill our stomachs, as well as fill the wombs of our women, in celebration to this great victory."

That said, Herodontus felt himself moving over the ruts, then along the smoother roadway. They thumped along the flagstones under the gates, and after another ten minutes came to a halt, supposedly in the king's court of celebration.

Horns blasted, tambourines jingled, and tin and animal-skinned drums beat. The crowd's roar surged and waned. Speeches were made. Dignitaries introduced one another. The ground bounced from dancers' feet. Laughter increased as it became clear someone had raided the deepest bowels of the wine cellars.

Herodontus squinted through the eye slits, seeing body-shapes twirling around the idols. Nearby braziers full of flames cast bronze reflections on the dancers. Herodontus felt himself cramping, and he had to pee like no tomorrow.

All of a sudden, a drum banged a brisk cadence, and the crowd stilled. "Mighty Trojans!"

That sounds very close, maybe a few feet away, and like the voice of King Amuwanda, Herodontus thought.

"We have much to announce. To begin, the gods have honored me with a beautiful Greek woman. Since the Greeks have abandoned her to our care, I propose to take Zenthe as my wife—she shall be only my thirty-fifth."

Someone sounding like Zenthe squealed, "Oh, my gods! I'm so excited! Thank you, my love. For this I have saved my virginity."

Virginity? What about her son back in Greece, Alexander the Average? Herodontus recalled seeing her round as a plum, not to mention, praying at the altar of Cyrus a dozen times.

Sounds like kissing made its way into the bull.

There was loud roaring from the crowd and clapping.

"As well, I decree lands, honor, and four wives of his choosing to our friend, Aophus of Macedonia. Let it be known that not all Greeks are beyond the grace of our gods if they serve us well."

"All hail, the great King of Troy, Protector of the Dardanelles, and Defender of all decent Hittites," some crier said and more clapping followed.

Herodontus nearly slipped up and laughed when he realized how completely Aophus had fooled the stupid Hitite king. Obviously their man had the run of the land and would have no trouble freeing them in an hour or two when the drunken Hittites started falling over into stupors. Aophus had even managed to get Alexander's dense wife, Zenthe, in on the act. He'd have to remember to reward both Aophus and Alexander the Small with a nut and date cake this coming Poseideon Day Festival.

"We also thank the Goddess Athena for providing us with this wonderful feast. As you know, we've been forced to live without meat, having run out of sheep ten days hence. The Goddess has seen this and provided us these three excellent examples of livestock."

The crowd again went wild with roaring and clapping.

Herodontus felt the funnel twisting and suddenly the head lifted off his bull. After squinting to get the sweat out of his eyes, he found himself looking up into the face of King Amuwanda. Zenthe stood beside him with both arms wrapped around his waist. In the distance, Aophus seemed to be staggering off with a woman under each arm.

How unmanly! Herodontus thought bitterly.

After squirming and banging his head all around the rim, Herodontus realized there was no way he could free himself from the bull. In fact, he could barely move more than his fingers.

The Trojan king stepped aside just as Herodontus' liberated ears heard a muffled scream. There before him, on a raised granite landing, glistened a bronze goose. Wood had been piled under it, covering the heavy base. Someone had set the wood afire. Two eunuchs in loincloths tended the flames, making sure the fire stayed small, but lit. Other slaves poured oil or water into the little opening at the top of the goose—now oven—before resealing it, no doubt to keep the steam in and the meat from sticking.

The goose vibrated in random jerks as Cyrus yelled and fought to break free. Herodontus noticed the vibrations, though quite violent, were not enough to threaten to topple the idol.

The screeching goose was distant, perhaps a couple hundred cubits off. Half as far away, on a second raised area, Alexander the Small's pig had both its head and back parts open. The man looked around frantically. "I'm Alexander the Small! You can't do this to me! Oh, Zenthe, tell them. At least tell them I'm your huthband. I have friends—men willing to pay to hath me back!"

Zenthe looked like she was about to faint from embarrassment. "Husband? I've never seen this man in my entire life. Why, any fool can hear from that lisp that he's never had a woman."

King Amuwanda laughed. A bit belatedly, others of his court followed suit.

A eunuch tweaked Alexander's privates, probably from envy. The pig's head went back on, followed by the butt end of Alexander's oven. Soon, kindling started under the pig, and as the heat picked up, everyone hushed so they could hear Alexander breathing heavily through the funnel. Both King Amuwanda and Zenthe took a trip over and put their heads down close while grinning. Finally, a little whimper and an, "Oohhh!" A few seconds later, "Oh my gods. Oh, ohh, ohhh. Ahh. Ahhhh!"

The king straightened and smiled upon hearing the first cries of discomfort from Alexander; Zenthe jumped up and down while clapping. The king went back to attending to the official ceremonies. He offered a toast to some general whose men had manned the walls faithfully for most of a year.

Cyrus, as usual, wasn't taking things in a manly fashion either as he whimpered, moaned, and put up a fuss while baking. After a while, the vibrating turned into hard bangs and long terms of silence were punctuated by deep moans as if Cyrus kept passing out and recovering to his same hell. One of the slaves opened up the top plug again and started pouring in a huge vase of what looked like orange puree.

As soon as Cyrus's goose stopped shaking and moaning entirely, the pig groaned up in earnest. Herodontus couldn't believe how much the pig wailed and shook, almost as if the bronze animal was alive and not made of beaten breastplates. He had deluded visions of the Goddess Athena coming down, shining her light, and causing the pig to become real and run off to safety. Shaking the sweat back out of his eyes, the Goddess' shimmering returned to simple reflections of fire off the bronze. The animal's shaking appeared to stem from knees, shoulders, and a head banging inside the pig like palms of a drummer. Even more earnest screams started and didn't pause for breath until a whole minute between each.

Steam began to continually blow out of the top hole on Cyrus's goose. One of the slaves had to remove one log because the king's cook told him the man was roasting too fast and he didn't want to be accused of serving the king tough meat. Alexander heard that, and the pig started shaking faster than ever. They opened the tiny top on the pig and poured in several little jugs of warmed lard then closed him back up. "Ahhh, ahh, ahh, aaaaah!" came out of the hole as well as out of the pig's mouth.

Herodontus was forced to watch all of this while he pleaded for mercy, insisting he'd be worth a fortune in ransom. Nobody seemed to care that he was a king though, probably because they were all mad at him for sealing them in the city for so long and causing them to do without meat for over a week.

After an hour, Alexander's pig stilled like Cyrus's had. The sounds of grease popping and water boiling replaced the anguished sounds and kicking. An appetizing aroma accompanied the smoke steadily streaming out of the top blowholes of the pressure cookers.

The time came to open up the goose. Oil, water, and vegetable paste oozed out after they unpinned the animal using the same hammer that had sealed them in. Once enough filtered out, they unhinged it fully and lifted the side all the way up. Eunuchs used spatulas to loosen the man from the bronze. They pulled him free, putting Cyrus on a portable table in the exact same position he'd baked in.

Herodontus had to look away when the movers cleared, offering him a better view. Cyrus didn't look anything like his former self, other than in general shape. His skin had shrunk back, exposing all of his teeth and both eye sockets steamed from the internal heat of his baked brain. In several places along his brown, scorched body, the skin had split, oozing juices.

The carvers came and cut a thin slice from Cyrus's back, set it on a plate garnished with vegetables, and took it over to the king who'd returned to his table only a few cubits away from Herodontus' bull. The table was adorned with fruits and vegetables, flowers and oils, and of course, his 'virgin' fiancé. Once the king ate the first portion of Cyrus, a plate was brought over and stacked with shank and ribs.

Zenthe licked her lips after a meaty bite of rib and leaned over to better be heard in the king's ear. "Darling. Would you mind?" She pointed. "That cow is looking at me while I eat."

King glanced over at Herodontus and chuckled. "Oh yes, my innocent little fawn, I nearly forgot." He waved the back of his hand in Herodontus' direction as if dismissing someone. Herodontus immediately figured out who, as the world went dark and the funnel once again rotated along his cheek until it lined up with his lips; he started hyperventilating.

His bull moved and seemed to be lifted onto some kind of raised area. The hole above his back opened, and something slippery and wet splashed across his body. Some of it trickled down his arms and legs. A drop or two made it all the way along his back and dripped off his chin.

Did I smell sulfur? he wondered.

Then the belly of the bull started feeling a wee bit hot. He lifted his chest off the metal, but his body only went a little ways before his back hit the top of the animal–he screamed.

"Darling, please do something about all that noise. I've heard enough already," a voice like Zenthe's said.

Someone unscrewed the head. Herodontus gasped for air when it came off. A eunuch presented an apple to the human bull's mouth while two others grabbed his chin and yanked his mouth open. The apple was shoved in with enough force to drive it past his teeth. When they finished, another slave ran an awl into the apple, piercing it through with a hole. Next, the head was put back on. Herodontus had to fight to get the hole in the apple lined up with the funnel opening, but once he managed it, he thanked the gods for the air. His mouth felt so full he couldn't even move his tongue.

Almost immediately the oven heated back up. The Greek king struggled to keep his breast off the surface, but then other parts of the oven got hot and he had to move pieces of skin away from individual oil-slicked surfaces and onto others. In time it became a challenge to shift his arms, legs, torso, and ass that touched the hot surfaces, ensuring that no part of his own body burned instead of cooked evenly. He realized he was seeing to his own even brazing, doing all the fine, detailed work of cooking himself, but he also knew he had no choice in the matter as the bull put up a continual buzz of self-vibration.

"Ummm, this chubby Greek who lied about being my husband is delicious," Zenthe said from outside where Herodontus was sure slaves fanned her and her new king with giant bird feathers.

"Ha. That's a delicacy, my little kitten," King Amuwanda said, laughing.

"Oh, you tricked me!" Zenthe said and giggled like a virgin. "Is this his naughty part I'm eating? They don't look threatening. My mother said they would look dangerous."

Lots of the cursed Trojans laughed after that.

The oven filled with smoke and steam, forcing Herodontus to close his eyes, internalizing every bit of the pain. All his screaming into the apple only made his head swim. Even though he willed an end to his breathing, he couldn't help but gasp for all he could manage through the funnel/mouth device.

His mind overheated and his thoughts became jumbled and confused as his brain cells died. The former king's intellect and memories reduced cell by cell until all that remained were the primitive brain stem and unbearable misery. A roar accompanied each intake and exhale, sounding like an animal.

Something in Herodontus' ears still worked though.

"Do you hear that, stud-muffin?" Zenthe asked. "It sounds like the bull is mooing. Are you sure it isn't a heifer?"

WHAT DEFILES THE MAN?

DANE T. HATCHELL

Haley Deucett was a man of dreams, mystery, and imagination. At least, that was how he thought of himself. He was a proud man of Creole descent and had lived in the same house since birth, near the Garden District of New Orleans.

He'd been working as a janitor at the Royal Sonesta in the French Quarter of New Orleans for the last ten years and had learned the basics of his profession while still in high school, helping his mother clean houses to meet their living expenses.

He'd found his calling in life when he'd seen a janitor cleaning up outside of the Hotel Monteleone. The gentleman was dressed in starched black slacks and wore black patent leather shoes. His black jacket was piped in red on the lapel, and his Remington hat was adorned with gold rope above the shiny black brim; a white shirt and black tie completed his outfit. The man looked like royalty, and he had the air of confidence and sophistication.

Haley had worked for several of the famous hotels in the French Quarter over the years and each one had their own unique staff uniforms. And believe it or not, he would switch employers when he tired of the uniform and wanted a new look. He'd always heard that *'clothes make the man'* and he liked to remake himself every so often.

Being a diligent worker, he was rewarded with a second shift–since the night maintenance man had given up his job. His first shift started at two P.M. and ended at ten P.M. It was near the end of his first shift when the head Chef from *Le Feu,* the hotel restaurant, exited the restroom and stopped when he saw Haley.

"Piss man!" Chef Barque roared boisterously. "I see you're working hard as usual."

"Yes, sir, Chef Barque," Haley said without looking up, but forced a grin as he continued to mop. He didn't like Chef Barque. He was impatient and ever since he'd taken over the night shift and was responsible for cleaning the kitchen, he couldn't do enough to please the Chef; he became more hostile toward him with each passing day.

"Since you started cleaning at night, the floors, they feel slick," Barque said with a slight French accent.

"No, sir, Chef Barque, I clean the floors super special. Why, you could eat off the floors after I've finished." Haley didn't like conflict, but his work was his reputation and he defended it proudly.

"And, piss man, someone helped themselves to the *Caciocavallo Podolico* last night. Did you have some cheese with your pork skin snack?" Barque asked accusingly.

"Chef Barque, I don't eat any of your food–that would be stealing. I don't eat any cheese other than American anyway," Haley said with annoyance.

Barque bent forward with his hands on his hips, "Eh, piss man, you watch your step or I'll get you fired."

"Chef Barque, you leave me be. Go on, get yourself home and let me get back to work," Haley said, even more agitated.

Barque taunted, "Yes, yes, you get back to work, piss man. I've left you a gift in the last stall to show you what I think of your…work."

Barque left with a laugh, and Haley could feel his blood pressure rising. In all his years of working, no one had ever treated him the way Barque did. The Chef did have the reputation of being overly demanding, which is why the previous guy had quit. Mr. Antone, the hotel's chief of staff, specifically asked Haley to take over the kitchen duties at night because of the quality of work he was known for. He'd been happy to do it, although it had cut down on his reading time at home. But he didn't want to give up his afternoon shift; he enjoyed meeting the people who stayed at the hotel. Plus, now that he was pulling two shifts, he was making more money and was saving for a newer car.

Haley pushed the bathroom door open and went to the last stall and looked inside–his worse fear was confirmed. Chef Barque had felt the call of nature to defecate and had left a smoldering pile of feces on the floor next to the toilet. Haley felt humiliated, but being a man of honor, he cleaned the mess up and left the bathroom in pristine condition.

His shift in the kitchen passed quickly while his mind was occupied with the mistreatment he'd received from Barque. He didn't let it interfere with his work though, and performed every task with the same care as always.

When he made the final pass with the mop, he was happy to see the clock showing four A.M. The floors were so clean that they reflected the florescent lighting fixtures as he made his final inspection; a job well done. He put away his cleaning supplies and made his way to his car for the short drive home.

He was allowed to park his car in the hotel's parking garage, although his spot was on the top level. He climbed into his 1981 Delta 88 and drove the six stories down, turning onto Bienville Street, toward home.

A red light brought him to a stop at the intersection of Bienville and Baronne, and of course, there was no traffic this time of the morning, but he still waited. He was still thinking about the good for nothing Barque when the passenger's door opened and a small, dark figure jumped in next to him and closed the door.

"Hey! What? Get out of my car!" Haley shouted–the invader bringing him back to reality abruptly.

"Hey, papi chulo, that's no way to talk to a senorita," said a petite woman with long dangling earrings.

"Are you crazy, woman? Get out of my car!" Haley demanded.

"Why should I get out of your car? You stopped for me," she said.

"I didn't stop for you. I stopped for the red light! I'm on my way home and I need to turn left here. Now get out," Haley countered.

"Not so fast, papi chulo, how about we party?"

"Party? It's four A.M.! I'm tired and need to go to sleep," Haley said incredulously.

"We party at your house, you know," the woman said, reaching her hand out and down onto his crotch, rubbing him gently.

"Miss! Get your hand off me!"

"Victoria, my name is Victoria," she said, with the 'is' sounding more like 'eese'.

"I don't care what your name is, I want you to take your hand off me and get out of my car!" Haley commanded.

"What's the matter, you don't like Latino girls?" she asked.

"I don't like Latino girls that jump in my car at four in the morning!" Haley snapped.

"Okay, I get out then," she said with a sigh, removing her hand.

"Good, now why don't you go home and get some sleep."

"I get out when you pay me," she added.

"Pay you for what?"

"Pay me for my time–give me fifty dollars and I get out."

"I'm not giving you fifty dollars, now out!"

Victoria grabbed his crotch, squeezing this time. "You give me fifty dollars and I give you your balls back."

"Get your... AHHHHHH!" Haley yelled as Victoria dug her boney fingers into his testicles. "Okay, stop. I'll give you the money."

Victoria squeezed harder. "You give me a hundred dollars, I stop."

Grabbing Victoria by the hair, he slammed her head into the steering wheel. She cried out and dug in even harder than Haley imagined possible. He wrapped his hands around her throat and squeezed as hard as he could; she made choking sounds, but didn't let go.

Haley repeatedly slammed her head against the steering wheel while choking her until she released her grip, and blessed relief washed over him. She was out cold; he pushed her back to her side of the car.

He looked in his rear view mirror and saw a car approaching from behind. His light had finally turned green, so he turned and parked on the side of the road. He looked over at Victoria–her eyes were open with a vacant, distant stare and his heart sank.

"Victoria! Wake up! Time to get out, Victoria," Haley said and tapped on her arm, but she wouldn't rouse. He reached for her wrist and felt around, but couldn't find a pulse.

She's dead! What am I going to do? How am I going to explain this to the police? How am I going to explain this to my boss at the Royal Sonesta? he wondered in a state of panic. He was going to have to hire a lawyer, miss work, maybe even spend time in jail–and going to jail was something he vowed he would never do.

He needed to get rid of the body. *She was just a prostitute*, he thought, *maybe no one will miss her.* What he needed was time to think, so he headed home to do his thinking there.

It was a short drive as he lived less than a mile down Baronne Street, in a house his grandmother had owned; Haley's mother had left him the house when she'd died thirty years before, and it still had the original curtains and was in bad need of painting.

Haley pulled into his carport and was glad he'd forgotten to replace the burned out bulb that normally lit the area. He didn't think any of his neighbors were awake yet, but it was best to be safe. He thought better of leaving the body in his car and moved her to the house while still under the cover of night. Fortunately, she weighed no more than ninety pounds so he had little difficulty dragging her in.

He entered the living room and closed the door and the curtains before turning the lights on. The illuminating glow revealed a wall of bookshelves, filled with hardback and paperback books. In one corner sat a desk with a black and white picture of JFK and an old IBM Selectric typewriter that had a half-typed page still in it. The rest of the room was sparsely furnished with a chair, couch, and a rug–all very old, but clean.

Haley grew up watching old monster movies on a TV show hosted by Morgus the Magnificent. Each week Dr. Morgus and his sidekick Chopsley would work on experiments during breaks in the movie, with the experiments always leading to disaster.

This led him to read novels and collect comic books of the horror genre. He treasured his, *Tales of the Zombie* collection, along with reprints of the comics from the 1950's. In New Orleans, you grew up hearing about voodoo and zombies. Marie Laveau was the most famous voodoo practitioner, and his Grandmother used to scare him with stories of her.

Haley decided he would put Victoria in the bathtub, ice her down, and deal with her later. He held her under the arms and was pulling her into the hall when his eyes caught the cover of a classic comic, *Crime Suspense Stories #22*. The cover picture was a graphic display of a man holding the severed head of a beautiful blond in one hand and a bloody hatchet in the other, with her body and exposed legs lying flat on the floor. This caused something to tingle in the back of his mind as it gave him an idea.

He had to get rid of the body and considered his options–he could chop her up or try to find a pile of fire ants and let them pick her bones clean, but didn't feel that he could get away with it. He considered throwing her away in a garbage dumpster and felt that he could probably get away with that.

Or...he could satisfy a certain curiosity he'd had ever since he'd heard a certain song on the radio.

The name of the song was, *Timothy*. It was a catchy little tune that dealt with three men trapped in a coal mine. They were *'hungry as hell with no food to eat'*. When a rescue team arrived, two satiated miners were found–Timothy was not. Ever since Haley'd heard the song, he'd wondered what human flesh would taste like. He'd even read up on ancient and modern cannibalism, but had never felt compelled to kill and eat anyone to find out. Now, here was an opportunity that might not ever come around again.

He continued his backwards walk as he dragged her into the bathroom. Her body was still limp and her head flopped from side to side in an eerie way as he removed her clothing. He lifted her into the old, cast iron tub, started the water, and gave her a quick wash down. He didn't want whatever filth and grime she'd picked up in the French Quarter to contaminate his meal.

He made a trip to the kitchen and retrieved a meat cleaver, a boning knife, some plastic trash bags, and returned to begin his work.

Applying skills he'd learned while spending time at his cousin's deer camp, he started off by removing her feet and hands and tossing them into the trash bag. He then removed the limbs at the joints, until only the head was connected to the torso. The blood draining out of the severed limbs was making a mess of things, so he turned the water back on and washed it down the drain before rinsing each limb and adding them to the trash bag.

The limbless torso of Victoria reminded Haley of the movie, *Boxing Helena*. "Now that was a woman who had to really trust her man," he said and chuckled to himself.

He made another trip to the kitchen for a serrated blade and sawed though the neck and removed her head. Retrieving the brain was a little messy–he used the meat cleaver to chop around the top of the skull. Finally–through the icky combination of blood and hair–he cut through enough bone that he was able to crack the skull open and remove the brain. It was smaller than he'd thought it would be, and decided it was what he'd eat first.

He laid the heart, liver, and kidneys aside as he gutted the torso, throwing the remaining organs away. He washed up again, removed the ribs, and decided her ass was too skinny to make a worthwhile roast.

He contemplated her genitalia, and a dark, perverse feeling flushed through him. It didn't look like a taco, and he was sure it wouldn't taste like one. And despite all the stories he'd heard about Cajuns eating anything, he'd never seen female animal genitals in a jambalaya.

What would it taste like? he wondered. *'Eating's not cheating'* popped in his mind and he chuckled to himself again.

How would I prepare it if I did want to eat it? "I don't have a recipe for cat, and I don't think it would go well mixed in with mayo and pickle relish," Haley said aloud, cracking himself up.

Eventually, he snapped to and decided just to throw the rest of the body away. He did one final clean up, changed his clothes, and brought the meat and the trash to the kitchen.

By now Haley had worked up quite an appetite and he decided to eat breakfast before putting the meat away.

He pulled out a large, cast iron skillet and began to heat it on the stove, cracked two eggs in a bowl, sprinkled in some seasonings, and whipped it all together. He took Victoria's brain and cut it in half, and sliced one half of it into equally thick slabs.

A thin wisp of smoke rose from the skillet, signaling it was ready. He threw some butter on the hot surface and soon it was sizzling hot. He sautéed some chopped garlic in the butter for a couple of minutes and placed the brain slabs in the buttery mixture.

The brains heated quickly and emanated a heavenly aroma that filled the kitchen. He put two slices of bread in the toaster and set the heat to medium, poured himself a glass of orange juice, and drank a sip as he removed the brains. He dumped the bowl of eggs into the skillet and moved them around with a spatula until they were done.

He felt like a kid at Christmas because he was about to get a present he'd been wanting for most of his life. He scraped the eggs onto his plate just as the toast popped up; he buttered it and added them to his plate. Pulling a chair away from the kitchen table, he sat down to eat in eager anticipation and quickly sliced off a piece of brain and jabbed it with his fork—the moment of truth had arrived. He put the piece of brain in his mouth and chewed slowly, waiting for all the flavors to develop. It tasted...it tasted like, well, it sort of tasted like liver. He'd never eaten cow or pig brain, but when he was a child he'd once eaten squirrel brains; his grandmother had made a gumbo and she'd put the squirrel heads in it. Squirrel brains tasted a lot like the brain he was now eating.

The flavor was not unappealing. The garlic and spices livened it up a lot. In fact, the more Haley ate, the more he liked it. It was different, and it would be something he thought he could enjoy on an occasional basis.

But, as he ate, he started to feel that something was missing. Ah, he thought as he recalled that he usually ate his eggs with ketchup and a little Tabasco sauce. He retrieved the ketchup bottle from the fridge and the Tabasco sauce from the counter, and added some of each to his plate. After sitting back down, he dipped a combination of brain and egg in the ketchup and ate it, but it still wasn't quite the taste he was looking for.

He continued to eat and it wasn't until he swallowed his last bite that he realized what would have gone best with it–salsa.

Salsa? he thought, perplexed. He didn't even like salsa. He didn't care for Mexican food that much at all and never ate salsa. It had a strange taste to it–some of that green stuff in it tasted like stink bugs to him. *Why would I have a taste for salsa now?* Haley continued to wonder as he cleaned up the kitchen. He put some of the meat in the fridge and wrapped the rest in white freezer paper and put it in his deep freezer. After the meat was safely stored, he took a shower, set his clock for noon, and went to bed.

Haley woke, dressed for work, and left his house with the trash bag full of discarded Victoria pieces and parts. It hadn't started to smell yet, and he wanted to get it in the dumpster at the hotel before the trash pickup today.

He parked in his normal parking spot and walked down the stairs to the dumpster completely unnoticed. He heaved the bag over the top, and it just became another anonymous bag of trash.

Haley still had some time to kill and his stomach was growling, telling him to eat again. The human brains in his stomach had settled in well–he'd been afraid that they might not agree with his system. But even with his body handling the change of diet well, he didn't want to eat too much human too fast, just in case.

He walked to Decatur Street with the full intention of drinking a root beer and eating a foot long from a Lucky Dog vendor. But before he made it to the hot dog stand, he came upon a taco van parked on the side of the road–a thriving business of taco vans had sprung up during the rebuilding of New Orleans after hurricane Katrina. Latino music was blaring from the van's radio, drowning out the sweet sounds of the calliope from the steam boat Natchez on the river near by.

The ambiance of old New Orleans was changing and Haley was not happy about it at all.

There were five people waiting to be served at the van, and Haley for some odd reason couldn't resist going over to check the food out. The hand painted menu sign included tacos, burritos, tortillas–the usual fare–and all of it looked surprisingly delicious to him.

When it was his turn, he ordered a shredded beef taco. When he was asked if he wanted salsa on top, he asked if the salsa had that green stuff in it. The Vendor said, "Si, it has cilantro." Haley found himself saying yes before he had time to talk himself out of it.

The steaming hot taco was served on a brown paper towel, which did a poor job of absorbing the grease. But with just one bite, the missing taste he'd been searching for earlier was satisfied. The tangy tomatoes and onions flavored with the distinctness of the cilantro were just what his palate craved.

This was not like him at all. He was a red beans and rice, fried chicken, or seafood po-boy type of guy–New Orleans through and through.

As he chewed on his taco, he realized that his foot was tapping briskly in time with the Latino music.

What the hell? he thought–he was a blues man first, a jazz man second. He thought of Latino music as the type that would be played at the department stores to make people shop faster. And now, he thought he could swing his hips and dance to the beat right then and there. **What's going on?** he wondered.

He felt as if his subconscious was playing tricks on him. He'd just killed and ate part of a Latino woman–what was his mind doing to him? There were myths about ancient man eating the brains and hearts of the men they killed in order to inherit their strength, but that was just silly superstition.

There was also another story he'd read about worms learning a path through a maze, being chopped up and fed to other worms, which then were able to complete the maze the first time they went through it.

Was there some truth that feelings and memories could be passed on just by eating another person? His grandmother was a Jehovah's Witness and she'd always said, *The soul is in the blood.* He didn't really know what that meant. Was he now sharing the soul of that Latino woman because he'd eaten part of her?

*   *   *

The fruits of Victoria's body lasted Haley for almost two weeks. Some of the meals were better than others, but he was always a little on the giddy side when he sat down to eat.

One of the problems he faced was that he was used to using smoked meat and sausage in many of his dishes. Working two shifts didn't allow him much time to smoke any of the meat, or make homemade sausage.

His red beans and thigh meat were just plain bland, and no amount of Tabasco could save it. The ribs had a good flavor, complemented by a root beer sauce that was both sweet and hot. But there was hardly any meat on them—the girl had needed to gain a pound or two. The gumbo held its own with the help of some pork sausage, but it tended to overpower the natural, subtle taste of the human meat. And no, human did not taste like chicken. The heart, liver, and kidneys were perfect when served cut up into small pieces and deep fried. A large portion of the meat he ground up and used like hamburger. It browned well in the black, iron skillet, and he made a couple of taco meals from it. The burgers he'd made and cooked on the charcoal grill were his favorite. They too were on the lean side, so he added a little more mayo to the bun to help them slide down.

Haley definitely felt like he was different as a person. Eating Victoria had him looking at the routine things in life in a slightly different way. Even his dreams were different, although he couldn't remember much of the details from them. But one that stood out in his mind the most disturbed him the whole day after he'd awoke—in that dream everyone spoke Spanish.

The next day, Haley passed Ray Percy, one of the two-day doormen, at the front of the hotel. He gave him a habitual nod, and Ray responded in kind. Ray didn't fraternize much with the help, except for a widow called Mrs. Adele. Haley thought that Mrs. Adele was a fine-looking woman. She looked like a candy bar with the almonds in the right places, except maybe for a few too many almonds on her backside. Mrs. Adele worked the day shift also, as a chambermaid.

Those day shift people are too stuck on themselves, Haley thought. Mrs. Adele wouldn't even give Haley the time of day, and this bothered him greatly. And now that thought bothered him even more. In fact everything seemed to bother him more lately, which was not typical of the New Orleans *laissez-faire* attitude he'd once had.

Haley went through the motions of sweeping, mopping, and cleaning during his first shift; his mind was occupied with an endless chain of thoughts. It was as if he were re-evaluating his life. There was a certain disharmony in his spirit that he'd never felt before. He wondered if it had anything to do with the growing craving for human flesh—it had been over a week since his meager supply had run out.

After a short break between shifts, he pushed his vacuum into restaurant *Le Feu* and started flipping the chairs and placing them on top of the tables so he could clean. Not even half way through, Chef Barque burst through the kitchen door, wiping his hands on a towel.

"Ah, piss man! You're here to push the dirt around, no?" Barque asked.

Haley sighed deeply and loudly—he was not expecting this.

"No, Chef Barque, I'm here to do my job, which I can't do until you get outta here," Haley snapped.

"Eh, piss man? Don't you think you can have that attitude with me," Barque said arrogantly. "I'm a five star chef in a five star restaurant. Piss men don't tell me what to do!"

"Chef Barque, I don't tell you how to cook, so don't you tell me how to clean. Now, get outta here so I can get started," Haley said.

"Yes, yes, piss man, I'm leaving," Barque took the towel and threw it on the floor. "In fact, I will be on a two-week holiday. I won't be here to slide on your greasy floors." He walked to the entrance door and stopped, "Two weeks, piss man, two weeks. Two weeks I come back. Two weeks you be gone."

Haley had resumed picking up the chairs and froze. "Gone? What do you mean gone? I ain't going nowhere."

"Gone, piss man. I get you fired when I get back. I am five star chef. You are five star dog shit. I give you two weeks to find another job, piss man, I'm a compassionate man," Barque laughed and left.

That was it! Barque had pushed him over a boundary, and now he was able to focus through his internal fog. This was a fight that he was going to win, and he would win it on his own terms.

Haley worked double speed and left the floors and kitchen not quite as clean as usual—something he would have never done before, but his priorities were changing.

It wasn't hard at all to break into Chef Barque's tiny office. All he had to do was work a credit card under the tang of the lock—the spring popped and he was in. He rummaged through the desk drawers and filing cabinets until he hit pay dirt. Chef Barque lived at 2418 Chartres Street in the Faubourg Marigny district of the French Quarter.

Now a man on a mission, Haley gathered a variety of utensils and supplies from the kitchen, and placed them in a large trash bag. He made his way out of the hotel and into his car. His first stop was at a convenience store for an energy drink, some ice, and a case of beer. Then down the street to his house, where he removed his license plate and retrieved his ice chest.

Fifteen minutes later, he pulled up in front of Chef Barque quaint, little one story house. The houses on the street were separated by no more than twenty feet, and Barque's house was less than a thousand square feet inside. Still, it would have sold for ten times what Haley's house would bring.

He was uneasy with the houses being so close together. But at three A.M. on a Monday morning, he hoped everyone would be asleep. He slipped a knit cap over his head and pulled it down low–just above his eyes and as far over his ears as it would cover.

He eased out of his car–gently pushing the door shut after he exited–and walked casually around to assess the situation. The streets were empty and the neighborhood was quiet–the brightest light on the street was half a block away. And what porch lights were on were dulled by an accumulation of dead bugs who'd sought salvation in the night.

Convinced that it was now or never, he walked up to Barque's door and gave it a sound, authoritative rap. He waited exactly twenty-five seconds and knocked again with his eye pressed against the peep hole; on his fourth round of knocks a light came on inside.

An agitated voice came from behind the door, "Go away! I call the police!"

"Sir, I am the police," Haley lied in a deep voice.

"I didn't call for police, go away," Barque said.

"Sir, we have a report that you're holding someone hostage inside. We need to come inside and talk to you," Haley said, still disguising his voice.

"No one else is here–you go away," Barque demanded.

"Just let us come in and talk to you for a minute. If everything is cool, we'll leave," Haley continued.

"Step in front of the peephole, so I can see you," Barque said.

"We are in front of the peephole, now let us in," Haley lied, his thumb covering the small, one way window.

"Damn humidity," Barque huffed.

There was some mechanical clanking behind the door and the sounds of deadbolts turning. Then the door swung open with a jerk and Barque was face to face with a grinning Haley Deucett.

'Piss man?' were the last two words Barque ever spoke. Haley raised a sixteen-ounce meat tenderizing hammer and slammed it down between

Barque's beady, little dark eyes; he dropped like a ton of bricks to the floor without even a whimper.

Things went a lot easier than he'd thought they would, and he was glad he hadn't had to use the large kitchen knife he'd shoved between his belt and pants. But he wasn't home free yet, he still had to make his escape.

Haley quickly looked up and down the street again to find it was still clear so he walked out and opened the trunk of his car. He lifted Barque under the arms and dragged him to the car and lifted him into the trunk. Barque was a little more than five feet tall, but the little bastard was fat, and he was a lot harder to handle than Victoria had been.

He closed the trunk as quietly as he could and forced himself not to rush around to the driver's side, in case anyone had heard the slam of the trunk and was now looking out their window with curiosity. He wanted to give off the appearance of having the right to be there and of knowing what he was doing; it was when you rushed around and acted nervous that people noticed you.

His car started right up with the normal sputter and puff of black smoke. He gave it some gas and made his way onto the Pontchartrain Expressway and across to the West Bank; his cousin's deer camp was less than an hour away. It was Monday, Haley's day off, and the camp was the perfect place for him to spend the day.

It was still dark when he turned off the main highway and onto the old logging road that led to the camp. Fortunately the road was dry, otherwise he would have needed a four-wheel drive truck. Still, he had to keep his speed at a minimum–the ride exposing the age of his shock absorbers as he was tossed about.

The camp itself was nothing more than a fifteen by fifteen shack built with discarded building materials from a subdivision that was being developed. It offered few creature comforts and was just a place to roll out a sleeping bag, out of the weather, until it was time for the morning hunt.

Haley pulled up next to the weathered structure, opened his energy drink, and waited for the sun to come up.

The morning light and energy drink knocked off the dullness of the drive, reviving Haley before he opened the trunk and manhandled Barque's body onto the ground.

Get me fired, he thought. *Ha! I'll get you fired up!*

He dragged Barque by his feet over to a large oak tree. A chain hoist was situated above on a branch to lift dead deer by their legs for skinning.

He looped the chain around the chef's ankles and lifted him up until his head was a good foot off the ground.

First, he removed Barque's clothing, and then he slit Barque's throat. The pasty white body marbled with cellulite swung from side to side as blood pooled underneath him from his dripping head. Haley took a knife and gutted him just like he would a deer, and hollowed out the body cavity.

There were a couple of wooden picnic tables close to the shack that he needed to clean before he could use them. He was glad the old well hadn't run dry as he used the hand pump to wet some rags he'd found inside the shack. He cleaned the two tables and benches, moved one over underneath Barque, and lowered him down onto it–Barque was laid out on his back, his face covered in crimson.

There ain't nothing attractive about a naked man, Haley thought

From the supplies he'd taken from the restaurant, he gathered a jar of liquid seasoning and a large syringe. He opened the jar and sucked up the oily mixture through the thick needle. Injecting food with liquid seasoning had been popular for some time because it gave meat more flavor. The 'Cajun Injection' seasoning was used mainly on pigs and turkeys, and Haley considered Barque both. He methodically placed his injections equal distances apart throughout the carcass, and shot liberal amounts into the joints before he used garlic powder and a blend of Cajun spices as a dry rub, with plenty going into the body cavity.

While the chef was marinating, Haley began to prepare what his cousin called his 'Cajun microwave'. The two metal poles he'd used before were still standing upright in the ground, which the entire gutted and butterflied body would be chained to. He built two fires, one a few feet in front of where the body would be placed, and one a few feet behind it. Behind each of the fires he would stand a sheet of 4 x 8 tin, slightly upright, but tilted at a slight angle toward the meat so the heat from the fires would be directed toward the prepared corpse–this would allow the meat to roast using indirect heat from the fires and both sides would cook at the same time, so he didn't have to worry about turning the body.

There was still plenty of firewood left over from winter, so Haley stacked the wood for each fire and gathered some smaller twigs and branches for kindling. When everything was set to go, he doused the wood with kerosene and gave it time to soak in.

He found an old blanket inside the shack and used it to keep Barque free of dirt while he dragged him to the poles. With some difficulty, he stood Barque up and chained each wrist to a pole. He then chained each ankle in a similar fashion so that Chef Barque was spread out like a big fat X. Haley put a match to the wood and soon both fires were roaring. He waited a couple of minutes for them to die down a bit and then he added the sheets of tin and let the corpse cook.

He went back to his car and retrieved his book and reading glasses; it would be several hours before dinner was ready and he had a lot of reading to catch up on.

He set up a folding chair and a TV tray he'd found in the shack near the fire ring for a small table and readied another jar of the liquid marinade for periodic basting.

Haley popped the top on a beer and took a long drink, enjoying the late May weather. *Now, this is nice*, he thought.

The day grew long as he finished one short horror story after another—he'd found himself reading more short stories these days because of his work schedule.

Each beer went down faster than the previous. The smell of the roasting chef filled the air and his stomach growled and gurgled in anticipation.

Finally, after about the twentieth time basting, he made a small slice into the meat and the juice ran out clear; it was ready and Haley could hardly wait to eat, but he took the time to douse the fires to prevent the meat from over cooking while he ate.

Haley cut a big slab off of Barque's shoulder; the knife slid through like it was hot butter. The skin was delightfully crispy on the outside, while the meat was tender and juicy on the inside. It was still a little hot, so he had to take little nibbles so he wouldn't burn his lips. The skin crunched and the savory flavors of the marinade came alive in his mouth. It was the best tasting meat Haley had ever eaten; pig at a *Cochon De Lait* had never tasted this good. Haley grabbed another beer and took long swigs to chase the hot meat down. He ate, and ate, and ate—trying a piece from one area, and then a piece from another. Haley had become addicted to human meat ever since Victoria, but he'd never enjoyed eating her like he was enjoying Barque.

When he could eat no more, he cut up the chef and packed the parts away in his ice chest. Then he put everything back where he'd found it and cleaned up all of his trash, taking it with him. After screwing his license plate back on, he left for home.

While driving back, Haley was savoring a piece of meat stuck between his teeth when an odd craving came over him. He wasn't hungry at all, but there was a yearning for a flavor somewhere in his mind that he couldn't identify. What was it? What was... *Caciocavallo Podolico*, popped into his mind. *Caciocavallo Podolico? Hell, I don't even know how to pronounce that,* he thought. It was the cheese Barque had accused him of stealing–a cheese that he'd never eaten, never thought about, but now could remember its flavor.

This wasn't his mind playing tricks on him. This was a consequence of eating Chef Barque. Just like Victoria, he would be sharing some feelings of the soul with Barque. This was a consequence he hadn't given much thought to. But now, he was determined that whatever Barque passed on to him, he would use to his advantage.

* * *

Haley was about to start his second shift, cleaning the kitchen for Chef Chauvin. Chef Barque had never returned from his vacation and the police didn't have a clue what had happened to him. Chef Chauvin treated Haley with respect, and he liked that. Chauvin was always friendly and complemented Haley on his work. He was also a football fan and the two of them would talk about the New Orleans Saints every chance they had.

Mrs. Adele came walking down the hall with her head hung low, and would have crashed into Haley if he hadn't stopped her.

Haley gently put his hands on her shoulders as she came up to him, "Mrs. Adele?"

"Oh! My…my goodness. I'm sorry, Haley, I didn't see you there," she said.

"I know, Mrs. Adele, your mind has been elsewhere. Is there anything I can help you with before I get started on the kitchen?" Haley asked.

"No, no, Haley. I just need to get this shift over with so I can go home and get a few hours of sleep before I go out searching again." Mrs. Adele had given up the coveted day shift to devote her time to searching for Ray Percy, who'd been missing for two weeks.

"Now, don't you go running yourself down. You need to eat properly and get plenty of rest. Or you're not going to be fit to work or search for him," Haley said with concern.

"Thank you, Haley, you're so kind. I've been meaning to thank you for spending your last two off days helping with the search. I know it's hard to help on the days you pull two shifts. I really appreciate your kindness in my time of need," she said.

"I would do anything I could just to see you smile before like you used to, Mrs. Adele," Haley's eyes glistened as they filled with tears.

Mrs. Adele sensed his concern and started to see Haley in a different way.

"Mrs. Adele, both of us have tomorrow off–why don't we go out searching together and if we don't find Ray, I'll treat you to a nice dinner at my place."

"Well now, I…I don't know. I wouldn't want you to go to any trouble."

"No trouble at all, Mrs. Adele. Why, I bought some French cookbooks and I've been experimenting in the kitchen–everything is cooked and frozen. All I have to do is thaw it out," Haley said.

Mrs. Adele hesitated, but she felt an attraction toward him unlike before, "Well then, Haley, I guess it would be okay then. Pick me up at eight. We'll go to Ray's cousins and search with the others."

"Yes, ma'am, I'll be there on time," Haley said with a grin.

Mrs. Adele left and he continued with his work.

The next day Haley, Mrs. Adele, and four of Ray's relatives took an hour ride south to Shell Beach. Ray had mentioned the day before he went missing that he might go fishing, and Shell Beach was a favorite fishing spot of his. No one knew for sure if he actually made it there or not; both Ray and his car were missing.

The day was long and the flies and mosquitoes only added insult to their unfruitful mission. The police investigation came almost to a halt when they learned that Ray had sizable gambling debts. The family too had given up hope of finding him, but was willing to continue the search as long as Mrs. Adele felt the need.

By five o'clock, weariness had overcome the crew. Everyone exchanged hugs and made the drive back to the city.

"Haley, are you sure you're not too tired for this?" Adele asked.

"No, ma'am. Everything is ready, all I have to do is heat some things up."

Adele sat at the kitchen table, which was adorned with a beautiful, new white cloth and a dozen roses in a ceramic vase–roses were Adele's favorite flower.

"I'd like to begin the meal by serving an apéritif," Haley said and removed a bottle of Moet & Chandon White Star champagne from the fridge.

Adele didn't know what 'apéritif' meant, but she figured it out quickly when she saw the bottle and watched him pop the cork.

He filled two glasses and sat next to Adele, "A toast to you, Mrs. Adele, may you find happiness." Haley raised his glass in anticipation. Adele smiled embarrassingly and raised hers to his. The glasses clinked together and they each took a sip—Haley's eyes never leaving hers.

"Oh, the bubbles tickled my nose," Adele giggled.

"I have something I prepared to go with our champagne," Haley said and got up from the table, coming back with a covered dish and water crackers. He removed the top and sat the dish on the table and arranged some crackers around it.

Adele wasn't quite sure what the brown loaf sitting on the dish was.

"I've made us a pâté to have before dinner," Haley sliced the mixture of liver, fat, and spices into squares to accommodate the crackers' size.

Adele looked at it curiously before putting it in her mouth. "Oh, it tastes like liver cheese."

Haley winced for a microsecond and then forced a grin. "Yes, they do taste similar."

"This is so good! I've never had liver cheese that tasted this good before. I can't believe you made this," Adele said with a bit of cracker clinging to the corner of her mouth.

"The secret is really fresh meat. My butcher is a friend of mine and I get the freshest meat in town." Haley was glad Ray hadn't been a glue sniffer, and that his meat had been clean.

"I can't stop eating this, Haley, it's so good!" Adele gobbled another up.

"Let me get the next courses warming," Haley stood and removed two pots from the fridge, and started heating them on the stove.

Adele excused herself for eating so much and had another glass of champagne. Haley cleared away the pâté and crackers to get ready for the next course, and the two continued to talk like teenagers on their third date.

When the soup was hot enough, Haley filled two bowls and placed a piece of toasted bread on top of each. He then layered on two different cheeses and dashed on some paprika. After five minutes on broil in the oven, he removed them. The cheese had melted and cascaded over the side of the bowls, all bubbly and golden brown.

"French onion soup," he said, placing a bowl in front of her. "I made the consommé myself."

"Oh my, this looks delicious," she said scooping out the cheese, bread, and broth mixture with her spoon. "Mmm…Ha-ley! This is so rich and tangy. I've never had any soup like this before. How did you learn to cook like this?"

"I bought a couple of French cookbooks so I could cook like they do at *Le Feu*. But when I started, it just seemed to come natural. Maybe I have some French blood in me from my ancestors," he said, knowing that he'd had French *'in him'* for weeks.

After the two finished eating, Haley cleared the table and removed a bottle of wine from a cabinet. "This will complement our entrée perfectly," he held the bottle out for her to read the label.

"Zydeco Rosato...," Adele's voice trailed off. "That's the same wine Ray used to drink on special occasions." She bit her lip and tried to hold back her tears.

Haley smiled to himself, he had a feeling he'd made the right choice. "It's been my favorite for a long time too," he lied. "It's dry and will go well with the Beef Burgundy." Although no 'beef' was in the stew. Haley poured them each a glass of the wine, prepared two plates of the stew, and sat down to eat.

"Haley, you've been so sweet. I want you to know that you've come to mean a lot to me. Ray's gone, and I miss him so. But you've made him being gone easier," Adele said as she reached out and squeezed his hand.

"You mean a lot to me too, Mrs. Adele, you always have," he said, giving her a smile before he picked up his fork and began eating. He didn't want her to get too emotional, at least not now.

"You know, Haley," she said after finishing a bite of the meat, "I feel that when I'm with you, Ray is here too."

He's here, Haley thought. *And after he makes his way through your intestines, you can say hello to him when you pass him in the morning.* But he knew what she meant, and everything he'd hoped for was falling into place.

Adele had finished about three quarters of her food when she put her fork down and wiped her mouth with her napkin. "I just can't eat another bite. That was the best tasting food I've ever had—everything was special. I would be as big as a house if I ate like that every day."

"A man would be lucky to cook for you every day, Mrs. Adele," Haley said with a wanting in his voice.

She felt a wave of embarrassment and stood up to break the awkward moment, "Here, Haley, let me help you clean up. It's the least I can do after you went through all this trouble for me."

The two gathered the dishes and put them in the sink. Haley said he would let them soak and take care of them in the morning. Adele felt like she was watching a movie, as if she were waiting for the next scene to happen.

Haley spoke, breaking the silence, "Would you like some dessert, my *little boo*? I can make Banana's Foster."

"What did you call me?" she asked.

"What? My little boo. I called you, my little boo."

Tears rolled down Adele's face, "When we were alone, Ray used to call me his *little boo*." She reached out and hugged Haley, and cried on his shoulder; he hugged her and patted her gently on her back.

"I'm sorry. I don't want to be upset. I've had such a wonderful time tonight. I feel safe with you, just like I felt with Ray," Adele said, doing her best to choke back her tears.

Haley pulled back and wiped her tears with his handkerchief. He looked deep into her dark eyes and gave her a gentle kiss; she smiled. Then Haley gave her a longer kiss, and she kissed him back. He took her by the hand and led her to his bedroom. She didn't protest, and the two shared a night of passion.

Haley awoke when the sunlight shown though the bedroom window. He got up and went to the bathroom, leaving Adele to sleep in. He had a feeling she wouldn't want to go looking for Ray today.

He sat in his living room and selected another collection of short horror stories off the bookshelf, and his thoughts drifted to the past events of his new life before he turned a page.

He considered himself a cannibal and felt no shame in it. The unexpected personality traits that he'd inherited from eating his victims he'd once considered an unfortunate consequence as he wasn't happy with what he'd inherited from Victoria.

But that changed when he ate Barque and used the 'add-ons' to his personality to his advantage. Even more so with Ray—it couldn't have gone any better if he'd written it himself.

Hmm, written it myself, he thought. His eyes drifted to the old IBM Selectric typewriter on the desk and half-typed page yellowing in the carriage.

Years ago, Haley had attempted to write a horror story and it had taken him hours just to write that half of a page.

He'd always meant to go back and finish the story, but he didn't know how.

But now, now, he thought, *there just might be a way.*

Haley looked at the anthology he was reading, *The Horror Book* from Penguin Press–the editor's name was on the bottom of the cover. He had a few of man's novels, but mostly had a collection of his anthologies.

That bastard sure is a prolific writer, he thought with jealousy.

Then it all came together in his mind. Next month he was scheduled for his two weeks of vacation. Tomorrow, he would go to the public library, get on the internet, and find out where the man lived.

He had two weeks to find him, eat him, and hopefully return home and begin a writing career–he might even give up one of his shifts if it worked out as he hoped.

In addition to becoming a writer, he thought, *I might even pick up a few skills from him that would improve my cooking techniques.*

He laughed out loud. He could always crack himself up.

BITTER FRUIT

ANTHONY GIANGREGORIO

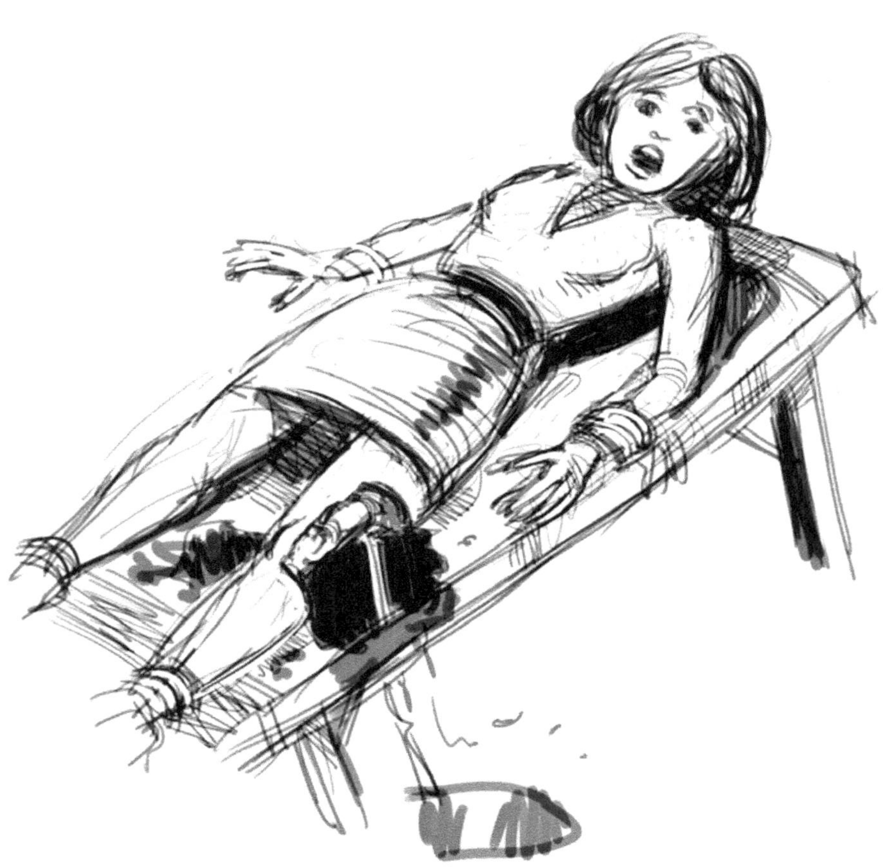

Martin cut into the plump steak on his plate, watching as the juices pooled around it. It was medium rare, just the way he liked it. The outside was charred and the inside was warm and pink.

He liked his meat the way he liked his women.

With the cut piece of meat on his fork, he slowly raised it to his lips and placed it in his mouth.

Ever so slowly, he pulled the meat off the fork with his teeth and let it roll around on his tongue. The juices began to coat his taste buds and he rolled his eyes in ecstasy.

God, this is better than sex, he thought.

When he bit into the succulent morsel and a burst of juices filled his mouth, he actually moaned in pleasure. Chewing ever so slowly, he swallowed, relishing the feeling as it slid down his esophagus and into his stomach.

He paused, letting the taste remain on his tongue, and then cut himself a new piece. He repeated the process yet again, until finally coming to the last piece.

It was with a heavy heart that he stabbed the morsel and ate it.

But he took joy in knowing there was more where that came from, and though he knew he should stop, he decided to have himself another steak.

What the hell, he thought. I deserve it. *I've been working very hard lately and this treat is mine.*

Placing his fork and knife on the table, he stood up and crossed the kitchen.

But he didn't go to the refrigerator to get another steak. Instead, he went to the basement door to the left of the fridge.

The door was padlocked with a combination lock and he quickly dialed in the combination, then opened the door.

A cool breeze wafted over him and he detected the smell of dampness.

But he detected something else in the odor, something that made his loins quiver with excitement. He took another dish from the nearby counter and descended the stairs leading into the dark basement.

A single light bulb hung from the ceiling. It was old, with a pull chain. When he pulled the chain, the naked bulb illuminated a twelve-by-fourteen foot room. Cinder blocks made up the walls and a thick rug covered the stone floor to help soak up noise. The cinder blocks were thick enough that sound couldn't penetrate to the outside world.

If he wanted to, he could scream his head off in his basement and his neighbors would never hear him.

There were no windows, the three having been bricked up years ago, and no light filtered in from outside.

In every respect the basement was a tomb, or worse, a torture chamber.

There was a butcher block table in the middle of the room and plastic sheeting was underneath it to protect the carpet from blood spray. Along the outer wall was a peg board, and on this were an assortment of tools.

Handsaws, hammers and screwdrivers were a few of the tools available. On a workbench below the peg board were more tools, these larger in size. A skill saw, jigsaw and an electric drill were the main ones, but an electric sander and nail gun were also there, both looking as if they hadn't been used in years, both covered in dust.

The saws however looked like they were used a lot, and there were small red dots on them, looking as if paint had splattered. It looked like paint, but it wasn't.

It was something far worse.

Martin walked over to the workbench, barely glancing at the table and what lay on its surface, tied down by all four limbs, the ropes wrapped underneath the table to hold it in place.

He ignored the whimpering and muffled cries for mercy behind the gag in the woman's mouth, but instead concentrated on the assortment of knives on the workbench.

Taking a large carving knife, he raised it to his face, seeing his reflection in its shiny surface. He smiled slightly at his visage and then turned to face the strapped and hogtied figure on the card table.

He stared at the naked and gagged woman, her eyes glaring back at him, both of her dark-blue eyes as wide as dinner plates. Tears ran down the sides of her face and pooled near her head, while her legs and arms spasmed as she tried to free herself.

On her left leg, at her thigh, a large piece of meat had been sliced off, leaving a running, bloody wound. Blood had collected and congealed on the table and some had dripped off to land on the plastic. There, catching in an impression in the plastic and the rug beneath, it made a small pool.

Martin said nothing to her as he crossed the short distance separating them. There was no need to speak. After all, when a man goes to the supermarket, he doesn't talk to the steak he buys, does he? Or at least he didn't.

No, it would be foolish to talk to his supper.

She began to kick harder as he reached her, the knife in his hand already coming down to her untouched right leg. Without hesitation, he began cutting and slicing into the meat of her thigh and then curving it up as he finished the cut.

When he finished, the woman now screaming in agony behind her gag, he had himself a six inch piece of human steak.

He carried the steak to a plate on the workbench, and after placing the tender flesh on it, he began wiping his hands clean on a towel. There was a bucket of water with a spoonful of bleach at the end of the workbench and he dropped the knife in it. He would clean it later with the others in the bucket, but for now he wanted to eat his prize.

More blood dripped off the table and he wondered if he had accidentally cut an important artery or vein in the woman's leg. Truth be told, he wasn't very good with medical stuff and could have easily zigged with the knife when he should have zagged.

With a slight shrug, he figured if she bled out then he would simply dispose of her sooner rather than later.

He gave her one last glance as he held his plate of raw meat. He eyed her naked form, not even the slightest hint of sexual arousal crossing his mind. Though her breasts were perfectly formed and the junction between her thighs shaven to a V, her stomach flat, her buttocks well-rounded, he didn't see her in that way. To him, she was merely a meal, a cow laid out for the slaughter.

As the woman cried behind her gag and shook her head in pain and fear, he left the basement, turning off the single light bulb on his way to the kitchen.

When he closed the basement door, the muffled sobs ceased…at least to his ears.

With the smell of cooking meat—reminiscent of pork—filling the kitchen, Martin daydreamed as he seasoned his meal. His stomach was content, but there was still room for more, and he knew he would really slow down and enjoy this second piece of heaven.

As he drifted off in reverie, he thought back to how he'd captured the woman now trapped in his basement. It had been so easy, really. He had wrapped his left arm in a sling and pretended it was broken, then had gone to the supermarket and waited until a half hour till closing. At that time of night, there was almost no one around and the lot was practically deserted.

He had then used his props of filled paper bags containing what looked like groceries, but were in fact empty cans and hollow packages of cookies and egg boxes.

He waited until a woman that caught his eye came out of the market, then he went to the rear of his van and made sure to drop the grocery bags sitting on the rear bumper onto the ground, spilling them everywhere.

With his arm in a sling and his small stature, no woman ever felt threatened by him and this woman was no different. As he dropped the groceries, she saw him, and as he bent down to try and pick them up one-handed, she came to his aid to help.

After she knelt down to help, he made a quick look around to make sure it was still clear, then he simply cracked her over the head with a small club he carried and rolled her into the rear of the van.

All this took less than a minute. Seconds later, he was driving out of the parking lot before the first can of soup had stopped rolling across the asphalt.

He always made sure to pick different supermarkets all across the state and sometimes he went further, driving to neighboring states. So far, the police had never put the multiple abductions together, and he always made sure to never leave a trace of the body when he was through with them. It was easy to get rid of the evidence when you ate most of it.

He flipped the meat in the pan over, the sizzle it made music to his ears. He sprinkled some fresh ground pepper and basil on it, then poured a tablespoon of olive oil over the top, the aroma heaven to his olfactory senses.

When it was cooked to his liking, he turned off the stove and slid the meat onto a fresh plate. He hated reusing dishes.

Sitting back down at the kitchen table, he poured himself a glass of red wine and began to eat, relishing the taste as only a true connoisseur of meat could.

He hadn't always been a cannibal, but after years of eating every meat known to man, he had become bored and had wanted something new. But there was nothing new to eat.

After eating everything from tiger from Africa to monkey brains from Nepal, he was craving something new.

That was when he heard about an underground club that served the juiciest meat of all…human.

It had taken a lot of money and favors to finally be invited to the exclusive club, but when he finally got in and sampled the ultimate cuisine, he found he was hooked for life.

Unfortunately, the club only met once a month. You see, it was extremely dangerous to take someone from the city and make them a meal. Homeless people were out because their disease-ridden bodies, so someone had to be taken from the middle class. The owners of the club usually tried to take single people, most often with no close family, but if an opportunity arose they would take anyone.

Martin didn't like this once a month thing. He found human meat was something he wanted more than anything to be a weekly if not daily basis, and to wait an entire month to savor the sweet juices was too much for him to take.

So he went off on his own and found it worked well for him. And best of all, he didn't have to share with others.

Finishing the last bite of his steak, he leaned back and sighed. He found human meat reminded him of pork butt, but with an aftertaste he'd never known before. It was gamey with a hint of sweetness.

Retiring for the night, he placed his dish in the sink. After checking to make sure the house was secure, he went to bed, already planning on dreaming about frying up the woman's breasts with bell peppers and onions the next afternoon.

His plans for a lavish lunch were destroyed when he walked down the basement stairs and pulled the cord to the light.

The woman was dead, having bled out hours ago. It seemed he had indeed severed an artery or vein and she had bled to death sometime in the night. As he walked over, he was careful not to step in the congealing blood pools. Bending over, he touched the tip of his finger to a wide puddle and tasted it. It was cold, she had been dead for many hours.

For just a moment, he wondered if he could eat her anyway, but no sooner did the idea cross his mind then he brushed it away.

No, he wouldn't eat meat from a dead body, it had to be alive. He wasn't a ghoul, after all. And besides, that was what made it so savory, knowing that minutes before cooking, the meat had been on a living, breathing body.

With a heavy sigh, he went to the workbench and began donning his gear. First was a white, Mylar jumpsuit similar to a hazmat suit. Next he put on a clear faceplate, similar to what coroners use when performing an autopsy, so when they saw into the body, blood spray doesn't hit them in the face.

He picked up the jigsaw, plugged it in, and played out the extension cord. After testing it to make sure it was in working order, he walked over to the corpse and began working.

He had to dismember the arms and legs, sever the neck from the shoulders, then slice the torso into four parts. When he was done, he would drive out to the desert and bury the parts in four different places.

As he began dismembering the body, he began to hum.

He lasted almost a week before he knew he had to go on the hunt again. He was craving human meat worse than a pregnant woman craves pickles and ice cream.

He got into his costume again—the sling on his arm making him look like a wounded baby bird—then headed off to a supermarket three towns over.

The capture went off without a hitch, and soon he was driving back home with an unconscious woman in the back of the van.

As he drove, he glanced in the rearview mirror to study the shapely form of his captive.

She was in her later thirties by the look of it, with large breasts, a thin waist and dark brown hair. She had on a little too much makeup, as if she was trying to hide her complexion, but Martin barely gave it any thought. Makeup could be washed off after all and soon he would have her naked and strapped to his table.

He licked his lips at the thought, deciding he would start with this one's breasts first, thus making up for the loss of the last woman.

Pulling off the highway and onto the back roads, he made his way home, his stomach already growling in anticipation.

Hours later found him in his basement again, with a new body on his table.

The woman was naked and strapped down, the same gag in her mouth as the previous woman. Martin didn't see any reason to change it.

He studied her curvaceous form and heaving breasts, his mouth salivating like a dog called to eat after missing a few meals. He couldn't wait to taste her.

He had been playing with the idea of drinking blood, wanting to savor it like a fine wine, and he decided this woman would be his first.

He used an ice pick and carefully slid the sharp tip into her left wrist, directly above the vein. As he slid out the ice pick, the blood began to flow, and he was waiting with a small basin. He let more than two glasses of plasma fill the basin before using a rag to tie off her wound. He didn't want her bleeding out…at least not yet.

The woman had yet to plead, beg or cry. All she did was stare at him, seeming as calm as if she was in her own bed. Martin decided it was shock and didn't pay it much mind.

He left her then, turning off the bulb and climbing the stairs.

Sitting by the fireplace, he sipped her blood from a crystal glass, smacking his lips at the coppery taste.

He decided he liked it and would now make it a habit each time he had a meal on his table. He also planned on using her blood as the base for a hearty sauce, figuring peppercorn would go with it nicely after he made a roast from a chunk of her well-formed thigh.

He loved the thigh and for good reason. It was one of the best places to take meat from a human being and he assumed all cannibals did it.

He watched some television, the news mostly, and he felt a nervous tingle when they began to cover an abduction from a local supermarket a few towns over. At this time there were no leads…just the way Martin liked it.

Two hours later and he was ready for the main course, a lovely sautéed piece of meat from the woman.

Rising from his chair, he went down into the basement and walked directly to the workbench. The knives were there, now cleaned, and he took a flensing knife. He crossed the room and hovered over the woman, who looked up at him with cold eyes.

She still didn't beg, didn't plead. It was as if she had resigned herself to death. They never did that. They always had hope that they would either be set free or escape. None had ever accepted they would die…at least until the very end.

Without pause, he carved a beautiful piece of flesh from her thigh and he saw she didn't cringe in pain. A single tear slid from her right eye, but otherwise she was stoic.

Not wanting to have to come back down for more later, he also carved off one of her breasts, thinking he could slice it into thick chunks and fry it up with vegetables.

He was about to leave when he went for a delicacy. With only two per captive, they had to be eaten and appreciated…savored like caviar.

Taking a soup spoon, he went to the top of the table and leaned over her face. With the skill of a surgeon or someone who had done this many times before, he slid the spoon into her right eye socket and carefully plucked the eyeball out. Done correctly, it barely caused the victim pain, though there was a lot of discomfort.

He planned on boiling it, and with some salt and pepper, it tasted a hundred times better than any hard-boiled egg he'd ever had. Three minutes would do nicely.

After placing his prizes on a small platter, he winked at her and left, the light going out as he pulled the cord to leave her in darkness.

He did hesitate halfway up the stairs for a few seconds, listening to her breathing hard through her nose. He expected to hear her crying now that she thought she was alone, but still there was nothing. He shook his head, not understanding.

Why was this woman so fearless when others were terrified?

Why didn't this woman beg and cower behind her gag, saying muffled prayers to God to save her?

And then he heard something that made no sense to him.

She began to laugh.

It was muffled, but it was definitely laughter.

He stood silently and listened for almost two full minutes before ascending the remaining stairs. He decided she must be mad with pain and fear, and instead of sobbing, was laughing instead.

That must be it. After all, what else could it be?

Closing the basement door when he reached the top, he shut out her laughing and carried his plate full of goodies to the kitchen to have himself a feast.

The next evening, after returning home from work, he felt his stomach rumbling and went down into the basement to carve himself a fresh piece of meat.

Reaching the bottom of the stairs, he turned on the naked bulb to see her looking right at him with her remaining eye. Even behind her gag, Martin could see she was grinning from ear to ear.

As he moved closer to her, she began to laugh again. It was crazed laughter, but it was definitely directed at him. He found himself growing angry.

His food wasn't supposed to laugh at him! It was supposed to grovel and beg for its life, not mock him. He was so angry he knew this would be the last meal he took from her before killing her.

He went to the workbench, chose a large carving knife, and went back to her. With a clean platter on the table beside her leg, he began carving off her remaining breast. He then sliced off more meat from her thighs and some from her upper arm. He didn't care for this part much, finding it tough, but had found with vinegar peppers and a lot of garlic, it made a nice stir fry.

When he finished taking what he wanted from her, Martin leered down at her still body. She had only stopped laughing to grimace at the pain she had suffered as he skillfully sliced her up like a Thanksgiving turkey.

It was a high point when she finally passed out from the pain. Her laughter was grating on him. It was as if she knew something he didn't and he felt terribly left out.

He took the knife and placed the edge to her neck. Though it wasn't really the best knife for the job, he knew it would do the trick. With one smooth motion, he slid it across her throat. Blood spurted forth to cover her chest and drop onto the table and then to the plastic covering the carpet. This was a new sheet of plastic, since replaced after the last 'meal' was disposed of.

As she bled out, he picked up his platter and left, already forgetting about the woman and looking forward to his meal.

He would take care of her tomorrow, what with cutting her up to destroy the corpse. It was Saturday and he would have plenty of time. He didn't work on Saturdays.

As he turned off the light and ascended the stairs, closing the door when he reached the top, in the darkness, only the soft sound of dripping blood could be heard.

When Martin returned to the basement the next morning after a restful night's sleep, he was surprised to see the woman wasn't dead, though she was close.

By the amount of blood congealing on the plastic, it was clear she wasn't long for this world, but the simple fact she was still alive defied logic.

Crossing the distance and avoiding the pooling blood, he stopped so he was standing behind her head. As he looked down on her, he found she was staring up at him with her remaining eye.

And then she began to laugh again.

It wasn't strong, as she was too weak to really get into it, but there was no doubt in Martin's mind that, yes, she was laughing at him again.

As he looked down to her neck, he saw where the blood had slowed and realized he must not have done a very good job at severing her carotid artery. So yes, she had bled out, but much slower than normal, the incision allowing less blood to pump through the wound each time her heart beat.

She began to choke behind her gag and Martin reached down and pulled it off. No sooner did he do this then she spit blood, coughing and hacking. Spasms wracked her body and Martin thought she would die right then, but she didn't.

Her eye had closed as she coughed some more, but now it opened again. There was no fear in the single orb, only hatred and something else…something he couldn't put his finger on.

Her blood-covered lips curved up into a wan smile and she began to chuckle, blood bubbling forth each time she breathed.

She was very close to death.

Martin could take no more, and though he had never spoken to one of his 'meals' before, this time he did.

"Just what the hell is so funny to you? Hmm? I've eaten half of you and taken one of your eyes, and now you're about to die. I promise you, no one will ever find your body. Soon, you will be one of thousands of women who disappear every year without a trace. So I ask you, no, I demand that you tell me…just what in God's name do you find so damn amusing?"

She laughed again but stopped when it turned into a coughing fit. Spitting blood across the basement, she said in a voice that was more of a hoarse cackle than a whisper, "I'm laughing, you bastard, because you don't know what I know. But you will." She began to spasm and her single eye rolled up into the back of her head, her neck wound leaking more profusely as it was torn open, the congealing blood broken free to allow fresh plasma to seep forth.

She was about to die.

No, she can't die, not yet! Martin screamed in his mind. *She knows something I need to know, I can feel it!*

As she began to fade out, he grabbed her head on each side and held it in his hands.

"Don't die yet, you bitch! Tell me what you know! *Tell me!*"

He began shaking her head back and forth, the neck wound squishing as blood seeped from it. The flow had slowed to next to nothing, there was no more blood inside her.

Suddenly, her eye snapped back to the center of the socket and it focused on Martin one last time. With her last breath she spit into his face, the blood striking him on the right cheek. He ignored it as he looked down on her now placid face.

She was dead.

And whatever she knew was gone with her.

His rage was so great he began to twist her head, turning it round and round like a corkscrew. With the neck already sliced open, it was easy for the head to slowly become separated from the torso, until with a dry *snap*, the spine cracked and split and he found himself holding her decapitated head in his hands.

Still filled with rage, he threw it against the wall. It slapped messily, leaving a semi-round red spot, the head rolling on the floor to stop with its left cheek facing down, droplets of blood dripping from the jagged neck.

Martin screamed to the ceiling, feeling cheated.

Eventually he calmed down, and when he was in full control, he began to chop up the headless corpse. He was so mad he didn't bother to don his gear. And soon, as blood splattered his face and he licked his lips clean, he found he was in a much better mood.

Four months later, and with many more bodies eaten, Martin found he wasn't feeling very well.

It had happened gradually over the past few months and now he was sluggish and barely had any energy to get out of bed in the morning. The worst part was his appetite had waned to next to nothing. Concerned there was something truly wrong with him, he went to his doctor to be examined.

The doctor had been rather quiet and had told Martin he would need to have him get some blood work done before he could say with any certainty what was wrong with him.

Once that was accomplished, the doctor would have a better insight into Martin's ailment.

The next week went by slow for Martin as he waited for his blood work results to come in. On the eighth day, he received a call from his doctor asking him to come to his office.

Martin had wanted to know right then what was wrong with him, but the doctor had been adamant about Martin coming in to see him face to face.

With nothing else to do, Martin did as he was asked.

"I don't know how to tell you this, Martin, so I'm just going to come right out and say it," the doctor said from behind his desk.

Martin, in one of the two chairs in the office, shifted uncomfortably as he waited for the news which he now knew wasn't good.

With a heavy sigh the doctor said, "I'm afraid you have a mutated form of AIDS. Not HIV either. It's progressed to a new strain of full-blown AIDS. Your white cell count is dreadfully low which explains your lack of appetite and low energy. Unfortunately this new strain hasn't been susceptive to the drugs AIDS patients have been taking. And so far it has a one hundred percent mortality rate." He shook his head slowly. "I'm so sorry."

Martin didn't know what to say. His mouth had fallen open and his eyes were wide. He felt like someone had punched him in the stomach with an anvil. He was floored. It was all too much for him to take.

He had just been handed a death sentence.

A painful death sentence.

"But how could this happen?" Martin gasped.

The doctor sat up straighter in his chair. "Well, surely you know the ways to acquire the disease. Have you had unprotected sex? A blood transfusion perhaps?"

Martin shook his head. "No, of course not. I haven't been with a woman for more than six months." His mind went back to the hooker he had paid to have sex with him. "And I haven't been to a hospital in years…well, until I went to get blood drawn last week."

The doctor nodded slowly. "I see. Well, what about sharing needles? Have you done drugs and shared a needle with another person?"

Martin was offended. "How dare you even suggest such a thing? I *do not* do drugs, Doctor," he snapped.

The doctor raised his hands in surrender. "I'm not judging, Martin, but I need to ask these questions if we're to figure out how this terrible thing happened."

Martin calmed down slightly. "Of course. Sorry for getting angry but it's just…"

"No apology needed," the doctor said. "I understand completely." The intercom buzzed and the doctor answered. "Susan, I told you not to disturb me, I'm in a meeting with a patient."

"I'm sorry, Doctor," the secretary's voice came over the intercom. "But Mrs. Carmichael is on the phone and she's in a panic over her blood pressure medicine. She really sounds upset."

The doctor sighed. "Fine, I'll be right out." He looked at Martin. "I'm very sorry about this, Martin. Mrs. Carmichael is eighty-three and she panics easily. Just let me calm her and we can get right back to discussing what will happen next for you." He stood up to go out to the secretary's desk to take the call there. "I'll leave you here to take all of this in. Maybe while I'm gone you can retrace your steps over the past year and try to come up with how you contracted the disease."

"Fine, fine, go," Martin said. "I could use a few minutes to myself anyway."

The doctor nodded and left the room, closing the door softly. A few seconds later and Martin could hear his distorted voice through the door as the man talked on the phone.

As he sat there, Martin began to wrack his brain for how this could have happened. He went over his movements for the past year and nothing came to mind. He worked and went home and other than eating the women he captured, he did nothing else that would…

Wait a minute, he ate other people. If one of them had been sick with the disease and he had eaten them, drank their blood, or had gotten it in his eyes, then that could only mean…

His mind raced back to months ago when he had that woman who always seemed amused. She had laughed at him, as if she knew something he didn't, as if though he was killing her, she somehow knew she would get her revenge, even from beyond the grave.

The doctor returned and sat down, mumbling more apologies. Martin heard none of it as the realization of what was happening hit him full force.

"Doctor, I have a question for you. Hypothetical of course."

"Please, what is it?" the doctor asked.

Martin chose his words carefully. "Well, if a person ate someone infected with this mutant AIDS virus, or say, drank their blood, could they contract the disease that way?"

The doctor laughed despite the morbid moment, thinking it was a joke. "Well, I suppose so, unbelievable as that sounds, but yes, if you ingested the blood or flesh of a terminally ill patient you would become infected yourself. But surely you're joking. Why, that would be insane, and the person ingesting the meat would be committing suicide by all counts."

Martin chuckled slightly, forcing a slight smile to crease his lips. "Of course, I was joking, and it's a bad joke at that."

He talked to the doctor some more, finding out what would happen next. From the progression of the illness, he had about four weeks if he was lucky, probably less, by the way the virus was eating into his body and had been for months. Then he would be too weak to take care of himself and would have to check into a hospice. Other than painkillers to make his death tolerable, there was nothing that could be done to help him.

Martin left the doctor, finding it ironic that he shook the doctor's hand, as if he was grateful to find out he was dying and would soon be dead. Or worse yet, would be suffering terribly. The doctor had let slip that it was a very painful way to die and many patients simply killed themselves before it became too much to bear, thus saving themselves and their families further suffering.

As he left the office building the doctor's office was in, and stepped out onto the sidewalk, he thought back to the laughing woman and how amused she was.

She had been dying, too, and though he had tortured her when he sliced meat from her body, in the end he had put her out of her misery by killing her. The pain she'd felt was nothing compared to what was to come when dying from the disease.

He finally understood what she was laughing about.

She was fearless because she had nothing to lose; she was already dying and had felt relief in knowing he was saving her from suffering further. And to top it all off, she knew she would get her revenge by infecting the man who was eating her flesh and would eventually kill her.

Unfortunately, there would be no one to do that for Martin.

ABOUT THE WRITERS

Rebecca Besser is a graduate of the Institute of Children's Literature. Her work has appeared in the Coshocton Tribune, Irish Story Playhouse, Spaceports & Spidersilk, joyful!, Soft Whispers, Illuminata, Common Threads, Golden Visions Magazine, Stories That Lift, Super Teacher Worksheets, Living Dead Presents Magazine, and The Undead That Save Christmas charity anthology. She also has multiple stories in anthologies by Living Dead Press, Wicked East Press, and NorGus Press, and one in an anthology by Pill Hill Press; and a poem in an anthology by Naked Snake Press.

Visit her website: www.rebeccabesser.com

Jim Bronyaur lives in Pennsylvania and writes horror. He's been published over forty times, all of which you can find on his web site: www.jimbronyaur.com. He's also socially addicted on Twitter @jimbronyaur.

Charles Day, has spent over twenty years working in the field of mental Health, 12 of those years locked inside a psychiatric hospital with some seriously ill patients. He believes the voices he still hears in his head today are from many of those he's frequented over the years in these secured facilities, begging for him to tell their stories through the power of the written word. You can find his works published with Pill Hill Press, Wicked East Press, Living Dead Press, Static Movement, and Blood Bound Books. Be sure to visit him at Charlesdayfictionwriter.blogspot.com or his new venture over at hiddenthoughtspress.lefora.com for more of his forthcoming Fiction and Non-fiction endeavors.

Mariah Deitrick currently resides in Iowa with her husband and four children. When she's not being a wife and mother, she's writing fiction for all ages. Her work can be found in various markets including, Living Dead Press, Static Movement and Stories That Lift.

Anthony Giangregorio is the author of 35 novels, almost all of them about zombies and has edited over 20 anthologies.

His work has appeared in Dead Science by Coscomentertainment, Dead Worlds: Undead Stories Volumes 1-7, and Wolves of War by Library of the Living Dead Press. He also has stories in End of Days: An Apocalyptic Anthology Vol. 1-5, the Book of the Dead series Vol. 1-6 by LDP, Zombie Zoology by Severed Press, and two anthologies with Pill Hill Press. He is also the creator of the popular action/zombie series titled Deadwater and his action/ horror novel Dead Rage is being optioned for a movie.

Check out his website at www.undeadpress.com.

Dane T. Hatchell has lived Baton Rouge, Louisiana all his life. In his youth he was a fan of old school horror movies, and a collector comics and magazines such as Creepy and Eerie. Now in his early fifty's, he is devoting his free time to writing to satisfy a lifelong passion. You can contact Dane at Enadious@gmail.com.

Mark M. Johnson is a horror and sci/fi fanatic known on-line as, The Black Empty. Mark enjoys writing as a hobby amongst other things he'd rather leave to your imagination. By the grace of good and extremely patient editors, his short fiction has appeared in numerous anthologies listed on his author page on Amazon. Born and raised in Detroit, he currently resides in Warren MI with his wife Cindy, one graduated daughter, one senior high school son, one crazy dog, three cats and a python.

Adam P. Lewis emerged on the horror-writing scene in early 2009. His work has appeared in anthologies and in print and digital magazines, all of which have shocked and entertained those who dared to read his work. Along with fiction, Adam has written articles on writing, book and movie reviews, essays on true crime, and lyrics recorded by nationally and world-wide touring musicians. For more information, please visit http://www.adamplewis.com.

Kevin Millikin has lived anywhere and everywhere in the last year, bouncing between the Pacific Northwest and Northern California. His stories have appeared in the Living Dead Press anthologies: Dead Worlds 6, Halloween Tales of Terror, Emails of the Dead, Christmas is dead…Again, as well as Rapid Decomposition (Library of the Living Dead). When he's not finishing up his debut novel you can find him online at face-book.com/Kevin.millikin

Brian J. Smith has been featured in The Horror Zine, Thrillers, Killers and Chillers, Drabblecast, New Voices In Fiction, Darkest Before The Dawn, Crooked, The Flash Fiction Offensive and Postcard Shorts. He was also featured in two previous Living Dead Press anthologies like E-Mails of the Dead and Book of the Dead 3: Dead And Rotting. He currently lives in Chauncey, Ohio with his mother, brother and six dogs and cheers on The Ohio State Buckeyes.

Alan Spencer has published the novels "The Body Cartel" (Damnation Books) and "Inside the Perimeter: Scavengers of the Dead" (Living Dead Press). In January 2011, "Ashes In Her Eyes," his third novel, will be released by Panic Press. He was recently nominated for the "Pushcart" award for the short story, "Suffering Begins in the Mouth and Ends in the Belly." Keep an eye out for his fiction in numerous Living Dead Press anthologies and the upcoming "Morpheus Tales Urban Horror" special issue.

Gary Wedlund escaped high school hell, only to become an Army slave for three years. He slipped the chains, soon working as a roofer, transferring funds to the Columbus College of Art and Design, where he graduated to the unemployment rolls. A teaching certificate, obtained at Otterbein College put Gary back into middle school purgatory. Almost incidentally, a major in math and an MBA at Ohio State qualified Gary to play guitar in several forgettable rock and roll bands. In the meantime, he fed his family on road-kill and Kroger food purchased by chits procured through employment as a radio system's specialist. He is blessed with a wife, four daughters, and one bathroom. Gary has several short stories to his credit, a shelf full of unpublished novels, and is the author of Living Dead Press's Zombies in Our Hometown. Which is non-fiction—metaphorically speaking.

PLAYING GOD: A ZOMBIE NOVEL
by Jeffery Dye

It was supposed to be a regeneration virus to help soldiers on the battlefield—regrowing limbs and healing wounds— but a simple act of carelessness unleashed it on an unsuspecting world.

For the virus was not perfected, and once exposed, the host quickly dies, only to rise again as one of the undead.

As countries are quickly overrun, scientists and military teams battle to contain the outbreak.

There is no other option.

If the infection continues to spread, soon the entire globe will be consumed. And perhaps that will be a just punishment for a mankind that dared to try to play God.

DEAD HOUSE: A ZOMBIE GHOST STORY
by Keith Adam Luethke

The old mansion on the edge of town, aptly named Dead House, has a history of blood, pain, and death, but what Victor Leeds knows of this past only scratches the surface of the true horrors within.

But when his girlfriend is attacked by a shadowy figure one rainy night, he soon finds himself caught up in a world where the dead walk and ghostly wraiths abound. And to make matters worse, a pair of serial killers are fulfilling carefully made plans, and when they are done, the small town of Stormville, New York will run red. The last ingredient to open the gates of Hell, and plunge this small upstate town into madness, is rain.

And in Stormville, it pours by the gallons.

The Lazarus Culture
by Pasquale J. Morrone

Secret Service Agent Christopher Kearns had no idea what he was up against. Assigned on a temporary basis to the Center for Disease Control, he only knew that somehow it was connected to the lives of those the agency protected...namely, the President of the United States. If there were possible terrorist activities in the making, he could only guess it was at a red alert basis.

When Kearns meets and befriends Doctor Marlene Peterson of the Breezy Point Medical Center in Maryland, he soon finds that science fiction can indeed become a reality. In a solitary room walked a man with no vital signs: dead. The explanation he received came from Doctor Lee Fret, a man assigned to the case from the CDC. Something was attached to the brain stem. Something alive that was quickly spreading rapidly through Maryland and other states.

Kearns and his ragtag army of agents and medical personnel soon find themselves in a world of meaningless slaughter and mayhem. The armies of the walking dead were far more than mere zombies. Some began to change into whatever it was they ate. The government had found a way to reanimate the dead by implanting a parasite found on the tongue of the Red Snapper to the human brain. It looked good on paper, but it was a project straight from Hell. The dead now walked, but it wasn't a mystery. It was The Lazarus Culture.

BOOK OF THE DEAD
A ZOMBIE ANTHOLOGY VOL 1
ISBN 978-1-935458-25-8
Edited by Anthony Giangregorio

This is the most faithful, truest zombie anthology ever written, and we invite you along for the ride. Every single story in this book is filled with slack-jawed, eyes glazed, slow moving, shambling zombies set in a world where the dead have risen and only want to eat the flesh of the living. In these pages, the rules are sacrosanct. There is no deviation from what a zombie should be or how they came about. The Dead Walk.

There is no reason, though rumors and suppositions fill the radio and television stations. But the only thing that is fact is that the walking dead are here and they will not go away. So prepare yourself for the ultimate homage to the master of zombie legend. And remember... Aim for the head!

REVOLUTION OF THE DEAD
by Anthony Giangregorio
THE DEAD SHALL RISE AGAIN!

Five years ago, a deadly plague wiped out 97% of the world's population, America suffering tragically. Bodies were everywhere, far too many to bury or burn. But then, through a miracle of medical science, a way is found to reanimate the dead.

With the manpower of the United States depleted, and the remaining survivors not wanting to give up their internet and fast food restaurants, the undead are conscripted as slave labor.   Now they cut the grass, pick up the trash, and walk the dogs of the surviving humans.   But whether alive or dead, no race wants to be controlled, and sooner or later the dead will fight back, wanting the freedom they enjoyed in life.

The revolution has begun!

And when it's over, the dead will rule the land, and the remaining humans will become the slaves…or worse.

KINGDOM OF THE DEAD
by Anthony Giangregorio
THE DEAD HAVE RISEN!

In the dead city of Pittsburgh, two small enclaves struggle to survive, eking out an existence of hand to mouth.

But instead of working together, both groups battle for the last remaining fuel and supplies of a city filled with the living dead.

Six months after the initial outbreak, a lone helicopter arrives bearing two more survivors and a newborn baby. One enclave welcomes them, while the other schemes to steal their helicopter and escape the decaying city.

With no police, fire, or social services existing, the two will battle for dominance in the steel city of the walking dead. But when the dust settles, the question is: will the remaining humans be the winners, or the losers?

When the dead walk, the line between Heaven and Hell is so twisted and bent there is no line at all.

RISE OF THE DEAD
by Anthony Giangregorio

DEATH IS ONLY THE BEGINNING!

In less than forty-eight hours, more than half the globe was infected.
In another forty-eight, the rest would be enveloped.
The reason?
A science experiment gone horribly wrong which enabled the dead to walk, their flesh rotting on their bones even as they seek human prey.
Jeremy was an ordinary nineteen year old slacker. He partied too much and had done poorly in high school. After a night of drinking and drugs, he awoke to find the world a very different place from the one he'd left the night before.
The dead were walking and feeding on the living, and as Jeremy stepped out into a world gone mad, the dead spotting him alone and unarmed in the middle of the street,
he had to wonder if he would live long enough to see his twentieth birthday.

THE CHRONICLES OF JACK PRIMUS
BOOK ONE
by Michael D. Griffiths

Beneath the world of normalcy we all live in lies another world, one where supernatural beings exist.

These creatures of the night hunt us; want to feed on our very souls, though only a few know of their existence.

One such man is Jack Primus, who accidentally pierces the veil between this world and the next. With no other choice if he wants to live, he finds himself on the run, hunted by beings called the Xemmoni, an ancient race that sees humans as nothing but cattle. They want his soul, to feed on his very essence, and they will kill all who stand in their way. But if they thought Jack would just lie down and accept his fate, they were sorely mistaken. He didn't ask for this battle, but he knew he would fight them with everything at his disposal, for to lose is a fate worse than death.

He would win this war, and he would take down anyone who got in his way.

MONSTER PARTY
Edited by Anthony Giangregorio

Zombies, vampires, werewolves and ghosts are just a few of the monsters in this anthology.

But this isn't any anthology, you see, this is a party.

Or to be more to the point…a *Monster Party*.

Ever wonder what would happen if a werewolf and a zombie squared off? Or perhaps a vampire and a Frankenstein monster? Or better yet, how about a world where every conceivable monster is real and humans are their prey?

If those burning questions have been driving you mad, then look no further than this book.

So go on over to the buffet table, grab yourself a plate (the shrimp looks good) and get yourself a drink, and enjoy the fun ride that is the *Monster Party*.

THE WAR AGAINST THEM: A ZOMBIE NOVEL
by Jose Alfredo Vazquez

Mankind wasn't prepared for the onslaught.

An ancient organism is reanimating the dead bodies of its victims, creating worldwide chaos and panic as the disease spreads to every corner of the globe. As governments struggle to contain the disease, courageous individuals across the planet learn what it truly means to make choices as they struggle to survive.

Geopolitics meet technology in a race to save mankind from the worst threat it has ever faced. Doctors, military and soldiers from all walks of life battle to find a cure. For the dead walk, and if not stopped, they will wipe out all life on Earth. Humanity is fighting a war they cannot win, for who can overcome Death itself? Man versus the walking dead with the winner ruling the planet. Welcome to *The War Against Them*.

DEADTOWN: A DEADWATER STORY
B OOK 8

by Anthony Giangregorio

The world is a very different place now. The dead walk the land and humans hide in small towns with walls of stone and debris for protection, constantly keeping the living dead at bay.

Social law is gone and right and wrong is defined by the size of your gun.

UNWELCOME VISITORS

Henry Watson and his band of warrior survivalists become guests in a fortified town in Michigan. But when the kidnapping of one of the companions goes bad and men die, the group finds themselves on the wrong side of the law, and a town out for blood.

Trapped in a hotel, surrounded on all sides, it will be up to Henry to save the day with a gamble that may not only take his life, but that of his friends as well.

In a dead world, when justice is not enough, there is always vengeance.

END OF DAYS: AN APOCALYPTIC ANTHOLOGY
VOLUMES 1-3

Edited by Anthony Giangregorio

Our world is a fragile place.

Meteors, famine, floods, nuclear war, solar flares, and hundreds of other calamities can plunge our small blue planet into turmoil in an instant.

What would you do if tomorrow the sun went super nova or the world was swallowed by water, submerging the world into the cold darkness of the ocean? This anthology explores some of those scenarios and plunges you into total annihilation.

But remember, it's only a book, and tomorrow will come as it always does.

Or will it?

ETERNAL NIGHT: A VAMPIRE ANTHOLOGY

Edited by Anthony Giangregorio

Blood, fangs, darkness and terror...these are the calling cards of the vampire mythos.

Inside this tome are stories that embrace vampire history but seek to introduce a new literary spin on this longstanding fictional monster. Follow a dark journey through cigarette-smoking creatures hunted by rogue angels, vampires that feed off of thoughts instead of blood, immortals presenting the fantastic in a local rock band, to a legendary monster on the far reaches of town.

Forget what you know about vampires; this anthology will destroy historical mythos and embrace incredible new twists on this celebrated, fictional character.

Welcome to a world of the undead, welcome to the world of *Eternal Night*.

DEAD HISTORY 2

A Zombie Anthology

Edited by Anthony Giangregorio

From the dawn of mankind, the walking dead have been with us.

The greatest moments in history are not what they appear.

Through the ages, the undead have been there, only the proof has been erased, documents destroyed, and witnesses silenced.

The living dead is man's greatest secret.

In this tome, are a few of the stories of what really happened all those years ago.

History isn't alive, it's dead!

INSIDE THE PERIMETER: SCAVENGERS OF THE DEAD

by Alan Spencer

In the middle of nowhere, the vestiges of an abandoned town are surrounded by inescapably high concrete barriers, permitting no trespass or escape. The town is dormant of human life, but rampant with the living dead, who choose not to eat flesh, but to instead continue their survival by cruder means.

Boyd Broman, a detective arrested and falsely imprisoned, has been transferred into the secret town. He is given an ultimatum: recapture Hayden Grubaugh, the cannibal serial killer, who has been banished to the town, in exchange for his freedom.

During Boyd's search, he discovers why the psychotic cannibal must really be captured and the sinister secrets the dead town holds.

With no chance of escape, Broman finds himself trapped among the ravenous, violent dead. With the cannibal feeding on the animated cadavers and the undead searching for Boyd, he must fulfill his end of the deal before the rotting corpses turn him into an unwilling organ donor.

But Boyd wasn't told that no one gets out alive, that the town is a death sentence.

For there is no escape from *Inside the Perimeter*.

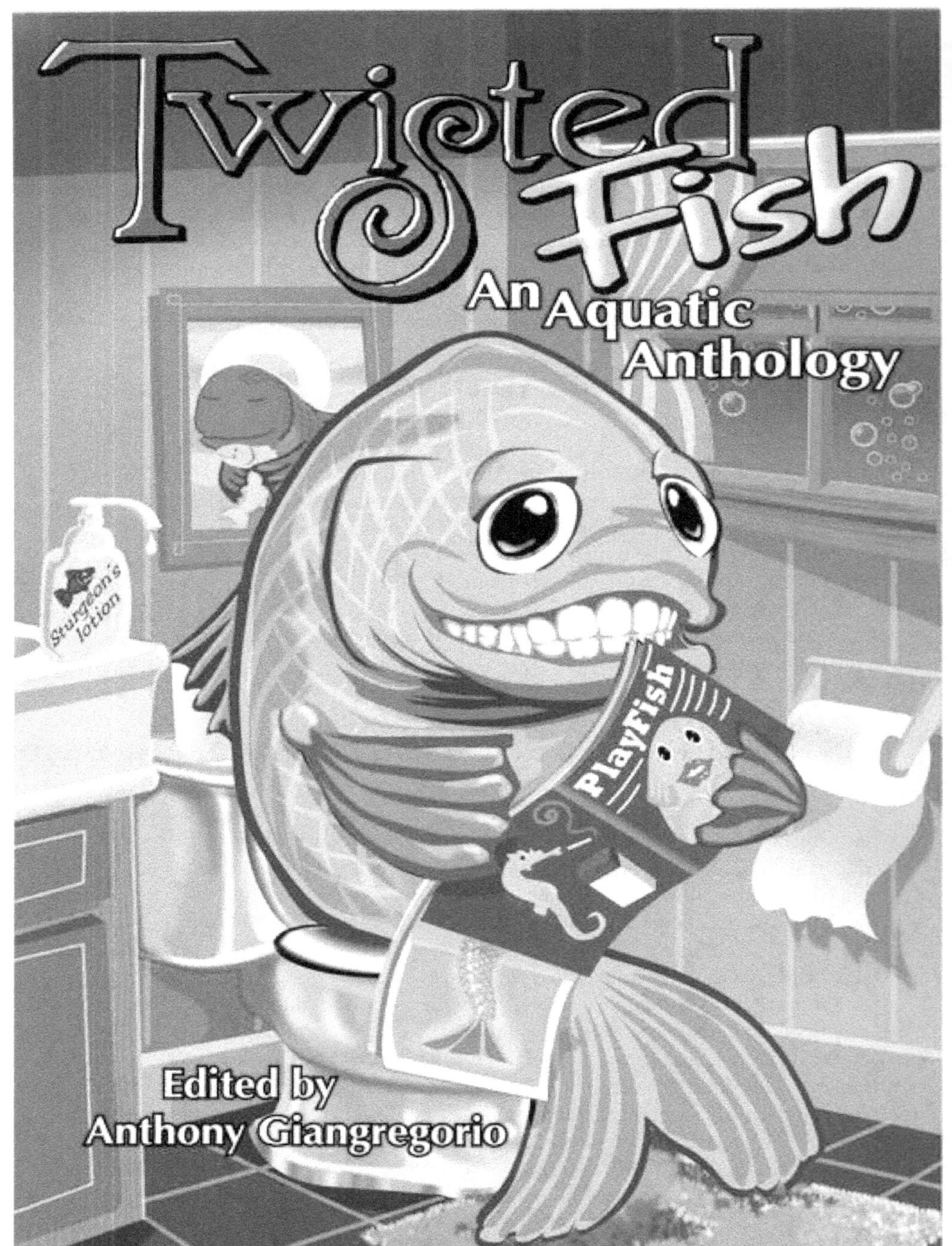
Twisted
Fish
An Aquatic
Anthology
Sturgeon's
lotion
PlayFish
Edited by
Anthony Giangregorio

THE BOOK OF CANNIBALS
ISBN 13: 978-1-935458-52-4   ISBN 10: 1-935458-52-3
STILL HUNGRY?